ALL FOR ONE

ALSO BY MELODY CARLSON

As Young As We Feel (Cook)

Hometown Ties (Cook)

Limelight (Multnomah)

Love Finds You in Pendleton, Oregon (Summerside)

A Mile in My Flip-Flops (WaterBrook)

The Christmas Dog (Revell)

ALL FOR ONE

BOOK THREE

MELODY CARLSON

transforming lives together

ALL FOR ONE
Published by David C Cook
4050 Lee Vance View
Colorado Springs, CO 80918 U.S.A.

David C Cook Distribution Canada
55 Woodslee Avenue, Paris, Ontario, Canada N3L 3E5

David C Cook U.K., Kingsway Communications
Eastbourne, East Sussex BN23 6NT, England

David C Cook and the graphic circle C logo
are registered trademarks of Cook Communications Ministries.

This story is a work of fiction. All characters and events are
the product of the author's imagination. Any resemblance
to any person, living or dead, is coincidental.

Unless otherwise noted, all Scripture quotations are taken from the Holy Bible, New
International Version®, NIV®. Copyright © 1973, 1978, 1984 by Biblica, Inc™. Used
by permission of Zondervan. All rights reserved worldwide. www.zondervan.com.

LCCN 2010942614
ISBN 978-1-4347-6493-5
eISBN 978-0-7814-0617-8

© 2011 Melody Carlson
Published in association with the literary agency of Sara A. Fortenberry.

The Team: Don Pape, Erin Healy, Amy Kiechlin, Caitlyn York, Karen Athen
Cover Design: FaceOut Studios, Tim Green.
Cover Images: Getty Images, #77502780 and #97829581, royalty-free.

Printed in the United States of America
First Edition 2011

1 2 3 4 5 6 7 8 9 10

122710

Chapter 1

ABBY

Holding her breath, Abby leaned across the bed and listened intently. Was Paul still breathing? The background sound of the high-tide surf outside made it difficult to hear. She held her hand about an inch from his nose and waited until a puff of warm air crossed her palm. With a sigh of relief she leaned back into her pillow. Paul was still alive. But Abby's adrenaline was flowing and she was wide awake.

She quietly slipped out of bed and tiptoed into the bathroom, where she picked up her prescription bottle of Ambien and blurrily studied the label. To take or not to take, that was always the question. So far she had resisted. Plagued with insomnia ever since Paul had come home from the hospital almost two weeks ago, Abby received the prescription from her doctor. And yet she was still afraid to take one. What if she fell so soundly asleep that she snoozed right through Paul suffering another heart attack?

"Don't be ridiculous," Paul told her when she'd confessed her sleepless nights to him—and that was after he caught her putting his mug of low-sodium soup into the freezer instead of the microwave. "I'm feeling great," he'd assured Abby. "You worry too much."

She had laughed off her faux pas and controlled her response. What she wanted to say was that she only worried too much because Paul didn't worry enough. He failed to take his recovery seriously. He'd already fallen off his exercise regime—a daily walk on the beach—which had been something she hoped they could do together. Plus, despite her efforts to reeducate herself to cook more healthfully, she had spied junk-food wrappers in his pickup just yesterday. It was as if he wanted another heart attack.

Naturally she couldn't say this to him, because she was also well aware that stress (i.e., domestic disputes) would only put him at greater risk. She was determined not to go there. As a result *her* stress levels seemed to be on the rise. Occasionally Abby wondered what would happen if she experienced a heart attack herself.

She set the Ambien bottle back in the medicine cabinet and went out to the kitchen to heat some nonfat milk. Nature's remedy. It sometimes worked, sometimes didn't.

With her cup of warmed milk in hand, she went into the living room and pulled out the notebook that she'd created for The Coastal Cottage, the name she'd finally settled on for her bed-and-breakfast. Filled with a collection of magazine photos, paint and wallpaper samples, fabric swatches, and lots of other fun things, this notebook seemed more like a dreamy escape than a real business these days.

Yet Abby knew the old house actually belonged to her now. Well, to her and Janie anyway. Janie, true to her word, seemed determined to remain something of a silent partner. However, Janie had begun some of the renovations needed to transform the basement into a law office. Abby was trying not to feel jealous over Janie's jump start, but sometimes it was a challenge to be friends with Janie. Not only did she have money to do whatever she liked, she also had the freedom. Of course, being widowed was a high price to pay for freedom.

Really, Abby reminded herself as she firmly closed the notebook, her number-one priority right now was to help Paul to fully recover from his surgery. According to his doctor that would take up to six weeks, or to right around Thanksgiving. She was determined to do everything in her power to ensure that Paul not only recovered, but that by Christmas he would be healthier than ever before. She just hoped that her own health could hold out that long.

Out of habit Abby picked up the remote and turned on the TV, tuning in to her favorite show—*Live in the Morning*—and she watched sleepily as the hosts did their usual chitchat, talking about their exciting lives, where they'd eaten dinner last night in New York City, and so on. Abby's ears perked up when it was time for the contest. She'd sent in dozens of postcards over the years, hoping that someday they would pick hers and call her and ask her the question of the day. Usually she knew the answers to the trivia questions, but lately her mind had been too muddled to remember. Today when they asked the question, Abby was clueless. She turned off the TV and hoped they wouldn't be choosing her postcard anytime soon.

* * *

"You look like death warmed over," Marley told Abby as the four friends met at Clifden Coffee Company on Tuesday morning. Thanks to an additional caregiver that Caroline recently found to look after her mom, their Four Lindas morning get-together had become a weekly event.

"Thanks a lot," Abby responded glumly. Then, as she slid next to Marley on the bench seat, she noticed that she'd forgotten to change out of her grubby sweats. Her friends always looked so stylish and well put together. Abby had promised herself to try harder in the fashion department. But she was just so stinking tired.

"Still not sleeping?" Caroline asked with concern.

Abby just shook her head, then took a slow sip of the steaming house blend.

"The Ambien's not working?" Janie scooted a chair closer to the table.

"I'm not taking it," Abby admitted. Then she poured out her tale, confessing her fears that Paul could possibly expire while she snoozed in oblivion. In the light of day and based on her friends' expressions, Abby suspected her story sounded rather silly.

"Poor Abby." Caroline patted her hand. "You need to go easier on yourself."

Marley nodded. "It's like you're playing God, Abby. Like you think you can control Paul's fate. But you can't."

"Besides that, you need to take care of yourself," Caroline said. "How can you possibly help Paul if you run yourself ragged?"

"Not only that, but sleep deprivation is dangerous to others," Janie pointed out. "Did you know that you're as unsafe on the road as an intoxicated driver?"

Abby just groaned. "Thanks for reminding me. I got a ticket for running a stop sign this morning."

"See?" Janie nodded vigorously. "You could get seriously hurt."

"Or hurt someone else."

Abby sighed. "I know, I know. You guys are right."

"It's only natural that you're concerned about Paul's recovery," Janie said gently, "but I'm sure he'd appreciate it if you were a bit more concerned about yourself, too."

"Otherwise you'll end up being totally codependent," Caroline added. "I've been learning a lot about that in my Alzheimer's support group. You don't want the purpose of your whole existence to be wrapped up in other people's needs."

Abby couldn't help but laugh at Caroline now. "Isn't that a little like the pot calling the kettle black?"

Caroline wrinkled her nose at Abby. "Hey, at least I'm working on it."

"How is your mom doing?" Janie asked Caroline.

"She seems to be going downhill. It's like her mind is just deteriorating." Caroline frowned. "This morning, before the caregiver arrived, Mom insisted on putting her slippers on her hands. She would not accept they were meant for her feet."

"Why not just get her another set of slippers?" Marley suggested. "One pair for her hands and one pair for her feet."

They all laughed over this. But even as she chuckled with them, Abby could almost relate to Caroline's befuddled mother more easily than to her friends. At the rate Abby was going, it probably wouldn't be long until she started wearing shoes on her hands too.

"How's your new law office looking?" Marley asked Janie. "Do you have any blank walls that are just begging for some art?"

Janie smiled. "Not a bad idea. We'll have to discuss that after the drywall guy is finished."

"Drywall guy?" Abby asked. As far as she knew the basement's walls were already finished. She was trying not to be territorial over her old family home, but what was Janie doing down there?

"Remember? I'm putting in that wall to divide the space into a private office as well as a waiting room."

Abby nodded. "Oh yeah. I forgot about that."

Janie tapped the side of her head. "Sleep deprivation will do that to you."

Abby forced a smile. "Okay, okay. I get the hint." Suddenly she remembered something—something really important. "Hey, Janie, I almost forgot what Paul told me. Is it true?"

"Is what true?" Janie looked like the confused one now.

"About Victor's ex-wife?"

Janie's brow creased. "What about Victor's ex-wife?"

Now Abby felt uncomfortable. What if she'd gotten her facts wrong? It wouldn't be the first time. And it wouldn't be surprising considering her mental state. "I … uh … I don't know."

"Come on, Abby," urged Marley. "What on earth are you talking about?"

"Spill the beans," Caroline pressed. "What did Paul tell you about Victor's ex-wife?"

"Furthermore, how would Paul know anything about Victor's ex-wife?" Janie stared at Abby with a curious expression.

"Victor stopped by to play chess with Paul last night," Abby explained. "Ever since Victor spent some time with him in the hospital, they seem to have become better friends."

"Yes …" Janie waited expectantly.

"Oh, well, I just thought you already knew." Abby twisted a

paper napkin between her fingers. Why had she even opened her mouth?

"Knew what?" Janie was getting impatient.

"Well, unless I've got my wires crossed"—Abby made an apologetic smile—"and that's possible—I'm sure that Victor told Paul that his ex-wife—isn't her name Donna?"

"Yes," Janie said, "Donna is correct."

"Well, Victor said that Donna is coming out to visit."

Janie cocked her head to one side. "Donna is coming out to visit? Who is she coming to visit? Ben perhaps?"

Abby shrugged. "Yes, I'm sure she'll visit Ben while she's here. But Victor told Paul that Donna was coming out here to visit him."

"Why would Donna come to visit Victor?" Janie looked worried. "I mean, that just makes no sense. Victor and Donna have been divorced for years. Donna is happily remarried and—"

"I guess the marriage wasn't as happy as Victor had thought."

Janie blinked. "Meaning?"

Marley and Caroline were both leaning forward, eagerly awaiting every morsel of this somewhat strange report. In fact Abby was almost beginning to wonder if she had imagined the whole thing.

"Come on, Abby." Caroline poked her in the arm. "Don't keep us hanging here like this."

"Yeah," Marley urged. "Out with the whole story."

"Please." Janie folded her arms in front of her.

"Now remember this is kind of secondhand," Abby pointed out. "But Paul said that Victor said that Donna experienced some kind of an epiphany or something and as a result she has split with her husband and she's coming out here to see if she can reunite with Victor."

"No way!" Caroline smacked the table. "That's crazy."

"Abby, are you sure of this?" Marley demanded. "Really, it sounds nuts."

"It does seem a bit far-fetched." Janie was absently fiddling with her phone now, as if ready to call Victor and question this bizarre statement.

"I know," Abby admitted. "I thought so too. It's possible Paul didn't get the facts straight. He seemed pretty surprised."

"Or maybe you got it mixed up," Marley suggested.

Abby nodded. "Yes, that could be. I'm not really thinking terribly clearly these days. Maybe I scrambled it somehow." Even as she said this, though, she didn't think so.

"Because if that was really true," Janie said carefully, "it seems Victor would've told me about it."

"Of course he would," Caroline assured her.

"Except that I think Victor just found out about this," Abby said. "Like maybe his wife—I mean ex-wife—had just called. In fact Paul said Victor seemed like he was in shock about the whole thing. Like he wasn't sure of what to do and wanted Paul to give him some advice."

"Victor is going to Paul for marriage advice?" Janie shook her head. "That's a little incongruous."

They all looked at Janie now.

"I mean … you know … you and Paul … you were having your problems before his heart attack. I know you've been doing couples counseling and all, but you know what I mean. Paul is not exactly an expert on marriage."

"Paul and I may have our problems," Abby admitted a bit tersely, "but we've also been married for thirty-five years. That's no small thing, if you ask me."

"No, of course not."

Caroline waved her hand. "Okay, enough about Paul's marriage expertise. What is really going on with Victor's ex? I mean seriously, does she think she can just waltz in here and demand that Victor take her back? Isn't that a little deranged?"

Marley nodded. "It sounds nuts to me."

"I don't know." Abby paused. Now she wasn't sure if she was just irked at Janie's comment about Paul's inability to give sound marriage advice, or perhaps she was jealous that Janie was already working on the old house that was going to someday be Abby's bed-and-breakfast, or maybe it was even the influence of sleep deprivation, but she opened her mouth knowing full well she was about to stick her foot in it. "If Donna has experienced a real epiphany—you know, like directly from God—it seems possible to me that God might want her to honor her original marriage commitment. You know the vow we all made on our wedding day. To love and to honor, yada yada, until death do we part. Maybe Donna wants to make good on it now."

The table grew silent and Abby saw the hurt in Janie's eyes. She wished she could rewind her words. Really, what was she thinking?

"That's an interesting theory," Marley said quietly.

"Well, you're divorced, Marley." Abby decided to redirect the conversation. "What if your ex did a complete turnaround? What if John came back to you, got down on his knees, told you he was sorry and that he wanted a second chance? What would you say to him?"

For a moment Marley just stared at Abby as if seriously considering this strange scenario. Then she threw back her head and laughed. She

chortled so hard that tears streamed down, and before long Caroline
and Janie were laughing hysterically too. Abby simply sat there and
watched as the three of them carried on like they were still in junior
high, like the time Bobby Reynolds walked out to the spring sock hop
with about ten feet of toilet paper trailing behind him. Perhaps Abby
should've been relieved by their merriment. Or maybe she should've
been laughing along with them. But the truth was, she felt more like
crying. Worse than that, she felt slightly betrayed by her three best
friends. She wasn't even sure why.

Finally she waved a hand at the giggling fools. "Go ahead and
laugh. Maybe I should just go and leave you to your jokes. I'm sure
you all think I'm crazy anyway."

"Don't go, Abby." Caroline looked like she was trying to sober
up now. "You're not crazy. But you are definitely exhausted."

"Yeah." Marley wiped her eyes with a napkin. "And slightly
delusional, too."

Janie nodded, but Abby was sure she spotted a trace of worry in
Janie's dark eyes. She was probably questioning Abby's sensibilities,
or even her loyalty as a friend or her dependability as a business
partner. Maybe such a reaction was perfectly justified. In fact Abby
was questioning some things about Janie as well. What if she'd been
wrong about her friend?

Chapter 2

JANIE

As she drove away from the coffee house, Janie wasn't quite sure what to make of Abby's strange bit of news. Was it really true? Or was Abby so sleep deprived that she'd gotten her facts mixed up? Really, Abby wasn't the most sensible person around. And it wasn't the first time Janie had second-guessed the strange partnership she'd entered into with her old friend. Of the Four Lindas, Abby and Janie probably had the least in common with each other.

While Janie had been living the fast-paced world of a corporate New York attorney, Abby had been a small-town homemaker. Where Janie was comfortable with facts and figures, Abby preferred flan and flowers. Really, they were an odd pair. A certain descriptive word flitted through Janie's head in regard to Abby. *Flaky.* She wasn't thinking about Abby's piecrusts.

At first Janie had attributed this flakiness to Abby's stress over her marital problems. Later on Janie figured that Abby was distracted by concern for Paul after his heart attack. Paul's recovery seemed to be coming along nicely, and yet Abby was still acting flaky. Not only that—though Janie might have been imagining this—it seemed that Abby was jealous of the work Janie was doing on the house. This made no sense; it was one of the main reasons Janie had partnered with Abby in the first place. She needed a place for her law practice. Now that her state license had finally been issued, she was ready to set up business.

It wasn't Janie's fault that Abby had been unable to make progress on her bed-and-breakfast. In fact, if anyone should have been aggravated, it was Janie. What if Abby's bed-and-breakfast idea fell by the wayside and Abby was unable to meet her financial obligations? Would Janie be stuck with a big old house and the mortgage to go with it?

Perhaps the most disturbing concern was their friendship. Would it survive a floundered partnership? Janie was well aware that partnerships between family and friends were often risky at best. Why hadn't she considered this before they bought the house?

She parked her silver Mercedes in front of the old Victorian home. Turning off the ignition, she looked up at the tall, stately house. This had been not only Abby's childhood home, but also the place where she and Paul raised their three daughters. Despite what was on paper, Janie knew that this house would always be more Abby's than hers. But at the moment, Janie had more finances invested. So, whether or not Abby did her part to turn the place into a flourishing bed-and-breakfast anytime soon, Janie intended to set up her law office. At least one of them would have some money coming in. She just hoped that Abby wouldn't let her down.

As she unlocked the front door, Janie felt guilty for these impatient thoughts. Perhaps she was being too hard on Abby. After all,

Abby had been through a lot these past few months. And Abby had helped with the renovations to Janie's home just a few months ago. Really, Janie needed to give her friend more time and patience. Patience was not Janie's strong suit.

"This isn't Manhattan," she said aloud as she closed the front door behind her. "It's okay not to move so fast in Clifden." Still, the idea of gearing down didn't come naturally to Janie. That was one big reason why Victor's influence was so beneficial to her, why she needed him. He knew how to take it easy.

Of course, thoughts of Victor took Janie back down the Abby trail again. Abby might be a bit mixed up in her facts, but she certainly couldn't have fabricated that entire story about Victor's ex-wife. Really, something had to be going on. The sooner Janie got to the bottom of it, the happier she'd be. She pulled out her phone and almost dialed his number, then stopped. No, it wasn't her style to be pushy. Some might call her old-fashioned, but she did not want to appear grasping or needy or even concerned. If something was going on with his ex-wife, she wanted Victor to be the one to initiate a conversation.

Janie puttered awhile in the basement. There wasn't much to be done until the drywall was finished. She looked at her watch. If she hurried to the fitness club, she could make it to the new Pilates class she'd seen advertised last week. Losing herself in exercise seemed highly preferable to fretting over Victor—or Abby.

* * *

"Hey, Janie, I didn't know you belonged to this club."

Janie turned to see Bonnie Boxwell at the opposite end of the dressing room. Dressed in sleek-looking navy sweats, Bonnie smiled as she placed a gym bag in a locker.

"Oh, hi." Janie waved at the younger woman. "Yes. I joined shortly after I moved to Clifden. I used to come in almost daily, partly for a workout, but even more to use the showers." She tossed a damp towel into the big canvas bin. "That was when my house renovation was still in progress and my bathroom was unusable."

Bonnie pulled her hair back with a headband. "I just joined last week." She patted her already slim waist. "With the holidays coming, I figured I'd get a head start."

"I know what you mean. My visits have been kind of sporadic. But I'd like to be more regular. I just did the Pilates class and it was really good."

"I've been doing the spin class."

"How's that?" Janie ran a brush through her shoulder-length hair.

Bonnie slapped her backside. "Painful at first, but it's getting better now."

Janie dropped her brush into her gym bag, zipped it, and hooked a strap over her shoulder, trying to think of a graceful way to end this conversation. It wasn't that she didn't like Bonnie. She did. It's just that she was well aware of Abby's feelings about the woman who once seemed to have attracted Paul's attention. "I guess I should get—"

"Do you mind if I ask you something before you leave?" Bonnie stepped in front of Janie, close enough that Janie could smell her perfume, an exotic spicy fragrance.

"Sure." Janie waited.

"I was wondering, how is Paul Franklin doing?"

Janie put on her best attorney smile, polite but cautiously cool. "He is recovering nicely."

Bonnie looked relieved. "Oh, I'm so glad to hear that. He is such a good man and a good friend, too. I wanted to call him, but then, well, I know that probably isn't the best thing. I realize his wife seems to have gotten, oh, you know … the wrong impression about me. But Paul and I have only been friends."

Janie shifted uncomfortably. Why was Bonnie sharing all this with her? "Well, I was just having coffee with Abby this morning, and Paul really does seem to be doing fine."

Bonnie smiled. "Good to know. You should come by the shop next week. I have a new shipment coming, and I have a feeling there might be a few interesting items that would be perfect for Victor's boat. You're still helping him with that project, right?"

"Yes." Janie nodded. "I'll make a note to stop by."

Bonnie's eyes lit up. "Maybe we could do coffee sometime. You know it's been a challenge making women friends in this town."

Janie felt the attorney smile again. "Yes. We should do coffee sometime."

Bonnie looked at the clock above the sinks. "Oh dear. I better get to spin class before they lock me out."

Janie felt guilty as she watched Bonnie's slender figure jogging down the hall toward her class. Janie felt badly for misleading her, especially after that vulnerable confession about needing friends. Really, Janie had no intention of becoming Bonnie's buddy. For one thing, Abby would throw a fit. And Marley and Caroline would probably back her on it.

To make matters worse, Janie suspected that Bonnie might be easier to get along with than Abby. As Janie got into her car, she was reminded of sixth grade, which was about the time the Four Lindas' friendships began to unravel. In some ways the circumstances hadn't been much different from this. "If you like me, you can't like her." So childish, so petty, so much like the situation between Abby and Bonnie. Wasn't it about time for everyone to grow up?

As Janie started her car, she wondered what would really happen if she befriended Bonnie Boxwell. Surely the world as they knew it would not come to a screeching halt. Yet even as she considered this, she knew it was a risk she was unwilling to take. Her friendships with Marley, Caroline, and Abby meant a lot to her, perhaps even more than her relationship with Victor, although it was hard to compare the two. Kind of like apples and oranges.

As she drove through the business section of town, Janie noticed city workers putting up flags along Main Street. It was an inspiring scene—stars and stripes rippling in the sunlight, lined up like soldiers at attention. But it was early November, the wrong time of year for the Fourth of July parade. Then she remembered: It would be Veterans Day next week. She was reminded of her father, and of the old war medals she'd found hidden in a drawer.

Janie wasn't sure what to do or how she would do it, but she was still determined to do something special to honor her father's memory. Perhaps Veterans Day would present this opportunity. As she pulled into the Safeway parking lot, her phone began to ring. Seeing it was Victor, she answered eagerly.

"What are you up to right now?" he asked.

"I was about to get some groceries. Why?"

"Have you had lunch yet?"

"No."

"Want to meet me at The Lighthouse?"

"As a matter of fact, I would."

"Ten minutes?"

"You got it."

Janie felt a slight rush of nerves as she drove toward the restaurant. Suddenly she was extremely curious. What was going on with Victor and his ex? Was he about to tell her? If Abby had gotten her facts straight—if his ex really did want to reconcile—what would Victor's reaction be?

Victor had been trying to live a godly life. He made no secret of that from the beginning of their relationship. In fact the strength of his faith sometimes challenged her own. Oh, she believed in God, and she felt like she'd been evolving spiritually, but Victor's level of spiritual maturity seemed a lot higher than hers.

"Just breathe," she told herself as she parked in front of the restaurant. She turned off her car, pulled down the rearview mirror and quickly touched up her lip gloss, fluffed her hair, and decided to simply hope for the best. Whatever would be, would be.

Victor was waiting for her in the foyer, but she could tell by his expression that he was uneasy. Like usual, though, he greeted her with a hug and a kiss on the cheek. "Sorry to be so last minute," he said as they were seated. "But I wanted to talk to you about something. Just as I called you, I realized not only had I skipped breakfast, but I forgot to eat lunch, too."

She smiled. "Works for me. I'm starving too." Even as she said this, she wondered if she'd be able to eat.

After they ordered, Victor put his elbows on the table and leaned forward, looking intently into her eyes. "Something a bit unusual has come up, Janie."

She felt the attorney smile coming on again, but she simply nodded. "Yes?"

"I can't remember if I mentioned to you that my ex-wife called a couple of weeks ago."

"I don't recall you saying anything." She waited.

"Well, it caught me totally by surprise at the time. She told me that she and Larry had parted ways."

"Oh?"

He nodded. "To be honest, I wasn't that surprised by that."

"Why?"

"Well, Larry was unfaithful to his first two wives. I guess I just figured history might repeat itself."

"So that's why they split up?"

Victor slowly shook his head. "Not exactly. Oh, I'm sure that had something to do with it, but there's more to this story."

Janie fiddled with the napkin in her lap and waited.

"Donna has had some kind of a spiritual awakening." Victor paused as if he was still trying to wrap his head around this. "She recommitted her heart to God."

"That's wonderful." Janie could hear the false ring in her voice.

"Yes. It really is wonderful." He smiled.

There was a long pause, and Janie was tempted to confess what Abby had told them this morning. Still, she couldn't bring herself to do it. *Let Victor do this in his own way and his own time.*

"Now I'm at the really weird part, Janie."

The waitress was putting their food in front of them now. Janie was thankful she'd ordered only the chowder. Hopefully she'd be able to get down a few bites. She took in a slow, deep breath as Victor bowed his head and said a short blessing. Then Janie picked up her spoon and dipped it into the soup. They both took a few bites, and then Janie decided to cut to the chase. "You mentioned something was weird," she prompted. "Right before our food came."

"Oh. Yes." He wiped his mouth with his napkin, then looked evenly at her. "The really weird part is that after Donna's reawakening, she read a book and talked to some spiritual adviser. Yesterday Donna called me." He let out a slow sigh. "Somehow she's gotten it into her head that God wants her to get back together with me."

Janie pressed her lips together, cocking her head slightly to one side and studying him closely. "How do you feel about that?"

He chuckled. "Well, besides being totally shocked?"

She looked down at her soup, slowly dipping her spoon again.

"I don't know," he said quietly. "I mean, I guess I'm still in shock."

Janie wanted to challenge him to define exactly what kind of shock he was experiencing. Was it the negative sort of shock, like someone had just pulled the floor out from beneath him (kind of how she felt right now)? Or was it the positive type of shock, like he'd just won the lottery?

"It's just so crazy," he continued. "I didn't even know how to react to her."

"I can understand that."

"It's such a bizarre situation." He shook his head. "I don't know how to react. I honestly am in shock."

Janie desperately wanted to ask Victor if he still loved his ex-wife. She really needed to know the answer, but she could not force that question past her lips. She couldn't force another bite of soup past her lips either. So she just sat there.

"I can see I've shocked you with this too," he admitted. "But I felt it was only fair to let you know, Janie."

"I appreciate that." She dabbed her mouth with the napkin.

"I told Donna that I felt blindsided. If God truly wanted her to get together with me, it seems like he would've let me in on the plan too."

"Good point." Janie put her hands in her lap, tightly clasping them together beneath the table.

"But Donna said she knew that God was going to show me the same thing, in time."

"Interesting."

He shrugged. "Interesting … in a freaky, psychotic, obsessed sort of way."

Another forced attorney smile.

"It gets weirder, Janie."

She watched him closely. "How so?"

"Donna plans to come out here."

"To Clifden?" She tried to look surprised, although this is exactly what Abby had said. He nodded. "To visit you?"

"More than just visit. Donna said God told her she needs to live here."

"*Live* here? Here in Clifden?" No faking it—she really was surprised now.

"Yes."

Janie reached for her water, took a small sip, and slowly swallowed. "Wow."

"Yeah. Wow."

"That's pretty intense, Victor."

"I know. I can tell it's troubling you, Janie. I'm sorry. I felt you needed to hear it … from me. But I don't want to upset you."

She took in a careful breath. "I don't think I'm upset. I mean, it's not your fault. Naturally I'm curious about it. And I won't deny that it's extremely weird."

"So you're okay with it?" He looked earnestly into her eyes. "All this nuttiness isn't putting you off?"

"Don't worry. I'm fine." Her smile felt almost real now. It seemed clear that he was concerned about her, that he still cared for her. Perhaps her initial reaction was overblown. After all, how could she hold Victor responsible for his ex-wife's neurotic behavior? What more could he do than what he was doing?

He sighed. "I'm so relieved that you understand."

Now Janie wasn't so sure that she really did *understand*. But she would do everything in her power to try to understand, and she would do everything in her power to hold on to Victor as well.

"When does Donna plan to come?" She tried to make her voice sound relaxed and natural.

He cleared his throat. "Next week."

A rush of panic surged through her. "Next week." She nodded, trying to act as if this was no big deal.

He nodded. "Two things you should know about Donna," he said slowly.

"Yes?"

He held up one finger. "She is very spontaneous."

That seemed fairly obvious. "And?"

He held up a second finger. "And she likes to speak her mind."

Janie considered this, then shrugged. "That's not a bad trait."

Victor laughed uncomfortably. "Well, not usually."

She smiled directly at him now. "I have a hard time believing you could've been married to anyone who wasn't a good person, Victor."

He sighed. "Yes, Donna is a good person. Just a bit unpredictable."

"I can't wait to meet her." And that was the truth. Janie was very curious to meet this spontaneous, unpredictable, outspoken woman. Who knew? Perhaps Janie might even like her. What would be wrong with that?

Chapter 3

CAROLINE

Certain that her mom was asleep, Caroline tiptoed from the bedroom and partially closed the door. Then, with the baby monitor in hand, she got Chuck's ball and took him outside to the front yard. Despite the dark clouds that threatened rain, she wished she had the freedom to take her dog to the beach. There they would run and run, even in the pouring rain, until they both grew exhausted. But that was a luxury she could not afford.

"You need to seriously consider putting her into a care facility now," the social worker, Beverly, had told Caroline that afternoon during their bimonthly appointment. "She's going down quickly now."

Caroline had not attempted to dispute this. Beverly's evaluation was not positive.

"The hospice nurse is concerned for her safety too, Caroline." Beverly placed a hand on Caroline's shoulder. "I know you're trying hard, but your mother needs more than you can give. You need to let her move onto the next stage of care."

"But the hospice nurse has only been here twice," Caroline pointed out. "And both times my mom was having a pretty bad day. It's not always like that."

"I know. But a bad day can lead to a bad fall, and then she'll need to go into residential care anyway. Wouldn't you rather be a step ahead rather than forced by an emergency into a hasty decision?"

Caroline considered this. "I guess that makes sense."

"I know you don't care for Mulberry Manor." Beverly handed Caroline a printed page. "Here are some other facilities in the area. I highlighted the ones I think would be most suitable."

Caroline studied the list, noticing that the highlighted ones weren't even in town. "Newport is a long drive from here," she said.

Beverly nodded. "I realize that. But it's a very good facility."

Caroline's mom let out a groan from her recliner, followed by a cry for help. "I'll think about this," Caroline had told Beverly as she went to see what her mom needed. "I'll read up on these places and try to figure things out."

"Good for you." Beverly had reached for her purse. "I know it's not easy, but it will be for the best." Then she said good-bye, and Caroline spent the next hour tending to her mom's toileting needs. After her mom was cleaned up, she picked at her dinner and eventually was put into bed.

Caroline felt a strange mixture of exhaustion and a kind of trapped, manic anxiety. She threw the ball to Chuck again, wishing she never had to go back into that house. It was like her prison, her torture chamber.

"Hey, you!" a woman called out. Caroline turned to see Janie walking down the street toward her. She looked neat and stylish in her jeans, boots, and suede jacket, complete with a silk scarf. Caroline tried not to think about her grungy sweats and haphazard ponytail. Instead she waved and waited for Janie to join her and the dog.

"Hey, Chuck." Janie leaned over and gave his head a rub. "Looks like you're getting your exercise too."

Caroline gave the ball another toss. "At least one of us will be in shape."

"How are you doing?" Janie peered curiously at Caroline.

"I'm okay I guess."

"You seem a little down."

Chuck bounded back, dropping the soggy ball at Caroline's feet. She threw it again, then turned back to Janie. "I am down."

"Need to talk?"

Caroline considered the raggedy appearance of her living room right now, mentally comparing it to Janie's chic, remodeled home only a few blocks away. What difference did it make? Janie had seen this place before. Besides, the house was Caroline's mom's, not Caroline's. "I'd love to talk," Caroline admitted.

"Me, too." Janie glanced up at the sky, which was quickly growing dusky. "But maybe I should run home and get my car. I can't believe how early it's getting dark now."

"Okay." Caroline nodded eagerly. At least this would give her a chance to pick up a few things, hide the diaper-changing kit, and maybe even make some tea.

"Have you had dinner yet?"

Caroline shook her head. "I have some Lean Cuisine meals in the freezer if you're interested."

"How about if I bring something over?"

"Oh, Janie, that'd be fantastic."

Janie smiled. "I'll be back in about an hour, okay?"

"I can't wait!"

They parted ways and Caroline took Chuck back into the house and quickly began to clean up. Thursday was always her hardest day. She had no caregiver or hospice nurse visits on Thursdays, and today had been further complicated by Beverly's visit. The place was a mess. But within the hour she made some improvements and even changed into some clean sweats and smoothed out her ponytail. Small victory. Her mom was still sleeping soundly, so Caroline closed the bedroom door to help cover the sound of their conversation and kept the baby monitor handy.

Janie brought Chinese food. "I wasn't sure what to get," she said as she began piling the white bags and boxes on the kitchen table. "So I just got an assortment."

"This is perfect." Caroline handed Janie a plate and soon they were feasting on egg rolls, broccoli and beef, sweet-and-sour pork, fried rice, and some other tasty things.

Caroline told Janie about Beverly's recommendation. "It's not that I love taking care of Mom," she admitted, "but I'd feel guilty for making her leave her own home."

"That must be hard."

Caroline looked around the cluttered kitchen. "This place isn't much, but it's all she's known for more than fifty years. It seems cruel to take it from her."

"Do you think she's cognizant enough to know the difference?" Janie asked gently. "I mean, if she were moved, would she even notice?"

Caroline shrugged. "Good question. Most of the time she seems pretty out of touch and confused, kind of lost in a fragmented time warp. But she occasionally has moments of clarity, and I know it's a comfort for her to see familiar things."

"But the social worker thinks she might be at risk?" Janie pressed.

Caroline nodded.

"That's a hard call." Janie took a piece of egg roll. "I don't envy you."

"If I were in my mom's shoes," Caroline said carefully, "I think I'd rather be allowed to stay in my own home. Seriously, even if I was at risk of falling, at least I'd be on my own turf. I really don't see what's wrong with allowing the elderly to spend their last days in their own homes. I mean, wasn't that what they did in the old days?"

"I guess so, although people might not have lived as long back then."

"Sometimes I wonder if caring for the elderly isn't turning into some big business scam. You force people into care, then keep them alive for as long as you need a bed filled. But who foots the bill?" Caroline used her chopsticks to pick up a spare rib.

"I do know it's not helping the national deficit."

"Okay, that's enough about me and my mom, Janie. I'll figure it out eventually." Caroline forced a smile. "What I want to know is what is up with you and Victor. I've been thinking for a couple of days now about what Abby said. Was there any truth to it, or is our Abby losing it?"

Janie made what sounded like an uncomfortable laugh. "Actually Abby was spot-on."

"Seriously?"

"In fact I should call her and let her know she was right after all."

"So Victor's ex is really coming here to Clifden? To get back with him?"

"That's what she told him." Janie filled in Caroline on the wild details.

"How do you feel about it?" Caroline studied Janie.

"I'm not sure. Mostly I'm curious to see what she's like."

"How is Victor taking it?"

Janie shrugged. "I think he's waiting to see how it goes."

"Wow." Caroline put her chopsticks down. "That's crazy."

"And a little unnerving."

"How about some tea?" Caroline stood and pulled out her tea tin. "I have green and jasmine and—"

"Jasmine sounds lovely."

Now Caroline reached behind the stove, struggling to plug it back into the outlet.

"What are you doing back there?"

"I keep the stove unplugged," she explained. "Safety issue." She filled up the tea kettle and set it on the burner. "I could nuke it, but for some reason I think tea is better when you heat the water the old-fashioned way."

"Right." Janie put some more fried rice on her plate. "So anyway, I've been coming to grips with the possibility that things could end between me and Victor."

"Really?" Caroline shook some loose tea into the teapot. "Do you seriously think he'd get back together with his ex?"

"I honestly hope not. It's not as if I'm giving up on him. I'm not.

But I have to be honest with myself. He and Donna were married for a fairly long time."

"Yes, but Victor really loves you, Janie. Everyone can see that." Caroline put a pair of china teacups and saucers on the table. These were from a set her grandmother once used. Now Caroline kept them safely tucked away on a high shelf.

"But keep in mind, Donna's the one who left the marriage. Victor hasn't really said so, but I'm relatively sure that she broke his heart. Plus they have two sons together, and a history. That's something to think about."

The whistling of the tea kettle made Caroline jump. She quickly turned it off, poured the steaming water over the loose leaves, then set the china teapot on the table. "Even so, Victor seems to have moved on. He has never struck me as the kind of guy who's pining away for his ex. He's happy with his life."

"I thought so too."

Using a tea strainer, Caroline filled the cups with the sweet-smelling amber tea. "I remember Victor saying how he and his wife were so different. It sounded like they were incompatible. He wanted a simple life, but she wanted all the bells and whistles. It seemed like the breakup was pretty mutual."

"Maybe." Janie took a sip of tea. "Mmm. This is good."

"So even if Victor's crazy ex-wife does want him back, I honestly don't think you need to be worried, Janie."

"I'm trying not to be, but I'm also trying to be realistic." Janie sighed. "Last night I had this dream: Phil showed up, and he was asking me to come back to him. I was so happy to see him, except that I knew he was dead. I was so confused."

"But that's different." Caroline put some more beef and broccoli on her plate, trying to think of a gentle way to say this. "Phil's gone, Janie. He can't come back."

"I know. I'm not saying it was rational, but I couldn't go to sleep after that. I kept wondering what I would do if Phil really did come back. What if I had to choose between him and Victor?" Janie looked close to tears.

"That's not going to happen." Caroline patted Janie's hand. "You shouldn't even think about something like that. It could drive you bonkers."

"But maybe that's how Victor feels right now. I mean I honestly don't know what I'd do if Phil were alive and I had to choose between those two men. I love them both. It feels terrible to admit that out loud. It seems like I'm betraying Phil. And then there's Victor."

"That's not going to happen," Caroline repeated. She felt slightly over her head. "It's impossible. You know that Phil is never coming back, and I'm sure he would want you to be happy."

Janie made a weak smile. "You probably think I'm losing my mind."

Caroline chuckled. "Hey, welcome to my life. When it comes to insanity issues, I'm becoming quite the expert."

"It's just that I'm trying to understand Victor's perspective."

"Then you should keep in mind that he loves you, Janie."

"I think he does."

"Victor is one of the good guys." Back before Victor and Janie were together, Caroline had entertained ideas of pairing up with him herself, not that he'd been particularly interested. But he'd been a good friend, supportive and honest and kind. It didn't take long for

Caroline to figure things out. She suspected he'd fallen for Janie the first day their paths crossed last summer—maybe even before that. "He won't let you down."

"But he might not want to let his wife down either."

Caroline didn't know what to say. "Hey, I've got some good raspberry sorbet if you're interested in a little dessert."

Janie grinned. "Sounds yummy. I could excuse a little indulgence since I had a lot of exercise today."

Caroline let out a little groan. Her favorite jeans had felt a bit tight this morning. The only kind of exercise she got nowadays was straining her back as she helped her mom in and out of things. "I wish I could say the same."

"So enough about Victor and me," Janie said as they took their sorbet and tea into the cluttered, lackluster living room. "How are things going with Mitch?"

"Same old, same old." Caroline sat in the easy chair opposite the sofa. "He was barely back from Italy and he had to head out to Singapore. He's supposed to be back next weekend, but then he leaves again. I'm not even sure where to this time."

"He really racks up those frequent flyer miles."

Caroline took a sip of tea. "It's because Dale, his partner, has a wife and kids, so Mitch gets stuck with most of the traveling."

"Will it always be like that?"

Caroline frowned. "I'm not sure."

"At least you're used to being independent. I mean, you've been single for most of your life."

"I guess." Caroline didn't want to admit that she'd never really liked being independent. She'd always dreamed of having a happy marriage with a guy who enjoyed being with her, enjoying beach walks, snuggling by a fireplace, watching old movies, taking fun vacations. She knew she probably sounded like a singles ad, but it was true. "I'm not saying I don't still want some of my independence, but it would be nice to have someone to grow old with."

Janie chuckled. "I hear you. At least we have the Lindas. Our girlfriends might be worth more than having a guy around anyway."

Caroline knew that if she could have her way, she would opt for both. She didn't know what she'd do without her girlfriends. How many times had the other Lindas come to her aid in the past few months? She held up her teacup in a toast. "Here's to the lasting friendships of a few good women."

"A few good women by the name of Linda." Janie held up her cup.

They sat there quietly for a couple of minutes. Caroline suspected they were both thinking about their guys and wondering what was going to come of the relationships.

"What if you put your mom in a nursing home," Janie said suddenly, "and you and Mitch got married?"

"Huh?" Caroline was caught off guard. "Well, he's not exactly proposing to me at the moment."

"But that might have to do with your mom, right? He knows you're kind of tied down."

Caroline considered this. Mitch had asked her to come with him to Italy last month. He'd also asked her to consider relocating to California to be near him. She supposed that was almost the same as a proposal. "I suppose you could be right."

"So if you your mom was in a good facility, do you think he'd propose?"

"Possibly."

"If you got married, and you didn't need to care for your mom, wouldn't you be free to travel with Mitch?"

Caroline nodded. "Well, yes."

"I've heard you say you want to travel."

Caroline frowned. "Sounds like you're trying to get rid of me."

Janie laughed. "Not at all. Selfishly I would make you stay right here in Clifden, but I can tell you're bummed about Mitch—and your mom. I'm just thinking there might be a light at the end of your tunnel."

Caroline thought hard about this. "You know what you said about your dream, Janie? About having to choose?"

"Yes." Janie set down her empty sorbet cup.

"I guess that's how I feel right now. I don't want to be forced to choose between my mom and Mitch. I mean, obviously my mom is a handful. But she *is* my mom, and I know she needs me. I'm all she has."

"What about Michael?"

Caroline grimaced to think of her MIA brother. On one hand she should probably try to reach him and give him an update. On the other hand he had the potential to make a difficult situation a whole lot worse.

"Do you ever hear from him? Does he take *any* responsibility for your mother?"

"The less we see of Michael, the better off we'll all be."

"But it's a heavy load for you to carry alone, Caroline."

"I know, but Mom won't be around forever. And in a weird way I've gotten close to her these past few months. You know, sometimes—like a couple days ago—she looks at me and I can tell that she knows me. There's this little spark of recognition and a tiny bit of a smile, and I'm just not ready to give that up yet."

Janie nodded. "You're a good daughter."

"Or a crazy one." Caroline picked up the baby monitor and listened. "Like I said, welcome to my world. Crazy kind of reigns around here."

===Chapter 4===

MARLEY

Friday morning the sun came out, and by noon the temperature climbed into the upper sixties, so Marley decided to take her paints and canvas outside.

"Hello, neighbor," Doris called from her bungalow next door. Doris was Abby's mother and a fellow artist. "What do you think of this delightful weather?"

"I love it." Marley set down her brush and went over to where Doris was watering her geraniums. "If this is global warming, I say bring it."

Doris laughed. "Sometimes we get days like this in the middle of winter."

"That works for me."

"So how's the painting coming?"

"Okay, I think." Marley glanced over to be sure her canvas was out of the wind. Despite the warmer temperatures, gusts still popped up sometimes.

"I don't know why I can't get more into art these days," Doris said.

"What's stopping you?"

Doris shrugged, tucking a strand of gray hair beneath her nylon sun hat. "I just haven't had the desire lately. Maybe by winter when I'm stuck indoors."

"You know, you were part of my inspiration for moving next door," Marley admitted.

Doris looked surprised. "You wanted to be like Abby's nutty old mother? The eccentric woman who lives like a beatnik on the beach?"

"Sounded good to me."

Doris laughed. "When's your birthday, Marley? Is it possible that you and Abby got switched at birth?"

Marley laughed. "Speaking of Abby, I've been a little worried about her." Marley had talked to Abby that morning, and the woman sounded just as tired and sleep deprived as before. When Marley asked about the Ambien, Abby changed the subject.

"You and me both." Doris set down her watering can, then eased herself onto a wooden deck chair, nodding to the chair next to her. Marley sat down too. "Abby is not herself these days."

"She's so worried about Paul's health that it seems like she's neglecting her own," Marley said.

"I know." Doris shook her head. "She's neglecting her business, too."

"You mean the bed-and-breakfast?"

"Yes." Doris exhaled loudly. "That was her big dream. She was so excited about it, but now it all seems to be falling by the wayside."

"It's like she doesn't even care about it anymore."

Doris rubbed her hands on the arms of the chair. "I wonder if

Abby realizes that she could be putting the bed-and-breakfast in financial jeopardy by not jumping on the opportunity right away."

"Oh dear. I hadn't really considered that."

"Well, if she doesn't get it up and running, and start bringing in some income, I don't see how she'll be able to stay current on her payments. Don't say you heard it from me, but that could put some serious pressure on her friendship with Janie. Partnerships between friends are tricky."

Marley thought back to the little rift between Janie and Abby on Tuesday. Perhaps the strain involved more than Abby's exhaustion. "I wonder if there's anything we can do to help Abby?"

"You mean besides slipping her a Mickey so she can get a good night's sleep?"

Marley chuckled. "That's a thought. Maybe I should show up tonight with a pitcher of margaritas and slip in one of her sleeping pills."

"Oh, I don't like the idea of mixing alcohol and drugs." Doris firmly shook her head.

"Just kidding."

"I've offered to spend the night at the house with her," Doris said sadly, "but Abby says unless I sleep with Paul, it's useless."

Marley snickered. "I'm sure Paul would just love that."

"Yes. You know how Paul and I get along."

"Maybe she should hire a nurse," Marley suggested.

"Can you imagine Paul agreeing to that?"

"Not really." Marley knew how stubborn Paul could be.

"I can't even blame him. If Abby treated me like that, all that hovering and concern, I'd tell her to go home. She's constantly nagging him to eat this and not that, and pestering him to walk with her on the beach. Why, I'm almost feeling sorry for the poor man."

"Maybe she needs some kind of a support group," Marley suggested.

"Or just a good night's rest."

"Or maybe an intervention."

Doris looked at Marley hopefully. "Yes, an intervention would be wonderful. Maybe you and the other Lindas could do something to help her. I think she'd listen to you—more than she listens to her old mother anyway."

"Well, it's worth a try. I'll call the others and see what we can do."

By the end of the day, Marley realized that an intervention with all the Lindas was simply not going to happen. Caroline didn't have anyone to watch her mother, and Janie had already committed to spending the evening with Victor. "I'd help you," Janie said apologetically, "but it's our last chance to be together before his ex-wife arrives tomorrow."

"So Abby wasn't just delusional?"

"No. Abby had her facts straight. Please tell her I will be there in spirit tonight. I back you 100 percent, Marley. Let me know if there's anything I can do later to help her."

So Marley went solo. She showed up at Abby and Paul's doorstep unannounced at eight o'clock. "Sorry to intrude," she told Paul.

"Is something wrong?" he asked with concerned eyes.

Marley wrinkled her nose at him. "Yeah, with your wife."

He looked confused.

"Abby is desperately in need of sleep," Marley stated as she pushed past him. "I am here to help."

Paul actually laughed. "Good luck with that."

"This was supposed to be a full-fledged intervention with all the Lindas present, but I'm the only one available."

Paul glanced over his shoulder. "Hey, it's not that I don't appreciate this or agree that Abby needs help, but how do you plan to do this little intervention of one?"

"I have a plan." She made a sheepish grin. "But it will require your full cooperation, okay?"

He shrugged. "Sure, whatever."

Abby emerged from the kitchen. "What are you doing here?" she asked Marley. Her eyes had dark shadows beneath them, and her slippers were shuffling.

"This is an intervention," Marley said with authority. "I'm here to ensure you get a good night's sleep, Abby Franklin. Caroline and Janie and your mother are all backing me, but they can't be here."

Abby made a lopsided smile. "Uh, right. What exactly did you have in mind?"

"Well, you have that lounge in your bedroom, and I plan to camp there tonight while you and Paul both sleep."

"Seriously?" Abby looked skeptical.

Marley held up a small white bottle. "To start with, you'll take two of these."

"What's that?"

"Valerian. It's an herb."

Abby frowned. "You mean those little pink flowers?"

"Exactly. I use it myself sometimes. It will help you relax."

"Okay." Abby nodded slowly.

Marley didn't mention that she also planned to make Abby take her Ambien tonight. One step at a time. "But first you're going to have a nice little bowl of cereal and milk." Marley pointed her back toward the kitchen, and Abby didn't resist as Marley fixed a small bowl of Cheerios, then watched Abby eat them.

"Now I realize it's only nine"—Marley glanced over to where Paul was sitting in the living room—"but I want you to go to bed now. I will keep an eye on Paul until he goes to bed."

"And then?"

"And then, like I said, I'll stay on the lounge chair."

"But what if you go to sleep?"

"I've been drinking coffee all afternoon, Abby. Trust me, I will not be going to sleep tonight." Marley took Abby by the arm and led her to her bedroom, then proceeded to help her friend get ready for bed.

"I feel like a three-year-old," Abby confessed after Marley reminded her to brush her teeth.

"That's what happens when you don't get your rest," Marley said as she handed a glass of water and the Ambien to Abby.

Abby looked slightly dubious, but like a good girl, she put it in her mouth and washed it down with the water. "Are you going to tell me a bedtime story?" she asked in a tired voice.

"Maybe." Marley pointed to the king-sized bed, where she'd already turned back the comforter. She waited for Abby to climb in, then leaned down and kissed her good night on the forehead. Then she turned off the light and sat in the lounge chair.

"No story?" Abby asked sleepily.

Marley did her best to tell a rather strange version of *The Three Bears*, but before the bears ever made it upstairs to discover Goldilocks, Abby was sleeping soundly. Marley tiptoed from the room and went to check on Paul.

"I see you haven't died yet," she said wryly.

He rolled his eyes. "Not yet."

"I know she's only doing it because she loves you." Marley sat down in one of the club chairs and sighed loudly. "But it must be driving you nuts."

"You got that right."

"Then you'll be happy to know she's asleep."

"You got her to take the sleeping pills?" Paul looked surprised.

"I did."

"And they really worked?"

"She's snoozing like a baby."

"So you can go home then, right?"

Marley shook her head. "Nope. I promised Abby I'd stay and make sure you don't kick the bucket in your sleep, and that's what I'm going to do."

Paul looked disappointed. "You're as bad as she is."

"We'll hope this won't become a permanent arrangement."

Paul gave her a sly look now. "Some guys would be envious of me, sleeping with two women."

"I don't plan to do any sleeping."

He just laughed.

"And I don't plan to get in bed with you either."

He feigned disappointment.

She adjusted her glasses and frowned. "You're not even my type."

He made a face at her. "Same back at you. In fact it would be like sleeping with my mother-in-law."

Now she laughed. "Thanks. I'll take that as a compliment."

They bantered for a bit, and by the time Paul decided to turn in for bed, Marley thought that she didn't dislike him as much as she used to. Oh, he was a bit obnoxious and slightly chauvinistic, but on some levels he was okay. Really, he wasn't quite the ogre that she used to imagine him to be.

As he was heading for his bedroom, she told him she'd give him thirty minutes to get ready for bed. "Then I'm coming in," she warned. However, she waited for more like forty minutes, and by the time she slipped back into their room, it sounded as if both Paul and Abby were soundly sleeping.

She made herself comfortable on the lounge. As she pulled a throw up over her legs, she couldn't help but feel this whole setup was a bit ridiculous. What people did for their friends! She was tired herself, but thanks to all that caffeine, she was not very sleepy. She decided to use this time to pray for Abby and Paul, as well as for all their kids and granddaughter, Lucy. Praying was still new to Marley. The idea that she could converse with the God of the universe and he would listen was truly amazing! After that she prayed for the other Lindas. And finally she prayed for her son, Ashton, and then for her good friend Jack and his family.

She wasn't sure what time it was when she felt herself slipping into slumber, but she knew it was hopeless to fight it.

Still, she was thankful to wake up before Abby. It appeared that Paul was already up—hopefully not off having a heart attack. She'd read somewhere that most heart attacks happened in the early morning. Feeling a tiny bit anxious, she tiptoed over to see that the master bathroom was unoccupied. Then she went out to the kitchen and found him quietly making coffee.

"Sleep good?" he asked as he filled the carafe with water.

"Please don't tell Abby," she pleaded.

He winked. "Our secret."

"Abby's still sound asleep."

"Hopefully she'll sleep in for a while." Paul turned on the coffeemaker. "Don't tell her, but I'm heading over to the golf course."

Marley frowned. "I thought you weren't supposed to do anything strenuous for six weeks."

"I'm just going to do a little putting. Don't worry."

"I won't, but Abby will."

"Tell her she can come and check on me."

"Well, I know you're supposed to get some mild exercise," she conceded. "But just don't overdo it, okay? I don't want Abby thinking I let her down."

"Abby can't control me." He poured a mug of coffee, offering it to her.

"Thanks." She took it.

He smiled as he filled another mug. "Thank you, Marley. I really do appreciate your help in getting the old girl to sleep."

"Hopefully she won't need any more help tonight, but if she does, I have a plan."

He looked a bit concerned. "You're coming back here again?"

"Not me. But I'll send Janie."

He took a sip of coffee. "Maybe after a good night's sleep she'll come back to her senses and realize that I'm perfectly fine without her round-the-clock supervision."

"I hope so. Besides, she needs to start focusing on her business. Doris pointed out that Abby has to make her payments on the inn, and the sooner she gets some money coming in, the better her chances of succeeding."

"That blasted bed-and-breakfast." He set his mug down onto the countertop with a clank. "I wish she'd never gotten it into her mind to do that. I can't imagine how she's going to make it work."

Marley's feelings on Abby's business venture weren't much different from Paul's, but she wasn't about to admit it. She was Abby's friend, which meant believing in her dreams, supporting her endeavors, and—when Abby was in need—stretching out hands to help.

"I'll hang around until Abby wakes up," Marley told Paul as he slipped out to the garage. She didn't mention that she'd probably catch a few more winks herself. But as soon as she heard his car pulling out, she climbed into the still-warm bed next to Abby and within minutes was asleep again.

Chapter 5

ABBY

By midmorning Sunday Abby felt almost normal. She also felt somewhat embarrassed. "I really appreciate how you and Marley helped me get some sleep," she told Janie as they sat in Abby's breakfast nook overlooking the beach. "I realize how badly I needed an intervention, but really, I'll be okay from here on out. No one needs to babysit Paul and me again tonight."

"That's right," Paul called out. He was sitting in front of the big-screen TV in the great room.

"You'll promise to take a sleeping pill if necessary?" Janie asked.

Abby held up three fingers, Girl Scout Promise style. "I give you my word."

"Okay then." Janie nodded, then took a sip of her coffee.

Abby stretched her arms up over her head and took in a deep breath. "I can't believe how much better I feel after getting two good nights of sleep." She looked out to where the sun was glistening on the rolling waves. "Good enough to go for a nice long walk this morning."

"A beach walk sounds good to me, too." Janie set down her coffee cup.

"How about you, Paul?" Abby called out hopefully.

"Not right now, honey," he replied in an automated way.

Abby made a face. "That's what he always says." She lowered her voice. "His cardiologist told him to walk or do light exercise about thirty minutes every day to help his recovery."

Janie frowned. "And he's not doing it?"

"Not regularly."

Janie stood now, strolling into the living room, where she casually shook her finger at Paul. Abby watched in wonder. Was it possible that Janie could get through to him when Abby could not?

"Paul Franklin!" Janie used a lightly scolding tone. "You need to get up and get moving, old man."

He glanced at her with surprise, then tossed a warning look in Abby's direction. "You two ganging up on me or something?"

"That's right," Janie told him. "Come take a walk with us, Paul. It's a beautiful day out there, and you could use some fresh air."

He made a pout. "But I'm really into this Green Bay game right now."

"You can TiVo it and watch it later," Abby said firmly.

He let out a low groan. "Give me a break, ladies, the game's tied and the Packers are about to score. Come on, Sunday's supposed to be a day of rest."

"Oh, Paul!" Abby scowled at him. "How will you possibly get well if you don't follow the doctor's instructions?" She turned to Janie. "See what I'm up against? See why I can't sleep at night?"

"Lighten up, Abby," Paul grumbled.

"I'm just trying to hel—"

"If you want to help, quit treating me like a child!" He turned up the volume on the TV.

"Quit *acting* like a child!"

"Hey, guys, guys." Janie formed her forefingers into a *T* shape. "Time-out. Really, this isn't worth fighting over."

Abby balled her hands into fists. "Well, at least you can see what I have to deal with, Janie—why I get so frustrated. It's like he doesn't even care, like he wants to just die or something."

"Oh, Abby, don't be such a drama queen." Paul stood and looked at her, softening his tone a bit as he continued. "I just want to watch this game, honey. If you leave me alone, I promise I'll get some exercise as soon as it ends. Just lay off me for now. Okay?"

Abby rolled her eyes. "Yeah, yeah, that's what you always say. It's always 'later,' but later hardly ever comes. You need some exercise, Paul. We both do."

"Hey, you guys should join the fitness club," Janie said. "They've got some great new classes starting up. And with winter coming, it would be a good way to get a workout regardless of the weather."

Abby grimaced. The idea of joining the fitness club was not the least bit appealing to her. She'd rather go beat her head against a brick wall. Oh, she'd gone in there once to check out the facility during one of its open houses, but she'd taken one look at all those young, thin, fit, scantily clad bodies and practically had a tizzy fit. No way was she going to strut her out-of-shape, fifty-something, flabby old self around that body shop.

"You know, I've been thinking about joining the club," Paul said.

"In fact one of my golf buddies gave me a free pass to try it out for a week."

"You should use it," Janie encouraged him. "Even if you just did the treadmill for thirty minutes a day, it would be better than sitting in front of the TV. Besides, they have TVs there, so you can catch up on CNN if you like. Plus, if you join the club, they'll give you a free consultation with a personal trainer who can set up an appropriate program for you. They coordinate with physical therapists and doctors. Really, Paul, it would be good for you." She turned to Abby. "And you, too."

Abby firmly shook her head. "Thanks, but no thanks. I'll get my exercise on the beach."

"What about when the weather's bad?"

Abby shrugged. "I don't mind walking in the rain."

Paul laughed like this was hilarious. "Yeah, right. That'll happen."

"I *do* walk in the rain sometimes," Abby defended. "I have a waterproof parka and rubber boots and—"

"Oh sure, Abby." Paul's tone was skeptical. "You're always out there walking in the rain. A regular duck."

Abby scowled, repressing the urge to pick up his newspaper and smack him on the top of his balding head.

He just grinned at her. "Come on, Absters, if I'm willing to join the fitness club, why won't you?"

Abby considered this. "I'll make you a deal, Paul. You take that free pass, and if you go steady for one week, I'll promise to look into it too. Okay?" She knew she was stepping out on a limb, but if this would get Paul to exercise, so be it. Besides, she only promised to "look into it," not to join. She had absolutely no intention of doing that!

"Okay, it's a deal." He reached out and shook her hand. "But we have a witness. You heard her, Janie."

Janie grinned. "I did. And I think it's a great idea for both of you."

"Now if you'll excuse us." Abby turned away from her couch-potato husband and went for her jacket. "We will go out and take pleasure in the fresh sea air and sunshine as we walk on the beautiful beach where our lifetime membership is already *paid in full.*"

"Enjoy!" he called out.

"We will!" she shot back. "Come on, Janie."

Janie laughed as they went outside. "Do you guys always talk like that to each other?"

"Actually I'd been trying very hard to be Miss Congeniality lately," Abby admitted. "I haven't wanted to get him ruffled up, you know, for the sake of his heart and health."

"How about for the sake of your marriage?"

Abby considered this. "Well, that, too. But, really, if what everyone is saying is true—if I've been overdoing it and obsessing over Paul's health too much—then I suppose I might as well start acting like my old fishwife self again."

Janie didn't respond.

"I know what you're thinking," Abby said as she led the way down the wooden stairs to the beach.

"Really?" Janie sounded surprised. "What *am* I thinking?"

Abby continued down the stairs until she reached the sand, then turned to look at Janie. "You think I'm not taking our marriage counseling seriously enough, and that I should practice talking to Paul the way the counselor has been recommending."

Janie gave Abby a surprisingly blank look. "And why would I think that?"

"Because you're the one who told us to get counseling in the first place." Abby started walking now.

"I merely suggested it."

"Well, you were right to suggest it."

Janie gave Abby a knowing smile. "Is it working for you?"

Abby felt a bit childish now. "Yes. It actually was starting to work, then the heart attack threw me off keel. When I remember to follow our counselor's advice, though, it does seem to improve things."

"What's the advice?"

"Oh, I'm sure you know the drill. It's okay to disagree, but keep our arguments clean. No personal attacks. No name-calling. No threats or ultimatums. Stop acting like overgrown children."

"That makes sense."

They walked for a while without talking. Abby shoved her hands into her jacket pockets and wondered why she was being so testy about Paul. She should be in good spirits after finally getting some rest. She looked out over the shimmering blue-green ocean, the curling waves capped with white foam, sun glistening on the water. She loved the comforting sounds of the rolling surf and the occasional screech of seagulls, like all was well with the world again.

But when she glanced at Janie, she noticed that her friend's expression was grim. Janie was being awfully quiet. Abby wondered if she'd hurt Janie's feelings somehow. Abby was good at sticking her foot in her mouth, sometimes without even knowing it. It wasn't as if her relationship with Janie had been terribly solid recently.

"Did I say something?" Abby asked carefully. "I mean, did I offend you without meaning to? We all know how good I am at saying the wrong thing."

"No. No." Janie shook her head in a convincing way. "Not at all, Abby."

"I know we've had some rough spots," Abby continued. "I have a feeling I owe you an apology."

"For what?"

Abby thought hard, wondering how much to say. If she and Janie were going to continue being friends and partners, she'd better just lay her cards on the table. "Well, the truth is I, uh, I think I've been jealous of you." Janie pressed her lips together, almost as if she'd been aware of this too. "It's hard seeing you working on the house, freely coming and going, doing as you please. Your life seems so carefree and fun, especially compared to mine."

Janie's brows shot up. "You think my life is carefree and fun?"

"Oh, I know you're a hard worker, Janie, and I know you've been through some hard things. It's just that, well, everything seems to come so easily to you."

Janie frowned. "You know what they say, Abby: Things aren't always what they seem."

Again they walked for several minutes without talking, but it didn't seem a comfortable sort of silence. Abby had probably really offended Janie this time. Really, why had she even opened her mouth? She looked at Janie as they walked. It was strange, but Abby thought she was seeing Janie more clearly than ever. She studied Janie's fine features, high cheekbones, straight narrow nose, the flashing copper color of hair as it blew in the sea breeze. Janie had been the ugly-duckling Linda back in high school, but she'd grown into a beautiful woman. Even that truth was slightly aggravating. Why did Janie get it all? Money, freedom, good looks ... it just wasn't fair.

Abby felt guilty all over again. Why was she being so hard on Janie? Was it just because Abby was jealous? How mature was that? She glanced at Janie again, this time noticing that Janie's brow was creased, as if she were deeply troubled. Probably thanks to Abby. "You're being awfully quiet, Janie."

Janie made what seemed a forced smile. "Sorry."

"It's because of me, isn't it?" Abby asked. "I know I'm a lousy friend. Jealous and cranky and unappreciative."

"What?" Janie seemed surprised.

"I'm sorry," Abby said. "I don't want us to be like this, Janie. I need your friendship. I really am thankful that you partnered with me in the house. It's just that my life seems so derailed recently. I don't want to be jealous of you. Please, can you forgive me?"

Janie smiled. "Of course I forgive you, Abby. And I'm sorry I was being so quiet. The truth is I was actually thinking about something else."

Abby felt relieved. "Oh, so it wasn't that I'd offended you by being jealous of your life?"

Janie kind of laughed. "No, Abby. I think I was simply caught up in my own thoughts. I'm sorry."

Abby considered this as they continued to walk. It was hard to remember exactly what was going on with Janie these days. Of course, she'd been working on her new law office. But what else was going on? Why would Janie be troubled about anything? Her life seemed picture perfect, at least from Abby's perspective. It was hard to imagine Janie with any problems.

Suddenly Abby recalled what Paul had said last week—that bit about Victor's ex-wife coming—and now she remembered how she had blurted it out at coffee on Tuesday. Marley had confirmed it later on. Of course that had to be what was troubling Janie. Why hadn't Abby thought of it earlier?

"So tell me, how are things with Victor these days?" Abby began.

"Oh, fine."

"And his ex?"

Janie sighed. "Ah yes, his ex."

"So is his ex still coming?"

Janie pushed a strand of hair from her eyes. "Actually she's probably here by now."

"Here?" Abby stopped walking. "Here in Clifden?"

Janie faced Abby and nodded with no show of emotion. "Victor drove over to Eugene to pick her up yesterday. Her flight was supposed to arrive around eight last night."

"You're kidding!"

"No, I'm totally serious." Janie shoved her hands into the pockets of her jeans and started walking again.

"Victor drove over there to pick her up?"

"That was his plan. Apparently she wasn't comfortable getting a rental car. I think she thought she couldn't return it." Janie made what sounded like a forced laugh. "As if Clifden were way out in the sticks or the ends of the earth or something."

"Out in the sticks? Well, that's ridiculous. What a foolish-sounding woman. I guess that means she'll be stuck here with no car?" Abby scowled as she bent down to pick up a whole sand dollar. She showed it to Janie.

"Nice." Janie nodded. "Anyway, Victor didn't seem to mind going to get her."

"So Victor's ex-wife is in Clifden now." Abby was still trying to wrap her head around this news. "Where is she staying?"

"The plan was for her to spend the night at Victor's."

"At Victor's?" Abby was truly shocked by this. "Just who does this hussy think she is, anyway?"

"Victor's ex-wife?"

"Well, that woman is asking for trouble. I have half a mind to go over there and give it to her." Abby shook her fist in the air.

Janie laughed at her, and although Abby was slightly offended, she was relieved, too. At least Janie's laughter sounded authentic. "Don't be too hard on Victor's ex, Abby. I have a feeling she's going through some hard things right now."

"That may be so. But why does she need to stay with Victor? I mean, there are plenty of other places in town. And yet she insists on staying right there in his house with him? Way out there on the beach? And she has no car, so it's not like she can easily get into town. Seriously, that seems a bit much, don't you think?"

"No, I actually think it makes some sense. Victor said Ben was going to drive down from college last night too. So they're having a little family reunion. Only their older son, Marcus, won't be there."

Abby didn't know how to respond to this. Something about it seemed all wrong to her. Something smelled fishy, and it wasn't the low tide.

"Janie, how do you feel about this? I mean seriously? You seem pretty calm and cool and collected. But if it were me, I'd be feeling jealous and left out. Oh, let's face it—if it were me, I'd be going bonkers. How can you stand it?"

"To be honest, part of me feels a little on edge today. I just keep reminding myself that Victor and I have something very special. And I trust him, Abby. Then I have to remind myself…. You know, the old *qué será será*. Whatever will be, will be."

"Do you *love* Victor?" Abby put a hand on Janie's shoulder, stopped her from walking, and looked deeply into her eyes.

Janie's lower lip quivered ever so slightly. "Yes, I think I do."

"So you're just trying to keep a brave front for his sake? Waiting for his ex to take a hint and go home, waiting for this nonsense to blow over?"

Janie nodded, but Abby thought her friend seemed close to tears. For some reason the display reassured Abby. Not that she wanted to see Janie break down and fall apart, but sometimes Janie appeared so controlled. She was such an expert at keeping up appearances and proper pretenses, like she thought she was still that Ms. Perfect Manhattan Attorney, like she could never reveal what lurked beneath her flawless surface. Anyway, although Abby didn't like to see her friend hurting, it was a comfort to know that Janie had feelings.

Suddenly Abby felt a maternal sort of love for her friend. In some ways Janie wasn't unlike Abby's daughters, who'd also suffered heartaches. Abby reached out and pulled Janie into a tight hug, just like she wished she could do with her strong-willed Laurie down in San Francisco.

"It's going to be okay," she assured Janie. "Don't you worry. Victor would be a complete fool not to know what he's got with you."

Chapter 6

JANIE

Monday morning, Janie decided to use Veterans Day and the parade as a distraction to her obsession over what exactly was going on at Victor's house. As Janie drove to town, she couldn't help but remember Abby's shock that Victor's ex had insisted on being his house guest. Really, Janie did not want to think about any of that today.

She was extremely glad she'd volunteered last week to help work on the local Veterans of Foreign Wars' float. It had seemed a little silly at the time. Seriously, how could her involvement with the VFW or this parade possibly reconnect her to her father? Still, she had felt it was right. Today her contribution to "The Patriots" float was to help put on the final trim: perishable decorations like flowers, as well as crepe paper and balloons. As it turned out, this mundane task of arranging streamers and inflating balloons was just what she needed today.

Unfortunately she'd been unable to coax, coerce, or even guilt any of the Lindas into joining her. Marley was playing grandma to Jack's seven-year-old granddaughter, Hunter, so that Jack and his daughter,

Jasmine, were free to man his art gallery. Veterans Day weekend was supposed to be profitable for them. Of course, Janie knew that Marley liked any excuse to spend time with Hunter. "I have to help Hunter with her parade costume," Marley had explained last night, "and then I need to get her delivered to the staging area and hooked up with the Clifden Mini-Majorettes, and then I'll remain on hand in case she needs me."

Janie hadn't meant to laugh as she wished Marley the best of luck. But the image of Marley, dressed in her usual beads and bright colors, hair sticking out as she traipsed down the street behind a bunch of hyper seven-year-olds, tying their tennis shoes or retrieving wayward batons, was rather amusing. "I'll be watching for you in the parade," Janie had told her.

Caroline's excuse was that Mitch was flying in for the day. And it turned out that Abby had her hands full with visiting relatives who were coming for their annual Veterans Day barbecue as well as to check on Paul's recovery. So today Janie was on her own. Just one Linda.

"So you say you lost your husband in Vietnam?" An elderly woman named Bitsy loudly asked Janie this question for the third time as they worked together on the flatbed trailer. Bitsy, it seemed, was not only hard of hearing, but a bit forgetful as well.

"No." Janie spoke clearly, hoping she might actually get through to her this time. "My husband died of cancer. But my father was in World War II. I wanted to help out with the float today in honor of his memory."

"What was his name again?"

Janie told her again, knowing full well that Bitsy wouldn't remember this either. Then Bitsy told Janie, for maybe the fifth time, about her son who actually did serve in Vietnam. "It was hard on him," Bitsy said sadly. "He came home a changed man." She slowly wound a roll of red crepe paper around the bumper. "Took him a long time to get over it." She shook her head. "I didn't know it at the time, but now I believe that was a war that never should've happened. No good came of it."

Janie wanted to question if good ever came out of any war, but because there were numerous veterans and survivors of veterans around, she decided it would be neither prudent nor kind. Besides, Janie knew that some wars had been waged for noble causes. "I think World War II was hard on my father," Janie admitted to Bitsy. "I think he came home a changed man too."

"Do you know my son?" Bitsy asked.

Once again Janie told her no, she hadn't had the pleasure of meeting Bitsy's son. Then she moved to the other side of the float. They had about an hour to put on the finishing touches of red, white, and blue crepe paper, balloons, and flags. Then about a dozen old veterans in uniform would take their places. Janie knew her contribution was a very small gesture, a feeble attempt to honor all the men who'd fought for their country, but when she'd called the local VFW hall a few days ago, this was the only volunteer opportunity they offered. As she wound crepe paper around a pole, she imagined she was part of past generations of women who had wrapped strips of cotton into bandage rolls for wounded soldiers on the field.

"My mother insisted I come over to speak to you," a deep voice said.

Janie was bent over, securing a piece of red crepe paper with masking tape. She looked up. "Yes?"

"Are you Janie?"

She stood up straight. "I am." She looked at this tall, sturdy-looking man with curiosity. With bushy gray hair peeking out of a Dodgers ball cap, his weathered face suggested he was at least in his fifties, perhaps even sixty.

"I'm Steve Fuller. For some reason my mother is convinced that I should know you. She told me to come back here and find out if we've ever met."

Janie smiled. "Let me guess, your mother is Bitsy?"

He nodded self-consciously. "You probably noticed she's got a little memory problem. That came with a stroke last year. Also, she has a little OCD and can get stuck on things. This morning she seems to be stuck on you, but at least she remembered your name. Has she been pestering you too much?"

"No, not at all." Janie glanced around the float to see if there was anything left to cover with crepe paper, but it seemed to be complete. "She just keeps getting confused, thinking it was my husband who was killed in the war. But it was actually my dad who served, although he passed away later." Janie wanted to add that in some ways it seemed like he had died overseas, but she stopped herself. "He was in World War II. I volunteered to help today in his honor of his memory."

"That's thoughtful of you."

"I never really understood until recently what a sacrifice my dad made," she continued, "or what a toll it took on his life."

Steve nodded as if he understood this. "Yes, war can definitely change a man."

"Your mother mentioned that you were in Vietnam." She waited, studying Steve's expression.

He pressed his lips together and nodded.

Janie set down the masking tape and stuck out her hand. "Well, I'd just like to say thank you."

He looked surprised, but he took her hand and shook it. "You're welcome. Thanks for saying that."

"I wasn't supportive of the Vietnam War back then," she admitted.

"Most weren't."

"But lately I've realized how tough it must've been for you guys, when you came home to angry war protests and antagonism. I know it happened a long time ago, but I feel really badly about it now." She looked down at her feet. "I was actually one of the war protestors in college. I don't think I understood the difference between hating the war and hating the ones who were forced to fight over there." She looked up. "I'm truly sorry."

"Yeah, it was hard being treated like a criminal back then, especially after you thought you were risking your life for your country. Then you come home to discover your country couldn't care less about that war … or you. First thing I did once I got stateside was to get out of uniform and grow my hair long." He shook his head. "Then I got hooked on drugs."

Janie tried not to look shocked. After all, she knew that many Vietnam veterans had used drugs or alcohol to escape the horrible memories of war. Really, who could blame them? "I'm so sorry," she said again.

Steve smiled. "Thanks. I really do appreciate that. Fortunately, and thanks to God, I got unhooked about twenty years ago."

She sighed. "Good for you."

"Yeah. Otherwise I'm pretty sure I wouldn't be standing here today."

Janie thought of her dad now. Instead of drugs he had built an emotional wall of protection around himself, holding everyone out and keeping all the pain in. "Hopefully today's soldiers get more help when they come home."

"You would hope so." But Steve's expression said he was doubtful.

Now Janie noticed that Steve, unlike the other vets, was not in uniform. "You're not planning on riding on the float today?"

He chuckled. "No thanks. I'm not ready for that yet."

She looked at her fingers, stained blue and red from the crepe paper. "I guess my work here is done then."

"Staying for the parade?"

"Oh, sure."

"Did you get a place to sit?"

"Sit?"

He shrugged. "Yeah, some of us old timers get tired of standing. But I parked my pickup over there." He jerked his thumb toward a white pickup surrounded by camp chairs and several older people, including Bitsy, already sitting down. "The chairs appear to be taken, but you're welcome to a piece of the tailgate if you like. I have a thermos of coffee, too."

She grinned. "Now there's an offer I can't refuse."

"Time for us to head over to the staging area," a veteran named Marv called out loudly. In charge of the decorations, he was also the driver of the float. "All aboard who's coming aboard."

Janie deposited the leftover crepe paper and masking tape into the supply box, then thanked Marv for letting her help today.

"Thank you," he said warmly. "You're welcome to help out any time you like, little lady." He handed her one of the small American flags. "We need you young people keeping patriotism alive and well."

She waved the flag and laughed at being called "young people," then followed Steve to his truck. Before long he had a stadium blanket folded and spread across the tailgate and was handing her a cup of coffee.

"That's her right there," Bitsy pointed proudly at Janie now. "The one who lost her husband in Vietnam."

The other old people sitting with Bitsy nodded knowingly, expressing their regrets. Janie decided to just let it go. Really, what did it matter?

"So if your husband didn't die in the war like my mom keeps telling everyone"—Steve glanced over his shoulder—"is he around here somewhere?"

Janie smiled sadly. "He actually died in the war against cancer a couple of years ago."

"I'm sorry. I know how that goes."

Janie wanted to tell Steve about Victor just then, and yet she couldn't find the right words. For some reason it seemed presumptuous to mention him. What would she say? Casually mention that she had a boyfriend—or what used to be a boyfriend—but that his ex-wife was in town to take him back? So she said nothing, realizing that Steve had said something to suggest he understood her loss.

"What do you mean?" she asked him. "About knowing how that goes?"

"I mean losing someone to cancer." He looked across the street as if he were looking across time. "I lost my wife about nine years ago."

"Oh, I'm sorry."

"Me, too."

As they waited for the parade to come down the street, Steve asked Janie about her past, where she'd lived, what she'd done, how she'd ended up in Clifden. She filled in the blanks and then asked him the same.

"I'm relatively new in these parts," he admitted. "My folks relocated here from Santa Barbara about five years ago. With my kids grown and gone, I just sort of followed my parents on up." The sound of a very loud fire-engine horn nearly blasted Janie out of her shoes. Steve laughed. "The parade has officially begun," he told her.

With marching bands, floats, old cars, clowns, and lots of candy, the parade took Janie straight back to childhood. She waved and called out to Marley when she spotted her friend marching in time, camera in hand, and keeping pace with the slightly out-of-step Mini-Majorettes. When the Clifden marching band played "The Stars and Stripes Forever," she felt her eyes getting damp. She wondered if her parents had ever come to one of these parades after she'd grown up. Despite her participating in the marching band, they had never attended any while she was at home. Perhaps it was too much for her dad, seeing men in uniforms, the National Guard with their tanks and jeeps. Who knew? It might've been her father's undoing.

During a quiet lapse about halfway through the parade—the antique car club was getting lined up while waiting for the Coast Guard float to move on—Janie told Steve about discovering her father's Medal of Honor buried in the bottom of a desk drawer.

Steve's eyes widened. "Wow, a Congressional Medal of Honor? That's quite an award."

"Yes. You'd think he might've been proud of it, kept it out for all to see…."

Steve got a knowing look. "Or it might've been filled with bad memories for him."

She wondered at this, but now the antique cars were putt-putting along, their drivers beeping horns and handing out candy to squealing children. This was followed by more parade entries, and finally the police cars came, raising and lowering their sirens to signify that the parade was over. Janie hopped down off the tailgate and thanked Steve for his hospitality.

"It was a pleasure to have you join us," he said as he began to gather up the camp chairs that the elderly folks had been sitting in, stacking them in the back of his pickup.

Janie said good-bye to the older people, including Bitsy, then decided to help Steve in gathering the chairs. "I was curious about what you said earlier," she said as she folded a chair and leaned it against the pickup.

"What I said earlier?"

"About my dad's medals, and how they might've had bad memories for him." She handed a chair to Steve. "How could a medal have bad memories?"

Steve frowned and scratched his head. "Maybe I shouldn't have said that."

"No, it's okay." She waited. "I'm curious to hear your thoughts. I'm sure your perspective on something like this is much broader than mine."

He put the last chair in the pickup and closed the tailgate. "Tell you what, you join me for a burger, and I'll tell you what I know and let you pick my brain."

She thought about Victor again. Eating lunch with Steve wasn't a date. It was simply two people sharing a meal and discussing a subject that interested both of them. Besides, Victor was probably with Donna and Ben right now, enjoying their impromptu family reunion. "Sure." She nodded.

"How about Barney's Diner?"

"I'll meet you there."

Steve's blue eyes brightened as he smiled broadly. "Cool."

Janie felt a little uneasy as she navigated through the parade traffic, slowly making her way to the diner. She knew that what she was doing was perfectly fine and respectable, but for some unexplainable reason she felt a tinge of guilt, as if she were cheating on Victor, which was completely ridiculous but irksome all the same. As she parked her car, she suppressed the urge to call Victor in an effort to explain everything to him, as well as to ease her conscience. A phone call wasn't merely juvenile, but unnecessary. They were both grown-ups, and Victor had other things to worry about at the moment. If needed, she could justify this unexpected luncheon with Steve Fuller at a later date.

To her surprise he was already there. She spotted him inside, waving at her from one of the old fifties-style booths by the windows. She'd only been to the diner a couple of times since moving back to town, but in junior high she had often come here with friends before her social life faded into oblivion.

"You certainly made good time," she said as she joined him.

"Took a short cut." He grinned. "Missed the traffic."

She slid into the vinyl seat across from him. "Even though I grew up here, I'm still figuring some of these things out."

"What was it like growing up in a small town like this?"

She ran a finger over the plastic-coated menu and smiled. "Good and bad."

"How so?"

"Well, everything was pretty good until I became a teenager. Then things got bad for a while."

He chuckled. "That sounds fairly typical."

"I suppose." She told him about the Lindas. "We were inseparable during grade school. But things changed in junior high."

He looked as if he was waiting for her to continue.

She glanced around to see if a waitress was coming, but the place was getting pretty busy. "Well, a couple of the Lindas suddenly got pretty and curvy and popular." She smiled uncomfortably, wondering why she was telling all this to someone who was practically a stranger.

"And some of them didn't?"

She nodded. "In particular, me. I got braces, my skin started breaking out, I grew too tall, and I had no curves."

He looked sympathetic. "The old ugly-duckling story."

"The upside was that I really honed in on academics. I became a nerd." She laughed. "Seeing the Clifden High marching band this morning brought back some memories."

"You were in the marching band."

She grimaced. "Yes. Some people called me Nerd Girl."

"But Nerd Girl turned out pretty nicely." He set his menu aside.

She laughed nervously. "Well, at least she went to law school and married well."

Then the waitress came, and, thankful for the distraction, Janie focused on the menu, finally deciding on a BLT and iced tea. Then as the waitress was leaving, Janie decided to redirect the conversation. After all, she was here on a mission. "So, you said something that got my attention," she reminded him. "Why would my father's distinguished Medal of Honor bring about bad memories? According to my research those medals were given for acts of true courage, usually for risking one's life during battle in order to save the lives of others. Is that correct?"

His brows arched. "You really do sound like an attorney."

"Sorry."

"Actually you're right. Your dad's Medal of Honor implies that he did something very heroic in the midst of a battle."

"It seems that would make him proud."

Steve shook his head. "You might think that, but the medal is only a very small part of the story."

"That's true." She thought about what she'd discovered through the letters. "My dad's plane went down and he ended up in prison camp. While that must've been terrible, he did survive. You'd think he would have some sense of pride and accomplishment in that, and yet he never spoke of it during his life. For all I knew, he'd been a cook during the war. But then I find out he'd received these distinguished honors!"

"You're still only seeing a tiny piece of the puzzle, Janie."

"Tell me what you think the other pieces are." She leaned forward eagerly. "I'd appreciate your perspective."

"Keep in mind this is speculation. But it's speculation based on real life. By the time your dad's plane went down, you can be sure he was among friends. Because you can't help but become friends when you're in the military. You have to understand that those guys become closer than brothers. You're watching their backs, and they're watching yours. It's hard to describe what it's like exactly. Most guys aren't good about talking about feelings. That might be one reason so many of us had difficulties when we returned home."

"That makes sense."

"So imagine your dad over there: His plane goes down, probably in enemy territory, and suddenly he's in the midst of a battle where there's a lot of, well, bloodshed. Your dad is doing his best to stay alive and to keep his buddies alive. I'm guessing he's putting his life on the line to save some of them. But let's be realistic. The battle isn't going well. He's probably seeing his friends being killed. That's usually how it goes in a really bad battle. It's not easy to watch a buddy die." He looked away, and Janie wished she'd never asked him to explain all this. Of course her dad had experienced some atrocities. So had Steve. Why hadn't she realized all this before?

The waitress set down their drinks. Janie took a cool sip of iced tea and waited.

"What I'm saying, Janie"—he looked earnestly at her—"is that even though your dad survived, and even though he must've saved the lives of some of his buddies, it's very likely that many others died right before his eyes. So for some veterans, some so-called war heroes, when they look at their war medals, all they can see is the unfortunate guys, the ones who came home in a pine box."

Janie felt a lump in her throat as she nodded. "I understand."

"Sorry to be so blunt."

"No." She shook her head, trying to hold back tears. "Thank you. It helps me to process this." She explained to him how hard it had been growing up in her home, how cold and removed her father seemed. "I had no idea what was really going on with him. In fact I believed I was the source of his unhappiness. I thought I would've made him happy if only I'd been a better daughter."

Steve reached across the table and put his hand on hers. "I'm sure your father loved you deeply, Janie. He just didn't know how to show it." Steve began to tell her how it was with his own kids after he came home from Vietnam. He fell into a depression and wasn't emotionally available to them. He pushed them and anyone who loved him away, and he got hooked on pain medications. "Thanks to God and a good woman, I finally came to my senses," he said as their food arrived. Then Steve bowed his head. "Father, please bless this food," he said quietly. "Bless all the veterans, those here on earth and those safe with you in heaven. And help them and their families to make sense of what often seems so senseless. Amen."

"Amen." Janie smiled at him. "Thanks for opening my eyes to what my father may have gone through during the war. I have a strong sense that he would appreciate you sharing your perspective with me."

=Chapter 7=

CAROLINE

"Don't you worry about a thing," the caregiver Joan told Caroline, practically shoving her out the front door Tuesday afternoon. "I know what I'm doing."

"But I didn't show you where the phone numbers are posted," Caroline protested.

"I'll bet they're right by the phone," Joan said a bit smugly.

"Well, yes. But my mom doesn't really know you yet."

"Does she know anyone?" Joan countered.

Caroline sighed. "No, I suppose not. Especially not recently."

"Really, everything will be just fine," Joan assured her. "I've substituted for Darlene several times. Some of our patients can't even tell us apart."

Caroline wanted to point out that her mom sometimes couldn't tell her own daughter apart from Darlene but knew it was pointless.

"You just take that big dog of yours for a nice long beach walk, dear. Just like you would have done if Darlene wasn't sick." Joan waved and closed the door.

"Okay." Caroline looked down at Chuck. His tail whipped happily back and forth. "I guess we're officially kicked out. It's just you and me, boy." She opened up the back of her mini SUV, and Chuck hopped in as if they did this sort of thing every day. Caroline wished that were the case, but the truth was she'd only been able to take Chuck to the beach once since she'd adopted him about a month ago. Usually she spent her time off from caring for her mother by doing errands, shopping for groceries, attending her support group, or occasionally grabbing coffee with the other Lindas.

Caroline worried as she drove toward the beach. It was always so hard to shake off her responsibilities, like she felt everything would fall apart without her. Darlene was the only one who seemed able to hold it together in Caroline's absence. But, like Darlene had told Caroline on the phone, it would be good for her mom to meet a new caregiver. "Joan is still relatively new to the agency," Darlene had explained in a hoarse voice. "So she might be more available for other times, too."

To reassure herself, Caroline mentally went over her safety checklist. The stove and the microwave were both unplugged. All chemical cleaners and aerosol cans were safely locked away. All knives, sharp objects, and breakables were well out of her mother's reach. She was much shorter than Caroline, so using the high shelves for glassware was ideal. Not that her mother wandered into the kitchen much these days, but Caroline could never tell what to expect.

That was the hardest thing about Alzheimer's: You could never tell. Just when Caroline thought she'd covered all her bases, her mother would pull a new trick out of her crazy bag, like the time she went out into the garage and attempted to start the lawn mower.

Why she thought she needed to mow the lawn in the middle of the night was a mystery, albeit no more mysterious than the time she thought she needed to take a boat ride in the buff. Then there was the time she sneaked into Caroline's room and attempted to cut her daughter's hair with a pair of manicure scissors.

Today, Caroline's bedroom door, garage door, and back door were all securely dead-bolted with two-way locks, and the master key was safely zipped in Caroline's purse. The front door had been trickier to secure. According to Beverly, one exit had to remain unlocked in case of an emergency. Caroline understood this, but she hoped that Joan did too.

"Of course she does," Caroline told herself as she turned down the road to the jetty. "She's a certified caregiver." Still, Caroline would've felt less concerned if Darlene, instead of this Joan person, were with her mother.

"You've got to quit worrying about her so much," Mitch had told Caroline just yesterday. "It's not doing either of you any good. You're always on edge, and your mother can probably sense this. You need to relax."

"That's easy for you to say," she'd retorted a bit defensively. Mitch had been dropping some not-so-subtle hints all day, and she had felt unexplainably weary just then. "You're not the one trapped into taking care of her 24/7."

"You don't have to be trapped," he reminded her. "You said yourself that the social worker has recommended that you put her in a home."

At that point Caroline decided to change the subject. What was the point of arguing about it with Mitch when Caroline could argue about it all by herself? Besides, it had been sweet of Mitch to make the effort to visit her despite knowing that Caroline's caregivers would be booked because of the holiday and she'd be stuck with her mom for the entire day.

She did her best to make it a good visit for him, going to the trouble of setting up a small barbecue picnic for them in the recently renovated backyard. This was no small feat, considering all the running back and forth to attend to her mother's increasing demands. By the end of the day Caroline was exhausted, and she fretted over the fact that Mitch left earlier than planned. He said he needed to get ready for his Tokyo trip, which was true, but she also suspected he was getting a bit fed up with their relationship. Who could blame him?

Caroline parked the car in the nearly empty lot and went around to let Chuck out. "It's just you and me, boy." She stroked his silky head as she clipped on his leash. "For all I know, you may end up being the only guy in my life." His tail wagged eagerly, as if this was perfectly fine with him. Really, he was a good companion. Always happy to see her. Never complained. Always appreciative. Enthusiastic, understanding, undemanding. And he never told her how to live her life. In fact he wasn't much of a conversationalist. In Chuck's case silence was golden. Like a golden retriever.

Caroline hadn't told anyone that Chuck had been sneaking into her bed at nights, or that she didn't mind. Something about the feel of that soft, warm fur and the sound of his canine snuffs and grunts … well, it was better than being alone!

She let him off the leash once they were out on the beach. Now was the time to run with carefree abandon, to chase the tennis ball she'd stuck in her pocket, to experience the thrill of the ocean, and to simply be free.

It seemed incredible to think of how many years she had taken her freedom for granted. Worse than not appreciating her independence, she had, at times, despised it. She spent hours, days, maybe even years lamenting the absence of a significant someone in her life. She had grieved over the children she would never mother. She had loathed the emptiness of living simply for herself, tending to her own necessities, obsessing over her own concerns, and basically being self-absorbed.

She'd tried to be a good friend to those around her, but so often her friendships were temporary. Naturally she'd had romantic relationships along the way, but never anything lasting. The men she attracted were usually takers, shallow guys who cared more about their needs than hers. That was typical of Hollywood culture, she supposed. All in all, she'd experienced an unfulfilled life down in Southern California. Independence, yes. Freedom, of course. But it had been very lonely.

Now she had someone who not only needed her but could not survive for one day without her help. Caroline was suffocating. She gave the tennis ball a hard throw and looked out to the ocean, where several surfers were making a go of it. The wave action looked rough, and she didn't envy them their youth, vigor, and vitality. She could accept that those days were long gone for her, and, really, she wouldn't turn back the clock. Not even if she could. In fact, by caring for her elderly mother, Caroline was finally coming to grips with aging.

Her hair beneath her highlights was graying, and wrinkles were inevitable. After seeing what happened to her good friend Shelby down in LA, Caroline had sworn off Botox for good. Now more than ever before, Caroline was starting to accept that, in her mid-fifties, things were changing, shifting, dropping, drooping, and sagging. But those were external things. The things that really mattered were interior things, for the most part unseen. According to her belief they were lasting things. She had spent most of her life focused on shallow priorities. For the remainder of her life she hoped to focus on what really mattered.

Right now all that mattered to her was being out here on the beach with Chuck, enjoying the ocean air, the sound of the thrashing waves, the clouds rolling across the horizon. *Be in the moment,* she reminded herself. *Live life fully. Relish every day you have. Be thankful!*

She checked her watch to make sure she hadn't walked too far. Her plan had been to allow forty-five minutes to walk one way before she turned back, but a bit more than that had gone by already. Her two-hour respite time always passed quickly, and she wanted to stop by McDonald's on her way home. Lately her mom's eating habits had been worse than ever. This morning Caroline couldn't even get her to sample what had once been her favorite protein drink. It was probably a long shot, but she hoped the old lure of a cheeseburger, fries, and vanilla shake would entice her mom to eat something.

On her way to McDonald's, Caroline heard sirens and pulled over to let a fire engine and a couple of emergency vehicles pass her. Silly as it seemed, her instinct was to dash home to check on her mom. Maybe mothers of infants felt the same while away from home. Instead Caroline pulled into the drive-through and waited to place her order. After she got the bag, she thought the aroma of those crispy fries would be just the thing to tempt her mom to eat. In fact they smelled so good that Caroline's stomach growled, and she considered sneaking a few herself.

When she turned down her street, her stomach forgot all about hunger. There in front of her mom's house were two fire engines, an ambulance, and a police car.

Caroline pulled over on the other side of the street, leaped out of the car, and ran to where firemen were spraying water onto the roof of the burning house. Caroline looked at the bystanders, searching for her mom but spotting only Joan. "Where is my mom?" Caroline screamed.

"Oh, Caroline!" Joan's face was white as she pointed to the house. "She's still in there."

Caroline started to run for the house but was blocked by a fireman in fire-resistant gear. "No, ma'am, you can't go in there." He held her firmly, walking her back to the sidewalk.

"But my mom!" she screamed into his face. "She's in—"

"They'll get her out," he told her. "They know what they're doing."

Caroline broke into tears. "Oh, Mom," she sobbed. "Please be okay."

After what felt like hours but was probably just minutes, two firemen emerged from the front door. One of them was carrying what looked like an oversized rag doll in his arms. The fireman continued to hold Caroline back as two paramedics raced over to tend to her mother.

"You need to stay out of their way, ma'am," the fireman said. "Let the professionals take care of her."

Caroline couldn't see her mom's face as they loaded her onto a gurney. But she did see one of the medics with an oxygen mask, which had to mean her mom was still alive. The fireman walked Caroline over to another medic, where she was told they were transporting her mom to the hospital.

"I'll follow in my car," she told them, and before long she was trailing the ambulance with its siren going and lights flashing. "Please let her be okay," she prayed as she drove. "Please help her, God. She is so helpless. Please help her."

Caroline parked near the emergency entrance as the medics rolled her mother's gurney into the hospital. They went directly into the ER, and Caroline went to the desk to give the receptionist her mother's information. Fortunately her mom was already in the computer system there, and the process didn't take too long.

"Can I go see her?" Caroline asked.

"Let me check." The receptionist picked up a phone, asked some questions, and then hung up. "I'm sorry," she told Caroline. "Until she is stabilized, there can be no visitors."

"Is she going to be okay?"

The receptionist's expression was impossible to read. "They will do everything they can for your mother. Please make yourself comfortable over there. I will let you know as soon as I hear anything." She pointed to the waiting area.

Caroline thanked her and, feeling like she was in a stupor, went over and sat down. It was the same place where Caroline had first waited with the other Lindas on the night of their class reunion after Cathy Gardener collapsed, and where they'd held their vigil for Paul following his heart attack—it felt eerily familiar. Fumbling through her purse, Caroline pulled out her phone and called Janie and quickly explained the situation.

"I'm on my way," Janie told her. "And I'll let the others know too."

"Thanks," Caroline mumbled. She closed her phone and just sat there wondering. What had happened? How on earth had a fire started? And where was that caregiver—Joan—while this was taking place? Furthermore, where was she now?

It wasn't long before Janie joined Caroline in the waiting area. So relieved to see a familiar face, Caroline hugged her tightly. "Thanks for coming."

"How is she?" Janie asked as they sat down.

Caroline shook her head. "No news yet."

"How did it happen?"

Caroline frowned. "I don't really know."

Janie looked confused. "Weren't you there?"

Caroline explained about Joan. "I was worried about going. I've never had that caregiver before."

"What did Joan tell you?"

"Nothing, not really."

"Not even how the fire started?"

"We didn't have time to talk."

"Where is Joan now?" Janie glanced around the waiting area.

Caroline shrugged. "I have no idea."

"That's odd." Janie's brow creased. "Maybe we should call Joan's supervisor and see what she has to say about this. It seems the caregiver on duty should have some responsibility to explain what happened."

"Yes. That's a good idea. I'll call the agency."

"Surely Joan was involved in filling out some kind of a report with the emergency crews."

Caroline waited as the phone rang. When a woman answered, Caroline explained the situation, then waited as she was transferred to the head of the agency. Just as someone said hello, a policeman came into the waiting area and called out Caroline's name. "Here," Caroline handed the phone to Janie. "Can you handle this for me?" Janie nodded with confidence and Caroline stood to greet the policeman.

"I'm Detective Alberts," he said as he shook her hand. "Very sorry to hear about your mother." He glanced toward the ER desk. "How is she doing?"

"I don't know." Caroline felt a lump in her throat.

He nodded. "I am a CFI, and I have some questions about the fire."

"A CFI?"

"Certified Fire Investigator." He nodded to some chairs by the door, indicating that they should sit.

"I thought you were a policeman." Caroline said as she followed him to the chairs and sat down.

"Since Clifden is a small town, some of us wear more than one hat." He opened a black notebook. "I understand you weren't present during the fire. Correct?"

"That's right. I had a caregiver watching my mother."

"Joan Wilson?"

"Yes. It was the first time she's stayed with my mom, so I was a little uneasy."

"Uneasy?" He peered at her.

"Well, because my mom didn't really know her." Caroline held up her hands. "My mom has Alzheimer's. She doesn't really *know* anyone."

"And you are the primary caregiver for your mother?"

"Yes."

"That must be exhausting for you." He smiled in a sympathetic way.

She nodded. "Yes. It can be pretty stressful."

"Have you been doing it for long?"

"Since August."

"Has she been difficult to care for?"

Caroline sighed. "Well, yes. She's in an advanced stage. She can be very difficult."

"I'm surprised you didn't move her to a nursing home."

"I've considered it."

"Of course, that can be very expensive." He seemed to be studying her closely.

"Yes."

"I had an elderly uncle with dementia," the detective continued in a rambling sort of way. "He was quite well-off, owned several houses, but he went into a care facility, and after several years there was nothing left of his estate." Caroline felt confused. Why was he telling her this story? "Anyway, do you know what caused the fire?"

"I've been wracking my brain," she admitted. "I keep the stove and microwave unplugged. There are no matches or candles or anything in the house. Even the lighter I use for the barbecue is kept safely locked in my room."

"I noticed there were a number of keyed locks on the doors." Again he peered curiously at her.

"That's because my mom wanders. If a door's not locked she will go right through it. She has no sense of boundaries. For safety reasons, I didn't have a lock like that installed on the front door. The social worker advised against it"—Caroline swallowed hard—"in case of an emergency."

"Like a fire?"

She nodded.

"Are you a smoker, Ms. McCann?"

Caroline blinked. "No. Not at all."

"Your mother?"

"No." Caroline frowned. "I mean she used to be. But that was ages ago."

"So those were not your cigarettes?"

"Cigarettes?" She stared at him. "What cigarettes?"

"And that was not your lighter?"

"You found a lighter and cigarettes?"

He nodded, but she sensed suspicion in his eyes, as if he didn't believe her about not being a smoker, which was ridiculous since it would be easy enough to prove. "The lighter and cigarettes were at the source of the fire, which begs the question—how did they get there?"

His dark eyes seemed to bore into her now, as if he thought she was about to make some crazy confession about being a closet smoker. Suddenly Caroline wondered if she might need some legal advice. She glanced at Janie, who was still on the phone, and considered waving her over.

"Look," she told him in a no-nonsense tone. "I do not smoke. Neither does my mom. If you found cigarettes and a lighter, they had to belong to someone else." A little light went on in Caroline's head. "Joan," she declared. "I'll bet those things were hers."

"Ms. Wilson denied that they belonged to her."

"Well, I deny it too." Caroline stood, waving to Janie to come join them. "That's my friend Janie Sorenson," she explained to the detective. "She's a lawyer and I'd like her to hear what you're saying."

"I'm not charging you with anything," he said. "I'm just gathering information."

Janie came quickly. Caroline briefly explained what was going on and how it seemed that Detective Alberts was questioning Caroline's honesty about being a nonsmoker.

"Caroline is *not* a smoker," Janie attested.

"And neither is my mom," Caroline said for the second time.

"It seems obvious that the cigarettes and lighter belonged to the caregiver," Janie said calmly.

"Unless someone else just happened to leave them in the house." The detective was looking directly at Caroline.

"Why on earth would I leave cigarettes and a lighter in the house?"

He continued looking at her. "I don't know. You tell me why."

"This is crazy," Caroline declared. "Do you honestly think I'd do something that stupid? I spend all my time trying to keep my mom safe. Why would I leave something dangerous around?"

He puckered up his lips as if thinking. "One more question, Ms. McCann. Is it safe to assume that you would inherit your mother's property in the event of her death?"

"What?"

"I think Caroline has answered enough questions," Janie interrupted. "If you want to question her further, I suggest you go through the appropriate legal procedures and that her attorney be present."

"Aren't you her attorney?"

"I am her friend." Janie stood straighter. "And if she needs an attorney, I am happy to represent her." Then she hooked her arm into Caroline's and walked her away.

"What just happened?" Caroline asked Janie.

"I could be wrong, but I think the detective was trying to pin something on you."

"But why?"

Janie sighed. "Who knows? Maybe he just wants to solve a case the easiest way possible. Or maybe he's having a slow week and wants to stir something up."

"Those cigarettes *had* to belong to Joan." Caroline tried to think. "Why would she deny it?"

"Did the detective say where the cigarettes were found?"

He was still standing by the door, still writing in his black notebook. "Maybe we should go ask him some questions," Caroline said.

"Good idea."

"Can you handle the question part for me?" Caroline asked as they hurried back.

"Gladly."

"Excuse me," Caroline said to the detective. "We have some questions."

"Yes?" He looked at them with renewed interest.

"Where exactly were the cigarettes found?" Janie inquired.

"In Mrs. McCann's bedroom."

"Is that where the fire started?"

"That's correct."

"And the lighter was in there as well?"

"That's right."

"So it's possible that Mrs. McCann somehow got hold of the cigarettes and lighter and took them into her room?"

"It's possible. Or else someone left them there." He glanced at Caroline.

Janie paused as if considering this information. "And you say the caregiver denies that they were hers?"

"She did. She assured me she is not a smoker."

"It seems that it would be easy to establish—I mean, whether or not the caregiver is a smoker." Janie waited for his response.

He nodded. "Yes, that should be easy to prove."

"And I can't imagine that caregivers are allowed to smoke on the job," Janie added.

"That seems reasonable."

Caroline opened her phone now. Moving a few steps away, she called the agency again. "I have a question about caregivers," she told the woman who answered.

"Yes, how can I help you?"

"I'm just curious, but caregivers wouldn't smoke in the homes of their clients, would they?"

"No. Of course not."

"This is a rule then?"

"Absolutely. Our caregivers would never smoke around their clients."

"Thank you." Caroline hung up and relayed this information to Janie and Detective Alberts.

Janie's brow creased. "So it's feasible that Joan broke this rule and is afraid to admit it."

"It's also feasible that Caroline left the cigarettes and lighter for her mother to find."

"Why would I do that?" Caroline waited.

"Because you know that your mother *used* to smoke. You know she might attempt to smoke again. You know that could cause a fire. You had locks on the doors. A person could become trapped and—"

"What are you suggesting?" Caroline demanded. "That I wanted my mom to burn the house down? With her in it?"

"It would be an easy way to get rid of someone. Someone burdensome."

Caroline was too angry to respond, and so she just walked away. Janie could deal with that creep. This was preposterous. Here in the hospital of all places, while she was worried sick about her mom, that cop had the nerve to practically accuse her of attempted murder.

Chapter 8

MARLEY

Sitting down across from Caroline in the hospital cafeteria, Marley could hardly believe what Caroline had just told her and Abby. "That is totally outrageous. The cops are accusing you of trying to kill your mom?"

"It certainly appears that way," Janie confirmed. "I witnessed the conversation."

"They seriously think Caroline would do something like that?" Abby demanded.

Caroline nodded sadly.

"How is your mom?" Marley asked.

"She's in critical condition," Caroline explained. "She's unconscious, which could be the result of stroke or heart attack or shock ... or pain. She has third-degree burns to the upper right portion of her body, and her lungs are damaged from smoke inhalation."

"It doesn't look good," Janie added.

"The doctor can't believe she survived." Caroline sighed.

"And the authorities have actually accused you of planting the cigarettes in your mom's bedroom?" Marley asked.

"It gets worse," Janie told her.

"How is that possible?" Abby asked.

"I am the sole beneficiary of my mom's life-insurance policy," Caroline said. "It's not a huge policy, but it's enough to make the cops even more suspicious."

"But what about that caregiver?" Marley persisted. "Why isn't someone calling her on the carpet?"

"She's not answering her phone," Caroline said. "For all we know, she might've left town."

"That alone should prove she's guilty," Abby said.

"She's a new caregiver," Caroline explained. "From what I can tell, no one at the agency really knows her that well."

"How did she get a job there?" Marley asked.

Caroline shrugged. "Who knows?"

"Someone there must know her," Marley persisted.

Caroline's eyes lit up. "You know, Darlene recommended her to me, and Joan mentioned that some patients mix her up with Darlene."

"Have you called Darlene?" Marley demanded.

"Not yet. She was pretty sick when we talked this morning. That's why she couldn't come today."

"Well, she can't be too sick to talk on the phone."

Caroline sighed and reached for her phone. Then, leaving the three of them in the hospital cafeteria, she stepped out a patio door and began to talk into her phone. Marley just shook her head. "Poor Caroline."

Abby frowned. "I've never seen her so stressed out."

"This whole thing is like adding insult to injury," Marley declared. "Here she's worked so hard, keeping her mom at home, trying to make that place safe, and *this* happens."

"You don't think there's any chance she really did put those cigarettes there, do you?" With a creased brow, Abby looked around the table.

"Of course not!" Marley shook a finger at her.

"That's ridiculous," Janie added.

"Yes, I'm sure she wouldn't have done that." Abby looked contrite.

"Unfortunately the investigator seemed rather stuck on the theory," Janie confided. "It's as if he's enjoying the drama of a potential murder charge."

"Small-town cops." Marley shook her head. "Instead of doing a real investigation, they take something sad and innocent and totally blow it out of proportion."

"Who was the policeman anyway?" Abby demanded.

"Detective Alberts," Janie told her.

Abby let out a groan. "Detective Alberts is a joke."

"What do you mean?" Marley asked.

"I mean he likes to *play* detective, but he's as clueless as they come." Abby shook her head. "Everyone in town knows it."

"Then why is he a detective?" Janie asked.

"Small-town politics. His father was chief of police before—" Abby stopped talking as Caroline rejoined them.

"Any luck?" Janie asked Caroline.

"Maybe." Caroline sat down with a thoughtful expression.

"Darlene didn't know if Joan smokes or not, but she thinks she lives in the Hyde Street Apartments."

"Hey," Marley said. "What if someone gave Detective Alberts a hand with his investigation?"

Caroline cocked her head to one side. "How?"

"Oh, you know." Marley stood. "Do a little snooping, ask a few questions, maybe collect some evidence. You know how I love a good mystery. I bet I'll be good at this."

"You can't be serious." Abby looked skeptical.

"Totally serious." Marley put one strap of her bag over a shoulder. "In fact I nominate you to be my assistant."

Abby looked shocked. "Me?"

"Yeah. You used to read Nancy Drew too."

"Even so, I hardly think—"

"Come on." Marley reached for her hand. "We have a crime to solve." Then she turned back to Caroline. "How about a little physical description of Joan, in case we run into her?"

Joan sounded like a nondescript woman a little older than they were, slightly overweight, with short hair that was light brown and gray, frumpy clothes, sturdy shoes. "And weird glasses," Caroline added.

"Weird in what way?" Marley asked.

"Kind of like they were from the eighties. Remember the oversized glasses with plastic rims? I think hers were tinted purple or pink. Sort of odd looking."

Marley nodded. "Okay then. I think we're set."

"Thank you both," Caroline said.

"Be careful," Janie called as they were leaving. "And smart."

"This is going to be fun." Marley grinned as she and Abby went outside. "I think you should drive so that I can keep my eyes wide open."

Abby actually giggled. "I can't believe I'm cooperating with you."

Even though it was cloudy, Marley put on her sunglasses. "I want to keep a low profile," she said as Abby cruised by the small apartment complex.

"Right." Abby chuckled. "No one will think it's odd that you're wearing shades with no sun out."

"Fine." Marley removed her sunglasses. Then she pointed to a sign. "Hey, it says there's an apartment for rent. Let's pretend I'm new in town and looking for a place."

"You want me to pull into the parking lot?"

"Well, we can't exactly make an inquiry in a drive-by."

So Abby parked. The two women got out and pretended to be interested in checking out the complex. They strolled around and assessed the landscaping, which was minimal, while keeping a lookout for Joan and her purple eighties glasses. Marley hoped to spy her smoking. When there was no sign of Joan, Marley led the way to the management office and boldly rang the bell.

"Are you sure about this?" Abby whispered as they waited.

Marley nodded. She was on a mission.

A short balding man answered the door.

"I'm looking for an apartment," Marley told him.

He opened the door wider. "You came to the right place. We got two different units available right now."

"Great." Marley asked him how much a unit rented for and then acted like the price was perfect. "Mind if I see one?"

"Not at all." He grabbed some keys. "Right this way, ladies."

As he led them up some stairs, Marley made small talk about being new in town. "I'm going to be looking for some work," she said. "How do you think the job market is here?"

He shrugged as he unlocked a door. "Pretty much the same as anywhere I guess. What kind of work are you looking for?"

"I've been a nurse's aide. I was thinking I might get back into that." Her hope was that this would jog his memory about another tenant.

He opened the door, waving them into the small, stodgy apartment. "The units are all the same. Two bedrooms, one bath, kitchenette. What you see is pretty much what you get." Then he explained about utilities and deposits.

"How about smoking?" Marley asked.

"You a smoker?" He frowned.

She shrugged. "Sometimes."

"Well, the owner charges an extra deposit for smokers nowadays. That's because we always end up needing to paint and clean more after they leave."

"What if I smoke outside?" Marley persisted, unsure of where she was going with this but wanting to continue the conversation. "Do you have some kind of designated smoking area?"

"Not really." He pointed out the window over the sink. Marley looked out to see a small grassy area with a rundown gazebo in the center. "Some of the tenants smoke out there. There are some benches."

She smiled at him. "Good to know."

"Hey," Abby said. "I think a friend of mine might live in these apartments."

Marley turned to her. "Really? You didn't mention that before."

"Her name's Joan Wilson."

The manager rubbed the top of his shiny head as if trying to remember. "Oh yeah, that's right. We got a tenant named Joan Wilson here. Just moved in last month."

"Oh, that's wonderful," Abby gushed at Marley. "If you take the apartment, you'll have a friend nearby."

"I wonder which apartment Joan lives in?" Abby persisted. "It would be nice if hers was near yours. You could be neighbors."

"She's on the other end," the manager told her. "Unit 132." He nodded. "Yeah, that's right." He turned back to Marley. "So would you like to fill out an application? You get a discount if you apply today."

Marley squinted as if thinking hard. "How about if I take the application with me? I want to look at one more place before I make up my mind."

"Don't forget that Joan is here," Abby said with a twinkle in her eye. "That would make this apartment really special."

"That's right," the manager agreed. "You'd have a ready-made friend."

They went down to get the paperwork then, and before they left, Abby turned to Marley. "I think I should introduce you to Joan before we go."

"Good idea," the manager said. "And remember, if you turn in your application today, you get that discount."

Marley thanked him and promised to keep that in mind. Then they told him good-bye and meandered on down to apartment 132.

"What should we do if we actually see her?" Abby asked nervously.

Marley shrugged. "I don't know, but don't worry, I'll think of something."

"Hopefully the manager won't come down here and blow our cover. He might call the cops or something."

Marley chuckled. "Just relax, Abby. There's no law against snooping."

The parking space marked 132 was empty, and the blinds in the corresponding apartment were closed.

"Now what?" Abby looked discouraged. "We might as well go."

"Wait." Marley pointed to a scraggly looking planter in the walkway that led to unit 132. There, mixed in with the dirt, were some cigarette butts. "Do you think?"

"Joan's?" Abby glanced nervously around, as if she expected someone to jump them from behind.

"Maybe so." Marley casually opened her purse, removed a clean tissue from the little packet she always carried, and, using the tissue, gathered up several of the butts, loosely wrapping them in another clean tissue. She slipped this little packet back into her purse, then zipped it closed.

"Well, it looks like nobody's home," Marley said loudly. "I suppose we should go."

"Yes." Abby nodded eagerly. "Let's go."

They walked quickly back to the car, but once inside, they both started to giggle like schoolgirls. And as Abby drove away, they burst into loud ripples of laughter.

"Oh, that was fun," Marley finally said. "It reminded me of sixth grade. Remember when we TP'd Don Gibson's house on Halloween?"

Abby nodded. "I do! And remember how we freaked out when

Mr. Gibson stood on the porch in his long johns, and how he was yelling that he had a shotgun and knew how to use it?"

"Caroline practically wet her pants, she was so scared."

They both started laughing again, recalling other details of that wild evening. Then the car grew quiet, and Marley began thinking about Caroline. She must be feeling awful with her mother's life hanging in the balance and the law treating Caroline like a criminal.

"Do you think those were really Joan Wilson's cigarette butts?" Abby asked as she turned toward the hospital.

"I sure hope so."

"I'll bet they could run a DNA test on them. Wouldn't that prove something?"

"Undoubtedly." Marley patted her purse. "Also, they can determine if the cigarettes are the same brand as the ones found in Mrs. McCann's bedroom."

Abby chuckled as she pulled into a parking space. "Nice work, Sherlock."

"You, too, Watson."

"I do feel a little guilty for lying to the manager," Abby admitted.

"All done in the line of duty," Marley assured her. "I think God will forgive us."

They hurried into the hospital to find that only Janie was in the waiting area. They quickly relayed their findings, and Janie told them that Caroline was with her mom. "Mrs. McCann's been moved to ICU. She's stabilized but not conscious. Caroline just went in there a few minutes ago."

"What should we do with the evidence?" Marley asked.

"Why don't you let me handle it," Janie suggested. "I plan to act as Caroline's attorney anyway. Hopefully she won't really need my help. But she has so much on her mind right now between her mom's injuries and the burned-out house. The least I can do is to cover the legal angles for her."

"Oh, I hadn't even thought about the damage to her mom's house," Marley said. "How bad is it?"

"Well, I poked around a bit when I took Chuck over there. I put him in the backyard with some food and water and he seems okay for now. But the house is definitely not habitable. Mrs. McCann's room is badly burnt, and the rest of the house has considerable smoke damage."

"Poor Caroline." Marley shook her head. "She so didn't need this."

"I know." Janie sighed. "I told her that she and Chuck can stay with me tonight."

"Or she can stay with us," Abby offered.

"Or me," Marley said, "although I'd have to put her on my couch."

"Well, my house is closest to the hospital," Janie pointed out. "We might as well stick with that plan for the time being."

Marley removed her precious evidence from her purse, handing the wad of tissues over to Janie. "I was careful not to actually touch the cigarette butts," she told her. "And these are clean tissues. I didn't have a plastic bag on me."

"Actually this is perfect." Janie looked at the small white bundle. "Plastic bags hold in moisture, and that can damage the evidence. This is great."

Abby patted Marley on the back. "See, you really are a good sleuth."

"Speaking of sleuths"—Janie glanced at her watch—"maybe I should pay Detective Alberts a visit while he's still on duty."

"And I should probably get home to start dinner," Abby said a bit reluctantly. "Otherwise Paul might use this as an excuse to run out and eat a triple cheeseburger or some other form of heart-attack-on-a-bun."

"I'll stick around here for Caroline," Marley offered. After Janie and Abby left, Marley sat down and tried to pass the time by perusing the old magazines in the waiting room. When Caroline joined her, Marley could see that she'd been crying.

"How is she?" Marley asked gently. Caroline began to cry even harder. Marley enveloped Caroline in a hug and let her cry.

After a while, once the crying stopped and they were both blowing their noses, Caroline described her mom's condition. "I just don't see how she can possibly survive this. Burns … damaged lungs … and the Alzheimer's." Caroline took in a jagged breath. "I don't like to question God, but the truth is, I wonder. I mean, why would he allow my mom to suffer like this? What is the purpose?"

Marley had no answer.

"The poor woman didn't have a great life to start with. She did get some peace after my dad died. But even that was cut short by the Alzheimer's. I just don't get it."

Marley thought hard, wishing for something to say that would comfort Caroline. Again she came up empty.

"Now she's just lying there all bandaged up, unconscious and possibly suffering in silence, breathing on a ventilator. It all feels so senseless. Really, she would be better off dead."

Marley remembered something. "Didn't you say that your mom had made a living will back before her Alzheimer's got bad?"

Caroline nodded sadly. "She did."

"Well, if it's like the one my parents had, wouldn't it mean that no one is supposed to use any artificial means of life support to keep her alive?"

"Something to that effect."

"So why are they keeping her alive on a ventilator? Why don't they allow her to die peacefully, like she wants?"

"Because of the police." Caroline wiped her nose. "Janie said that until the investigation regarding the fire is resolved, the police can get a court injunction instructing the hospital to keep my mom alive indefinitely."

"Oh dear." Perhaps the findings of Marley's investigation would change the law's perspective. She quickly told Caroline about the apartments and the cigarette butts. "In fact Janie is taking the evidence to the police right now."

Caroline threw her arms around Marley again. "What would I do without the support of my friends?" she cried. "You guys are the best. Better than family!"

Chapter 9

JANIE

"Honestly I think Abby is right about Detective Alberts. I'll bet he watches too many crime shows on TV," Janie said as she handed Caroline a cup of Sleepy Time herbal tea. It was past eleven, and even though she'd already made up the guest room with fresh sheets, silk pajamas, and a nice set of toiletries that she knew Caroline would appreciate, it seemed that Caroline was too wired to go to bed.

"Too many crime shows?" Caroline frowned. "What do you mean?"

"I mean it's almost as if he's hungry for crime. Like he's actually hoping for real murders to occur."

"That's seriously twisted." Caroline took a sip of tea and sighed. "He should be thankful that Clifden is a relatively peaceful town. If he wants excitement, he should head down to LA."

"Or New York." Janie sat down on the sofa.

"So what did he say about the cigarette butts?"

"You mean after he got over the shock of hearing that someone else was out there doing his job for him?"

Caroline's brow creased. "I hope that didn't rub him the wrong way."

Janie smiled. "I actually handled it rather carefully. I made sure that other police staff were around when I presented the evidence to him. And I made it sound like it had been his idea right from the start."

"He fell for that?"

"He seemed to. I mostly tried to act as if I'm simply trying to help him get to the bottom of this case."

"I wonder how long that will take."

"I'm not sure. It's not helping that Joan Wilson seems determined to make herself scarce."

Caroline nodded. "Yeah, I called the agency again, and they hadn't heard from her either. It seems like that alone would cast some suspicion her way."

"My thinking exactly. I even pointed that out to Detective Alberts." Janie pulled her legs under her on the sofa and leaned back. "How was your mom doing when you left her this evening?"

"The same." Caroline reached down to pet Chuck. He was lying on the oriental carpet that had been in Phil's family for several generations. Although Janie knew these old carpets were tough, she felt a little uneasy about having a dog in her house. Still, she was determined not to let Caroline know about this. Good grief, her friend had enough worries without adding that to the pile. "As I was sitting with her—just talking, you know, like she could understand me—I got to thinking that it might've been a blessing in disguise that the police intervened in regard to the living will."

"How so?" Janie took a sip of her tea.

"Well, I'm pretty sure that Mom would be dead. I just think there's no way she could survive without the ventilator. Even with it she might not make it through the night."

"I'm not quite grasping how that's a blessing in disguise."

"Because it allowed me to have more time to be with her, to talk to her. I know she probably can't understand a word I'm saying, but what if she can?"

"Good point. I've read some medical research that suggests there is sometimes a lot more going on in a person's head than it seems."

"Tonight I was telling myself to talk to her like she was really aware, to tell her how I feel, how much I love her, and how I really want to catch up with her in heaven someday." Caroline looked down at her mug of tea. "I even prayed the old sinner's prayer with her."

"The old sinner's prayer?"

Caroline nodded. "It's what they used to say in Sunday school when I was a little girl. Where you confess you are a sinner and you ask Jesus into your heart, and you accept his forgiveness. I kind of prayed it in proxy for Mom. Do you think God will honor that?"

Janie couldn't help but smile at this. "I don't see why not. And for all we know, somewhere in the deep regions of her mind, your mom might've been right with you and saying amen."

Caroline brightened. "That's what I'm telling myself."

"So maybe you're right. Maybe this injunction is really a blessing in disguise."

"It all feels so surreal," Caroline said. "This morning I was lamenting about how I have no life and feeling overwhelmed with my mom, and the next thing I know everything is different. I can't even wrap my head around it."

"I'm sure it will take a while to let reality sink in, and to sort it all out. Fortunately there's no hurry, Caroline. In fact what you probably need most is a good night's sleep."

"I'm keeping you up late," Caroline said. "Please don't feel like you need to sit here with me, Janie. I'm fine, really."

"I'm fine too." Janie took another sip of tea. "Trust me, if I wanted to go to bed, I would."

Caroline looked relieved. "Enough about me and my problems. I want an update on Victor and his ex. How's that going?"

Janie just shrugged. "It's hard to say."

"Hard to say in what way?"

"In that Victor isn't saying much."

"When did you last talk to him?"

"This afternoon. I called him. I thought, since he's your friend too, he'd be interested to hear about your mom."

"And?" Caroline waited expectantly.

"And, well, I don't know how to say this except that he seemed a bit distant." Janie felt a small ripple of fear to hear her own confession aloud.

"Distant like he didn't want to talk to you? Or distant like maybe his ex was right there listening and he didn't want to say too much?"

Janie hadn't really considered that possibility. She did now. "I'm not sure," she admitted. "But my gut feeling was that he wasn't himself."

"Oh, I'll bet it was because his ex was in the room with him, Janie. He's in a pretty uncomfortable spot. Just give it some time."

Janie nodded like maybe Caroline was right. But deep down she didn't think so. Janie was fairly sure that whatever she'd had with

Victor was coming to a slow but certain death. Maybe it was for the best. Maybe the purpose of her relationship with Victor was simply to show her that it was possible to have feelings for a man again. But even as she tried to convince herself of this possibility, she felt sad. It was going to be hard to let go.

"Have you met his ex yet?" Caroline persisted.

Janie shook her head.

"Aren't you curious?"

"Actually I am."

"If I weren't in the middle of my own mess, I would try to think of a way that we could all meet Victor's ex. You know, like a dinner party or something."

Janie waved her hand. "I don't think so. And, like you said, you need to focus on your own life right now."

Caroline held up her mug. "Your herb tea must be working, because I think maybe I can go to sleep now."

Of course, Janie felt wide awake. She said good night to Caroline and went into the kitchen to clean up the tea things. Then she turned off the lights, but instead of going to bed, she returned to the darkened living room and sat down and just thought. What if her relationship with Victor really was over? Was she okay with that? Or was there something else she needed to do to keep the relationship alive?

She went round and round in her mind, replaying scene after scene between her and Victor. Up until quite recently the scenes were lovely and memorable—almost a storybook sort of romance, which only left her feeling more confused and sad.

Finally she replayed her last conversation with Victor. She'd called him from the hospital this afternoon, and when he answered the phone, he had sounded like his usual upbeat self, but when he realized it was her, she felt certain that his voice turned just a bit formal, perhaps even frosty. She quickly relayed the information about Caroline's mom. Though he displayed what sounded like genuine concern for Caroline, the tone of his voice sounded oddly impersonal and almost detached.

"Well, I'm sure you're busy," she had said after a silent lapse of several seconds.

"I'm sure Caroline needs you," he responded.

"So take care," she said in what she knew was her business voice, although she'd only been following his lead.

"You, too."

Something between them had definitely changed. Something truly was wrong. Janie felt certain that something could only be Donna.

Janie stood and began pacing. By the light of the street lamp outside, she walked back and forth in the shadowy living room, trying to figure this thing out. Maybe Victor had realized that he still had feelings for Donna. Maybe he had even decided he wanted to be with her. Who could blame him for wanting to reunite his family? Holidays, birthdays, weddings, even funerals—all would go much more smoothly with the original family back together again. Ben and Marcus would have their parents back together too. Really, it was a wonderful thing. Janie should be happy for all of them. Truly she would be—once she got over her own personal loss.

She stopped pacing and stared out the front window. Even so, why wouldn't Victor do the noble thing and be up front with her? Why wouldn't he take the time to explain his change of heart? Was that too much to expect? After all, they were adults. These things happened. Why not simply be open and honest about it? Full disclosure.

Janie sighed. She really was tired. Rehashing this over and over really wasn't a healthy use of time or brain power. It was possible she was blowing the whole thing out of proportion. She needed to let it go, at least for tonight. Perhaps she'd see it all differently in the light of morning.

What Janie saw in the light of morning was a big hairy dog drinking out of her toilet. "Hey, Chuck," she gently scolded him, "why don't you go drink out of the other toilet?" He looked up with innocent eyes and a dripping mouth, then meandered on out, making his way to the other end of the house, where Caroline was staying. As Janie cleaned the drips from the toilet and the marble tiled floor, she wondered just how long she'd be comfortable housing Caroline and her dog. After seeing the condition of Caroline's home yesterday, Janie felt certain that Caroline would be homeless for a while. It wasn't that Janie wanted to kick them out anytime soon, but eventually Caroline would have to find another place to live—a place that catered to large dogs.

As Janie made coffee, she considered how to stay on top of things with the police. Hearing the back door open made her jump, and she was relieved to see Caroline come in.

"I took Chuck over to my mom's backyard again," she told Janie. "Gave him food and water. He should be okay for most of the day while I stay at the hospital."

Janie nodded. "He seemed comfortable there yesterday."

"I poked around the house some more." Caroline sighed. "It's such a mess. I don't even know where to begin with it."

"You might want to begin with an insurance claim." Janie slid a mug of coffee toward Caroline.

Caroline blinked. "Oh, you mean for the house."

"Your mother must've had homeowner's insurance."

Caroline frowned now, as if thinking hard.

"You did have guardianship of her, didn't you?"

"Yes, of course."

"So you handled all the bills and things?"

"Yes, I'm just not sure that there was insurance on the house. I mean since the house was paid for."

"Surely she had a homeowner's policy."

"I honestly don't know. I've been handling her finances since summer, but I never paid for homeowner's insurance."

Janie considered this. On one hand it could help Caroline's case if there was no fire insurance. That would remove some motivation for causing a fire. On the other hand, without insurance, how would Caroline afford the repairs? "Well, I'm sure you'll figure it out," Janie said.

"Eventually." Caroline finished her coffee, then rinsed her mug and set it in the sink. "I called the hospital. It sounds like there's been no change in my mom."

Janie wasn't sure how to respond.

"Anyway, I'm heading over there now." Caroline jangled her keys. "Guess I'll see you later."

"I plan to go have another conversation with Detective Alberts this morning," Janie informed her. "Then I'll swing by the hospital to give you an update. Maybe we can have lunch."

Caroline nodded. "Sounds good."

After Caroline left, Janie decided it might be wise to dress more like an attorney today. She suspected that Detective Alberts wasn't taking her as seriously as she would've liked. She pulled out her favorite gray suit, an exquisitely cut St. John that was both classic and authoritative. No-nonsense. She even combed her hair into a neat French twist and pulled out her best briefcase of sleek black leather trimmed in sterling. She usually reserved it for court. It went nicely with her black Stuart Weitzman pumps. Yes, she was overdressed for their small coastal town, but her goal was to get some attention and then show the Clifden legal system that she meant business.

She parked in front of city hall and had just entered the building when she found herself face-to-face with Victor. "Oh!" She gave him a surprised smile. "Fancy meeting you here."

He looked even more shocked. "Janie—what are you doing here?"

"I'm here on some legal business for Caroline." Now she looked past Victor to see a petite blonde standing beside him, smiling with interest.

"Uh, Janie"—Victor cleared his throat—"I'd like you to meet Donna Lewis. Donna, this is my good friend Janie Sorenson."

The two women shook hands, and Janie took a quick inventory. Donna was very pretty in that soft, delicate, feminine sort of way. Wearing a blue cashmere sweater set and tweed wool pants, she looked casually chic and stylish—nothing like Janie had imagined.

"You must be the New York attorney I've been hearing about," Donna said as she studied Janie. "You look as if you're about to try a very important case."

Janie forced a smile. "I'm on something of a legal mission."

"How's Caroline's mother doing?" Victor asked.

"The same as yesterday," Janie told him.

He nodded. "Well, give Caroline my best."

"We'll let you get on with your mission," Donna said brightly. "Lovely to meet you, Janie."

"You, too." Janie nodded primly. "I hope you're enjoying our little town."

"Oh, I absolutely adore Clifden," Donna gushed. "It's a delight."

Janie glanced at Victor. His eyes looked troubled, but she wasn't sure if the source of his angst was his ex-wife or Janie. Maybe both. Janie wanted to ask what they'd been doing in city hall, but a deep-down sense of dread told her that she might not like the answer. What if they'd been in to get a marriage license? Or worse yet, what if they'd already remarried? "Well, nice to see you both," Janie managed to murmur.

"Good luck," Victor said a bit formally.

She thanked him and said good-bye, but as she walked to the reception area, Janie felt as if someone had pulled the floor from beneath her. Her worries were totally ridiculous, not to mention completely unfounded. Really, what were the chances that Victor and Donna had already decided to remarry? It wasn't only preposterous, it was paranoid. And yet …

=Chapter 10=

ABBY

Paul was hunched over, sitting on the bench by the door and taking far too long to tie the laces of his athletic shoes.

"What did you just say?" Abby demanded.

He looked up. "Hey, don't chew my head off, Abs. I was just asking."

"You honestly expect me to have lunch with Victor and you as well as *Victor's ex-wife?*" With hands on hips Abby frowned down at him. Seriously, had he lost his ever-loving mind? "Did I hear you correctly?"

"Fine, don't come if you don't want to. But you don't have to shoot the messenger. I'll tell Victor that you can't make it. It's not that big of a deal, Abby."

"Maybe not to you." She pressed her lips together and thought hard. "Honestly, do you expect me to go along with you, socialize with Victor's ex, and act like Janie's not one of my closest friends?"

"Of course not." He stood and pulled on his sweatshirt. "Victor just wanted to introduce Donna to some of the locals. I think it would help to take some of the pressure off of Vic. Poor guy, he's trying to accommodate this demanding ex-spouse, and I have a feeling he's a little overwhelmed."

Abby envisioned a domineering woman, outspoken and bossy as she tried to force Victor to conform to her unreasonable whims and harebrained plans. The image made her feel a little sorry for Victor. He probably felt trapped between a rock and a hard place. The more she considered this, the more she realized she might be doing both Janie and Victor a favor to meet the ex-wife today. At the very least she could gather information about Victor's ex, and then she could reassure Janie that there was nothing whatsoever to be worried about.

Besides all that, Abby was just plain curious. Who was this woman?

Abby sighed. "Well, I suppose I could go to lunch with you guys. Just this one time probably wouldn't hurt."

"Great." He picked up his gym bag. "I plan to do my workout, and then I'll sit in the sauna for a while. I'll meet you at The Chowder House at noon. Okay?"

"Okay." But she could hear the doubt in her own voice.

He frowned at her. "You will be civilized, won't you, Abby? No dramatics."

"Good grief, Paul. What do you think I am?"

He grinned. "Well, I know how you can be sometimes, though usually you save it for me."

She gently smacked his forehead with the heel of her hand. "That's because you ask for it." She watched as he got his truck keys and put on his ball cap.

"You're still taking it easy at the fitness club?" she asked with concern.

"Like I already told you, my fitness program is doctor approved."

"I know that's what you said, Paul, but I also know how guys can act."

He cocked his head to one side. "How can guys act?"

"Oh, you know, you see another guy who's about your age, or maybe older, and he's doing a vigorous workout—or maybe it's a cute chick you want to impress—and so you decide to push yourself a little harder. And instead of using a twenty-pound weight like you're supposed to, you go for a fifty-pound one, and the next thing you know you're taking an expensive one-way trip to the emergency room."

"You certainly have one vivid imagination." He leaned over and pecked her on the cheek. "Don't worry, my macho-man days are a thing of the past."

"Okay, just don't you forget it."

"See you at high noon."

As soon as Paul left, Abby was tempted to call one of the Lindas to confess what she was about to do, but Caroline had her hands full, and no way was she calling Janie yet. Abby would have no problem filling her in after the fact, but not before. She was just about to call Marley when she stopped herself. No, she didn't need to phone a friend to bolster her confidence. Instead she would simply put on her big-girl pants and do this thing herself. She could report back to the Lindas later.

She went to her closet and looked for something appropriate to wear. For some reason she felt she should put her best foot forward.

Of course, with Abby's lackluster wardrobe, this was always a challenge. Eventually she settled for her best jeans, an oxford shirt, and her favorite fisherman-knit cardigan. So she wasn't the epitome of fashion. Clifden was her town, and she had no problem showing this interloper Donna that she was perfectly comfortable in it. For that matter so was Janie. Not that Abby planned to mention this, but it would be going through her mind.

Abby got to the restaurant at noon, but Paul's truck wasn't in the parking lot. She considered waiting for him in her car, but it was possible he'd parked on the street. So she went inside. There, waiting in the foyer, was Victor with a very pretty blonde woman next to him. At first Abby assumed the blonde was the hostess. She appeared to be maybe in her late thirties or early forties, and she had the pleasant smile of someone totally comfortable in her own skin.

"I'm so glad you could make it." Victor clasped Abby's hand.

"Paul must still be on his way," Abby told him. The next thing she knew, Victor was introducing her to this pretty woman, who was not the hostess but his ex-wife, Donna. Abby shook her hand and tried not to look overly surprised, but Donna was nothing like what she'd imagined. Almost as disturbing was the fact that Donna seemed very nice. Quite likeable, in fact.

"I just love Clifden," Donna told Abby as they were led to a table. "Every single thing about it. It's absolutely charming. I honestly think if the rest of the world got word of it, this town would be overpopulated by Thanksgiving."

"I told Donna we try to keep it our little secret," Victor said as they sat down.

"I don't think Paul would agree with that," Abby told him. "He's on the chamber, you know, and they do all they can to bring positive publicity to Clifden."

"Who can blame them?" Donna said pleasantly. "When you have something this lovely, this delightful, well, you can't help but want to share it with friends."

"At least the friends with deep pockets," Abby said. "Our town could use some more development."

"That's exactly why I encouraged Victor to go to city hall this morning," Donna said with bright eyes.

"City hall?" Abby was confused.

"To discuss the possibility of a farmers' market."

Abby nodded. "Oh yes, I remember that idea you had, Victor. So are you really getting serious about it now?"

Victor kind of shrugged, and for a moment Abby remembered him as the shy schoolboy, brainy but nerdy.

"He should be serious about it," Donna answered. "It's a brilliant idea. The city manager we met with this morning whole-heartedly agreed." Then Donna went on to tell Abby she'd worked as a publicist in Chicago and was eager to use her publicity skills in Clifden.

Victor waved at someone, and Abby turned to see Paul making his way toward their table. Before long they were all chatting like old friends. Although Abby felt guilty for Janie's sake, she couldn't deny that she liked Donna. As Paul told Donna a bit about the chamber's priorities in regard to business development, Abby turned her attention to Victor.

What was going on in him? He definitely seemed different from his usual relaxed and easygoing self. Was it because he was torn? Had he rediscovered his love for his ex? If so, where did Janie fit into this new scenario? Though he was being polite and congenial, it seemed he was holding something back. Abby suspected—or maybe just hoped—that Victor wasn't as comfortable with his ex-wife as Donna appeared to be with him.

It was impossible to ignore the loving gestures Donna made toward Victor: a touch of the hand, a warm and engaged smile, a merry laugh at his wittier comments. No doubt, this woman was seriously putting the moves on her ex-husband. Why shouldn't she? Wouldn't Abby do the same thing in the same situation?

But what about Janie? Abby felt like a traitor. Really, where were her alliances?

"So where will you be living in Clifden?" Abby asked Donna when the conversation came to a lull.

"That's actually one reason I wanted to have lunch with Paul today," Victor said quickly. "I thought Donna might like to hear about some of his spec houses. You still have some on the market, don't you?"

Paul nodded eagerly. "I do have a couple of houses for sale. One is nearly finished. The other should be done by Christmas."

"That's great." Victor smiled eagerly. "Paul is the best builder in town. You should see his home—it's really well done. I'm sure his spec houses are equally nice."

"Oh yes," Abby said. "Paul only uses the finest materials, and yet his designs are practical for the Oregon coast. If you decided to go with the one that won't be done until Christmas, you could probably pick out some of your own finishes for floors and cabinets and such." She turned to Paul. "Right?"

He nodded. "Absolutely."

To Abby's surprise Donna looked unimpressed.

"Of course, there are lots of other lovely properties for sale in Clifden," Abby said. She hoped she hadn't been too pushy about Paul's houses. That wasn't her usual mode, but she'd been caught up in the moment. "In fact I could introduce you to a realtor friend of mine. If you'd like, I mean." Abby felt like backpedaling. Why was she being so aggressive?

Donna made a stiff smile. "Well, it might be a bit premature for that. But I will definitely keep all this in mind."

Victor glanced directly at Abby. "I actually had another idea." He cleared his throat. "It might be a crazy one, but I thought I'd toss it out anyway, just in case."

Abby was curious. "Sure, what is it?"

"Well, I know you purchased that property for your bed-and-breakfast, and I know you probably won't be opening it for a while, but I wondered if—"

"If I could rent a room to Donna?" Abby finished for him. He looked a bit sheepish, but Abby nodded eagerly. "That's a fantastic idea, Victor."

"Seriously?"

"It really is." She glanced at Paul, but his expression was hard to read. "I want to get it running, but, well, as you know I've been distracted with Paul—"

"*Distracted* is not the word," Paul inserted. "*Obsessed* is more like it. Abby's been like a cat on a hot tin roof, sneaking around the house, always checking on me, acting like I'm going to kick the bucket at any given moment. It's creepy."

Abby filled in Donna about Paul's recent heart attack. Donna, bless her heart, was rather understanding. "I don't blame you a bit," she told Abby. "My father died young from a heart attack. I would take my husband's recovery very seriously too if I were you." She shook her finger at Paul. "You need to accept that Abby's concern is only because she loves you."

Paul made a half smile. "Yeah, I know."

Abby was liking Donna more and more.

"Would you really be interested in renting a room before you officially open the B and B?" Victor asked.

"It would be a great way to get the whole thing rolling," Abby assured him. "My plan had been to attack one room at a time. The master suite is actually in great shape." She turned to Donna. "If you're interested, I would be happy to let you use it until you figure things out. My house isn't far from here. In fact it's very conveniently located to town."

"That's right," Victor said. "It's near the library and post office and lots of other things. In fact, if you got a bike, you wouldn't even need a car."

"I don't know." Donna looked unsure.

"I'm sure it doesn't sound very inviting," Abby admitted. "But the house is nice. I mostly just want to make some cosmetic changes. You know, a little paint here and there, fresh curtains, the right furnishings, good linens, some nice touches. In fact we could run over there after lunch if you like. I could show you around."

Donna still looked disinterested, and Abby tried not to be offended. Victor spoke up. "That's a good idea, Abby. I've only seen the outside of the house, and I'd love to see the interior." He turned to Donna. "It's an appealing old Victorian. I'm sure you'd love it. I remember how you used to love old houses."

"I'm just not sure about this." Donna frowned. "Living all by myself in a big old house. It sounds a bit sad and lonely."

"Janie will be there sometimes," Abby said quickly. Perhaps a bit too quickly. She realized too late whom she was talking to.

"Oh, you mean Janie the lawyer?" Donna looked interested.

"Yes, she's going to use the basement as her law office. So, really, you wouldn't be all alone. I'll be there a lot too." Abby smiled hopefully. "You know, working on the place."

"I was curious as to where Caroline is going to live," Victor injected. "I hear that her mom's house is uninhabitable."

"Oh, Victor, what a fantastic idea! I hadn't even thought about Caroline staying there, but it would be perfect." Abby turned to Paul. "And you were worried about how this was going to work. My bed-and-breakfast is already filling up."

Paul looked a bit doubtful. "Just don't count your chickens before they hatch, Abby. You never know."

After Abby gave Donna and Victor the full tour of the house, she thought Paul was wrong. She was ready to count her chickens. After all, Victor had been effusive in his praise, and after Donna saw the master suite, which was actually rather cozy, it seemed that she warmed to the idea too. Abby strongly suspected that Victor was eager to get Donna out from under his roof. She couldn't even imagine what that last few days must've been like for him. Abby was starting to see that, as sweet as Donna came across, this woman was determined—determined to get Victor back.

What Abby couldn't quite discern, though, was Victor's position. At times he seemed to respond to Donna's affection, and at other times his jaw hardened and his eyes looked troubled. That had to be hard on Janie. As Abby drove to the hospital to check on Caroline, she realized that her own efforts to convince Donna to live at the bed-and-breakfast could backfire. How would Janie react to the possibility of having her law office in the same house as Victor's ex?

=Chapter 11=

CAROLINE

"There's been no change in her condition," Caroline told Mitch on the phone. She stood outside the hospital cafeteria, where they could talk without bothering anyone. He'd just called from Tokyo, where it was around eight in the morning *tomorrow*. Caroline always had a hard time wrapping her head around the time differences.

"Do you want me to come home?" Mitch asked for the second time.

"No," she said quickly. "Of course not. I know this trip is important. And you only just got there yesterday … or today … or whenever that was."

"But I would come home if you needed me, Caroline. You know that, don't you?"

She was slightly shocked by this. The truth was, she didn't know that he would actually drop everything and come halfway around the world to be by her side. A part of her was tempted to test him on this, but she wouldn't.

"I really appreciate that," she told him, "but don't worry, I've got the Lindas here for moral support." She told him about Janie's legal help and how Marley and Abby had done some sleuthing. "Really, I'm in good hands."

"It's a lot to deal with," he said sadly. "I wish I could be there for you."

"I promise that if I really need you, I'll call, okay?" Of course, even as she said this, she doubted it.

"I'm with you in spirit," he said gently.

"Thanks."

They talked a while longer, but then it was time for him to go in to a meeting. She wished him good luck, and he told her to keep him posted, then they hung up. She returned to the dining room, where Abby and Janie were waiting for her. The three of them had been on their way to get something to drink when Caroline's phone had rung.

"How's the traveling man?" Abby asked as Caroline sat down with them.

"He seemed very concerned," Caroline admitted. "Even willing to come home."

"Wow." Abby nodded. "Impressive."

"I got you some green tea." Janie slid a cup in front of Caroline. "Hope that's okay."

"Perfect." Caroline opened a sugar packet and poured in half of it, then stirred the tea. "I almost called him on it."

"Called him on what?" Abby asked.

"You know, asked him to leave Tokyo and come home to help me. But that seemed unfair. Besides, I told him I have my Lindas as backup." Caroline smiled at them. "No one could expect more than that."

"Marley was here earlier," Janie told Abby, "but she had to leave because it's her afternoon to play grandma to Hunter."

"Janie tells me that the police are getting a little more cooperative," Abby said to Caroline. "That's something."

Caroline chuckled and pointed to Janie. "That's because she went in there wearing her power suit and talking legalese. I'm sure she must've shaken them up a little."

"I only wanted to get their attention," Janie defended, "and to have them take me seriously."

Caroline patted her hand. "And for that I am truly grateful." Now she turned to Abby. "You'll never guess who Janie met at city hall!"

Abby's brows arched. "Who?"

"Victor's ex!"

Abby got a funny look now, like she knew something but wasn't going to say it. Caroline continued, "But our big question is—what were Victor and Donna doing at city hall this morning?"

Janie made what sounded like a forced laugh. "Yes, I told Caroline I was worried that they were in there getting hitched, but I have to admit that's a bit far-fetched."

"Don't worry. They weren't getting hitched," Abby declared.

Now both Caroline and Janie turned to Abby. "How do *you* know?" Caroline asked.

Abby held up her hands in a flustered way. "Well, I … uh … I just happen to know."

"Come on," Caroline demanded, "spill it."

Janie's eyes looked worried.

"Well, I was going to tell you," Abby began slowly. "You see, uh, it was Paul's doing." She paused and took a sip of tea.

"Paul's doing what?" Caroline persisted.

"Paul asked me to go to lunch with Victor and Donna today."

"You went to lunch with Victor and his ex-wife?" Caroline exclaimed.

"Don't look so scandalized," Abby said quickly. "I didn't *want* to go."

"But you went anyway?" Caroline frowned at her.

"Why don't we let Abby explain?" Janie said gently.

"Yes," Abby agreed. "Let me explain." She said Victor wanted Paul and Abby to have lunch with them so that Donna could meet locals and learn about some of the housing opportunities in town.

"So she's sticking around, then?" Caroline asked.

"I think so." Abby sighed. "Anyway, I'll just cut to the chase. I kind of asked Donna if she wanted to rent a room at my bed-and-breakfast."

"But your bed-and-breakfast isn't even running," Janie said quietly.

"I know. Not officially. But there's no reason Donna can't rent a room from me and—"

"Abby Franklin!" Caroline had to stop herself from saying, *You Benedict Arnold!* "What were you thinking?"

"Hear me out," Abby protested. "It sounds like Donna is trying to make herself a permanent fixture in Victor's life, and I got the impression that Victor isn't really comfortable with it. I was merely trying to help Victor out of a sticky situation."

"I don't know." Janie sighed. "I got the impression that Victor and Donna were rather comfortable together."

"By the way," Caroline added, "what *were* they doing at city hall?"

Abby explained Donna's support for Victor's interest in the farmers' market. "Donna is really gung-ho about Clifden. She has a marketing or publicity background, and it sounds like she's determined to put our town on the map."

"We are on the map," Janie pointed out.

Abby looked frustrated.

"I'm sorry," Caroline said to Abby. "I didn't mean to sound so accusatory. But it's kind of shocking to hear you getting all buddy-buddy with the enemy."

"Donna's not the enemy," Janie said. "In fact she seems quite nice."

"You know what I mean," Caroline told her.

"I don't want to turn this into some kind of a battlefield," Janie said calmly. "We are all grown-ups, and this is a small town. If Abby wants to rent a room to Donna, we shouldn't make her feel guilty about it."

"Speaking of renting rooms," Abby said. "I thought you might like to use a room there too, Caroline. I mean rent-free."

"You want me to live with Victor's ex?" Caroline frowned at Abby.

Janie laughed. "Oh, come on, Caroline. It's not like you and Donna would become roommates. And don't forget, my law office is downstairs."

"It seems a bit odd." Caroline tried to imagine the whole thing. "What about Chuck? Is he welcome there too?"

"Why not?" Abby smiled. "I read that pet friendly B and B's are becoming quite popular."

Caroline looked at Janie now. "I appreciate your hospitality, Janie. But your house isn't exactly pet friendly. I mean it's friendly enough, but ..."

Janie seemed relieved. "I'll understand if you and Chuck want to stay at the B and B. In fact it seems like a handy solution. You'll be even closer to the hospital."

"I don't think I can have the rooms ready for a few days," Abby told Caroline. "But it would really motivate me to get moving if I knew someone was going to live there."

"Count me in," Caroline said. "Maybe I can get some of my things moved from my mom's house so you—"

"What about the smoke damage?" Abby asked. "We don't want—"

"My room was closed up during the fire," Caroline told her. "I think most of my stuff will be okay with some laundering and dry cleaning."

Abby nodded. "Well, okay. But I want to get some beds and furnishings and things. So, other than your clothes and personal items, you shouldn't need much."

"Maybe I can help you out with the laundry and dry cleaning," Janie offered. "I could stop by on my way home and pick up your—"

Caroline pointed at Janie's nice suit. "Not in those clothes."

"Oh, right." Janie nodded. "But I can check on Chuck and get some of your things if you want."

"Thanks," Caroline told her. "I'd appreciate that."

Abby stood. "I'll start getting some things together for the B and B. I'm actually getting excited at the prospect of the house being used. It's lighting a fire under me."

Caroline rolled her eyes. "Please, Abby, spare me the fire metaphors."

Abby grimaced. "Oh yeah. I forgot. Sorry."

They all stood and hugged, then Abby hurried on her way.

"Call me if you need anything," Janie told Caroline. "If you want, I'll fix us a late dinner tonight. I know you'll probably want to stick around here until visiting hours end."

"Thanks." Caroline sighed. "Not that it makes much difference."

"You never know," Janie assured her. "What if your mother can hear you?"

"That's what I keep hoping for."

As Caroline headed back to the critical care unit, that's what she told herself. *Maybe Mom really can hear me.* Wouldn't that make all this worthwhile? Most of the time that Caroline sat by her mom's side, she had to wonder. In some ways it seemed like her mom was already dead, and yet circumstances refused to give Caroline permission to grieve. Those machines just kept going, as if they could go on like that forever, sustaining a life that wasn't even there.

"Oh, Mom," Caroline said as she watched the motionless features of her mother's pale, wrinkled face. "I wish there were a way I could release you to move on, to go to a better place, but that's for God to do. It's up to him. Please trust him, Mom. Feel his arms around you and surrender yourself to him. He loves you, Mom. He wants to take care of you. He wants to heal your mind and your heart and your soul. He wants to give you a new body. Just let him." She sighed. "Maybe you already have." She reached over and touched her mom's forehead. "Maybe you already have."

Chapter 12

MARLEY

"Are you going to marry my grandpa?" Hunter asked Marley as they were leaving the craft store. Marley had just bought some sculpting clay.

"What?" Marley looked down at Hunter's serious-looking, big brown eyes.

"I said, are you going to marry Grandpa?"

Marley chuckled as she ran her fingers through Hunter's red curls. "What makes you ask that?"

"I'm just wondering."

"As far as I know, I am *not* going to marry your grandpa."

"Why not?"

Marley laughed as she unlocked her car. "Because I'm not."

"You don't like my grandpa?" Hunter sounded offended as she buckled herself into Marley's backseat.

"I like your grandpa, Hunter. You know that."

"Then why won't you marry him?"

Marley had to think hard now. "Marriage is a big thing," she explained as she started the car. "It's not something I would ever jump into. I did that once, and it didn't work out too well."

"You were married before?" Hunter sounded surprised.

"Yes. I told you that. Remember? And remember that I have a son, Ashton—the one who makes drums for a living?"

"Oh yeah. But you're not married now, right?"

"Right."

"So you could marry my grandpa if you wanted to."

"Right." Marley was trying to think of a way to derail this conversation.

"But you just don't want to?"

"Like I was saying," Marley tried again. "I was married once, and it wasn't so great. If I ever get married again—and I'm not planning on it—but if I do, it will only be after I've carefully thought about it, and after I've prayed about it, and only if I know absolutely, positively that it's the right thing to do."

"And then you might marry my grandpa?" Hunter sounded hopeful.

"I'll tell you what, Hunter."

"What?"

"If I ever do decide to marry your grandpa, you will be the first one to know. Okay?"

"Okay."

"So let me explain to you how that clay works," Marley said in an effort to swing their conversation well away from the subject of marriage. "It's not like Play-Doh, you know."

"I know," Hunter said. "You can bake it."

"Yes. So I want you to start thinking about what you want to make. We only have a couple of hours before I take you back to your grandpa, and we want to make the most of it." They began discussing the possibilities of creating jungle animals, clowns, teddy bears, and all sorts of things.

Before long they were in Marley's beach house, working at her kitchen table, using the colorful clay to create a tiger and a giraffe. Then they moved on to making Christmas-tree decorations. "Do you really think I can sell these in Grandpa's gallery?" Hunter asked hopefully. The prospect of earning money was appealing to her.

"I don't see why not, if we do a good job and make a cute display. I know I would buy something like that." Marley pointed to the sweet snowman that Hunter had just finished. "With that crooked smile and carrot nose, he's charming."

Hunter frowned. "His smile is crooked?"

"I mean a good kind of crooked," Marley explained. "It's part of his charm, like he's not perfect. I like that sort of thing."

"Like my grandpa?"

Marley was caught off guard again. "Huh?" she asked as she rolled out a strip of lime-green clay.

"His leg," Hunter said, like Marley should know what she was talking about.

"His leg?"

"Yeah, his wooden leg. Only it's not really wooden. He just says that."

"Your grandpa has a wooden leg?" Marley tried to say this carefully, not wanting to sound shocked in case it was true, nor confrontational if it wasn't.

Hunter peered at Marley. "You didn't know about Grandpa's leg?"

Marley thought hard. Jack had a slight limp. She had assumed it was caused by arthritis or an old sports injury. It didn't really slow him down much, and she'd never heard him mention anything specific.

"Do you know why his gallery is called the *One*-Legged Seagull?" Hunter persisted.

"Because it's a clever name?"

"Because it's my grandpa," Hunter explained. "He's the One-Legged Seagull."

"Really?"

"You didn't know that?"

"I'm not sure," Marley confessed. "Maybe I knew that and forgot somehow." But the truth was she did not recall hearing this before, and, even now, she wasn't totally sure that Hunter wasn't pulling one of Marley's legs. "How did your grandpa lose his leg anyway?"

Hunter was rolling out a white ball for another snowman. "It's a pretty good story."

"Yeah?" Marley stopped sculpting the clay to listen.

"Yeah. He was working on this boat back when he was a lot younger. Like I think he was nineteen, but I'm not sure. It was a crabbing boat. I know this for sure because when I was really little I thought that Grandpa got his leg bit off by a crab. And I used to be really scared of crabs because I thought one was going to bite my leg off too."

"That does sound frightening."

"But it wasn't a crab that bit off his leg. It was some kind of a machine on the boat. It was really wet and slippery on the deck when it happened, and Grandpa slipped and fell, and his leg got caught in this big machine-thing. They were way, way out in the ocean, and he had to be rescued by the Coast Guard helicopter. I think he almost bled to death too."

"Oh my!" Marley shuddered.

"Yeah, you should have Grandpa tell you the story. He can tell it really, really scary, especially if he thinks I'm not listening."

Marley had to smile. "Well, the way you told it sounded scary enough for me." For a while they both worked quietly, but now Marley was curious as to why Hunter had asked all the questions about whether Marley would ever marry Jack. Was it possible that Hunter had heard something? Well, Marley didn't want to know. What she had told Hunter was true. She intended never to marry again unless she could be 100 percent sure it was the right thing to do.

If she ever got to the place where she was actually considering marriage—and who knew, maybe it would be with Jack—she would do it differently. She would definitely ask God for some direction.

* * *

After Marley dropped Hunter at the gallery, she couldn't quit thinking about Jack. He was such a great guy, such a good grandfather to Hunter, such an encourager to Marley in regard to her art. As she drove away, though, she felt uneasy. Whether it was Hunter's questioning or Marley's own imagination, she knew that she had acted differently around Jack that evening, and she suspected he noticed. She'd been slightly cool, aloof, and standoffish, even as she gave him simple information about Hunter and a quick update on the painting she was finishing. Then she'd turned and left. That was not like her.

In the past she usually lingered a bit, visiting with Jack or Jasmine or both of them, hearing about the latest comings and goings in the gallery or in town. Sometimes they'd even grab a bite to eat. Today she ran out of there like a scared rabbit, which made her mad. She wasn't mad at Hunter, although she wished the little girl hadn't questioned her so much about the whole marriage issue. She wasn't mad at Jack either. Poor guy, he had no idea what was bugging Marley tonight. The truth was, she was simply mad at herself. Why hadn't she just acted normally?

As she turned into the hospital parking lot, she considered blaming her bad behavior on her concern for Caroline and Caroline's mother, even though that hadn't been on her emotional radar at the time she was scurrying away from the gallery. Although it provided a believable excuse, it was disingenuous. She didn't want to do that to Jack. No, the next time she saw him, she would simply strive to be herself.

Marley spotted Caroline coming out of the women's restroom. She looked so weary and worn out, as if she'd aged by ten years in the past week. "How are you holding up?" Marley asked her after a quick hug.

"Okay." Caroline made what looked like a forced smile.

"And your mom?"

"The same."

Marley just nodded. "You've been here all day again?"

"Yeah." Caroline sighed. "I know, it's probably futile. I mean, my mom seems totally oblivious. In fact I almost feel like she's already gone. It makes me wonder if the spirit really can leave although the body is still down here."

"I've read accounts of people who experienced the afterlife, then returned to life," Marley told her as they sat down in the waiting area.

"So maybe some people do leave here? I mean, before their bodies do?" Caroline looked hopeful.

"Maybe."

"I hate to sound like I want her to die. I really don't. I just don't want to see her suffer anymore. If she did come back, well, she'd have all those burns, and the treatment for it, and then there's still the Alzheimer's." Caroline almost brightened now. "Unless the frightening experience of nearly being burned to death could've shocked the Alzheimer's out of her. Do you think that's possible?"

Marley didn't know what to say. "I'm no expert, but I kind of doubt it."

"Yeah, it sounds a little nutty. Even to me."

To distract Caroline, Marley told her about Jack's wooden leg.

"You're kidding me."

Marley shook her head. "I don't think so. Hunter told me a very believable story this afternoon. In fact she said that's why the gallery is called the One-Legged Seagull."

"Wow, I never would've guessed that about him." Caroline frowned. "Does that change how you feel about Jack?"

Marley had to chuckle. "I don't even know *how* I feel about Jack."

"Well, you know what I mean. You guys spend a lot of time together. It could develop into something more. Would him having lost a leg change anything for you?"

"No, of course not." Marley laughed. "If anything, I find it charmingly attractive."

Caroline looked surprised. "Seriously?"

Marley nodded. "I actually do. I mean, Jack kind of reminds me of an old sea captain. The fact he has a wooden leg, or whatever it is, well, I find it rather romantic."

"Romantic?" Caroline made a funny face. "Wow, you and I have some very different opinions about what's romantic."

"I mean romantic in the storybook sense," Marley clarified. She didn't tell Caroline about Hunter's inquisition. For some reason she just wasn't ready to talk about that. Instead she let Caroline fill her in on the latest news about Janie and Victor.

"Oh my." Marley shook her head. "Victor's ex living in the same house where Janie's got her law office? That should be interesting."

"I'm going to live there too," Caroline said. She told Marley all about Abby's plans to get the B and B started as soon as possible.

"Man," Marley just shook her head. "I'm out of the picture for a few hours and I miss out on all kinds of things."

They talked for about an hour, then Caroline wanted to go in for her last visit of the day with her mom. Marley was ready to head for home, but first she hugged Caroline. "I'll keep praying for your mom. I really believe that God is at work with her. Whether you can see it or not, I believe that God has your mom in his hands. God is big enough to handle this."

Caroline nodded with a grim expression. "It's not always easy, but I'm trying to believe that too."

As Marley drove back toward the beach, she did pray for Mrs. McCann, and she prayed for Caroline, too. Although Marley's faith still felt relatively young and new and perhaps even a bit naive, she sensed it was growing stronger. By the time she got home, she felt certain that both Mrs. McCann and Caroline were going to be just fine.

══Chapter 13══

JANIE

It was hard to believe that Caroline's mother was still alive after seven long days—especially long days for Caroline, who spent most of her time at the hospital. Janie had quite a long week as well. It was bad enough feeling like her relationship with Victor was in limbo and possibly finished. Having houseguests—including an oversized, overly friendly dog that shed hair all over the place—was no picnic either.

Still, when Monday arrived, Janie could hardly believe that Mrs. McCann was still hanging on. Even the medical staff was surprised, and most acknowledged that only the machines were keeping her alive. Yet the court injunction remained fixed, and the police investigation crept along at a snail's pace. Despite the mysterious disappearance of Joan Wilson, Detective Alberts refused to admit that the missing caregiver was the most likely cause of the fire. To make matters worse, the DNA results for the cigarettes seemed to have been misplaced somewhere along the line. The lab blamed the police, the police blamed the district attorney, and the DA maintained the innocence of his office.

"Look," Janie said to Detective Alberts on Monday morning. "I know you care about justice as much as I do."

He nodded.

"I'm not blaming you for the loss of the evidence."

"I know you're not." He shuffled the papers on his desk and sighed. "You know I feel bad about it."

"I know." Janie sat up straight in the chair. "But I am asking you to do everything you can to find out if Joan Wilson was a smoker, which I'm sure you'll discover to be true, and then find out what brand of cigarettes she smokes, and then, please, let my client off the hook."

"I've tried to locate Joan Wilson," he explained. "But the agency claims she's gone to visit her sick sister in Texas, and they don't know when she'll be back."

"I know that already." Janie took in a slow breath to steady her nerves. She felt like yelling at the thickheaded detective. They'd gone over all this last week. But her goal was to earn his trust and respect, and she didn't want to jeopardize that with a confrontation. "I realize that the agency is being careful to distance itself from any responsibility in the fire," she continued. "But it would help my client if you could encourage the agency to be forthcoming with any information. I've already told them that Caroline has no intention of pressing charges of negligence against them, but we can only guarantee that for as long as the agency cooperates with your investigation."

"Yes, I understand that."

"It would be helpful if you could back me in that, Detective."

"I can do that."

"And it would be helpful if you could question the other care-giver, Darlene Kinsey, about Joan Wilson. According to Caroline they were friends, and Caroline suspects that the agency is pressuring Darlene to keep her mouth shut."

The detective made some more notes and then nodded. "Okay. I'm on it."

She smiled as she stood. "Thank you, Detective Alberts. I really appreciate your work."

"I'll let you know if I find anything."

"Or if the DNA evidence shows up?"

He gave her that apologetic look again. "Yes, I'm on that, too." He tapped his pen against his computer keyboard. "I honestly don't know how that happened, and I'm as upset about it as you are."

"I know." Janie nodded, and she believed him. Even so, it was aggravating. "Thanks again for your time."

On her way to her car, Janie decided to get a coffee at the kiosk around the corner, but as she stepped up to Crabby's Coffee, she realized that Victor was there too. As much as she wanted to avoid him, which she'd done successfully since their brief encounter the previous week, there was no graceful way to do it now. She put on her best attorney smile, the same one she'd been giving Detective Alberts. "Victor," she said in an even tone.

His eyes widened. "Janie."

Before she could stop herself, and feeling foolish for doing so, she stretched out her hand to shake his. "How are you?" she asked in her attorney voice.

"I'm fine." He shook her hand and offered an uncomfortable smile.

"I'm just getting a quick coffee," she said as she stepped up to the counter. With her back to him, and not sure if he would linger, she ordered a latte, then took her time to pay and count out a tip. As the girl began making her coffee, Janie turned to see that Victor was still standing there. As childish as it was, she feigned surprise. "Oh?"

"Are you too busy to talk?" he asked in a serious tone.

She considered this. They really needed to talk. At the same time, she wasn't ready to hear the words she was expecting him to say. "Sure." She forced another smile. "I'd love to talk."

He nodded to the picnic table near the kiosk. "I'll wait for you to get your coffee."

She turned back to the kiosk, and while she watched the girl steam the milk, Janie braced herself. *You can do this*, she told herself. *You can do this. Just be a big girl, get it over with. You can do this.*

With her coffee in hand she slowly walked over and sat down across from Victor. "It looks like it might rain," she said as she looked up at the gray sky.

"Is it too cold out here for you?" he asked uneasily.

"No. I'm fine." She'd dressed more warmly today, but even so, she felt a chill run down her back. She wrapped both hands around her cup and simply waited. If he wanted to talk, she would let him.

"I'm sorry it's taken me so long to speak to you," he began in a formal way.

"We've all been very busy this past week." This was true, but she also knew that they hadn't been too busy to talk. Instead Victor had not wanted to talk. She knew he'd been avoiding her, just as she'd been avoiding him. And she was pretty sure she knew why.

"Yes, I know. It's been a hard week for everyone. By the way, how is Caroline holding up? And her mother?"

Feeling like a newscaster dishing out the morning report, Janie gave him a quick update, then listened to his sympathetic response, then waited for him to get back on topic. She wasn't trying to be difficult, but she had no intention of helping him out with his little talk. She wanted him to get it over with. It would be like pulling off a bandage. Faster was probably better.

He took a quick sip of coffee, then looked directly into her eyes. "I've known for a while that we need to talk, Janie. And I feel irresponsible for not making the time for this sooner."

"Well, at least you're getting to it now," she said crisply.

He seemed to stiffen a bit. "Yes, right."

She sat up straighter, looking at him expectantly.

"So, anyway, last week …" He paused and frowned. "Was it really only last week? It feels like it must've been a month ago."

She let out an exasperated sigh. "I'm not sure *what* you mean exactly."

"Right." He set down his cup, then, placing his elbows on the table, he leaned forward, looking intently at her. "It was on Veterans Day," he began slowly. "I guess that really was only a week ago."

She nodded with impatience. "Yes, a week ago."

"Ben and Donna and I went to the parade."

Feeling slightly lost and somewhat edgy, she just stared at him. She wanted to demand that he just get on with it, but there seemed to be no rushing this man. "It was a nice parade," she said quietly, hoping that might encourage him to continue with his saga.

"After the parade we were walking down Main Street, and Ben noticed you in the diner." Again he stopped. His brow was furrowed as he looked at her.

"Barney's," she filled in for him. But as she said this, a little light bulb started to dimly glow in her head.

"So there you were in Barney's."

She saw something else in his eyes, something she hadn't noticed before, or perhaps she was imagining it now. But Victor seemed really troubled, perhaps even genuinely hurt. "What is this about?"

"You were sitting there with Steve Fuller," he said quietly.

"Yes," she said a bit eagerly. "I was sitting with Steve. Do you know him?"

"Not well. But I know enough to know he's a good guy."

"Yes, he is." She nodded, then waited.

"And you two were, uh, holding hands," he said in a slightly gruff voice. "And Ben asked me if you were dating him. And I … well, I didn't know what to say." He looked at her with worried eyes.

"Holding hands?" She frowned. "What?"

"You and Steve were holding hands and you were looking into his eyes, and he was looking at you and—"

"We were *not* holding hands," she declared.

"I *saw* you, Janie."

"I'm not sure what you saw, but I know it wasn't anything like *that*. Steve and I had been working on a float for the parade, and we got to talking—"

"Hey there," called a woman's voice. Victor frowned and Janie looked up to see Donna strolling their way. Wearing a pale gray parka and blue jeans, she had a couple of shopping bags in hand.

"Coffee," Donna said happily as she set the bags down on the bench next to Victor. "What a lovely idea." Then she smiled at Janie. "And how are you doing?"

"I'm well," Janie said a bit stiffly.

"Great. I'll be right back!" Donna opened her purse and headed over to the kiosk.

Janie exchanged glances with Victor. The kiosk was less than ten feet away and well within hearing distance. Janie had no intention of continuing this awkward conversation with Donna around. At least not openly. "What you saw on Veterans Day," she began carefully with her eyes locked on Victor's, "was not what it appeared to be."

He looked toward Donna then back at Janie. "In that case I'd definitely like to hear more about it."

"I'd be happy to discuss it with you sometime." Janie pressed her lips together.

"Maybe we can arrange that."

"Yes, I would appreciate it."

They sat there quietly, looking at each other, and Janie wondered if all the assumptions she'd been making about Victor and Donna were completely wrong. As she gazed into Victor's eyes, she felt certain he was looking at her with the same warmth and longing that she felt toward him—unless it was just her hopeful imagination running amuck.

"Here we go," Donna chirped as she held out her coffee like a trophy and sat down next to Victor. "So, Janie, what have you been up to lately?"

Janie told Donna and Victor a bit about her visit to city hall, making the latest incident seem bigger than it was. She explained about the lost evidence and how she was trying to get some cooperation from the police. "I decided that it made more sense to befriend them than to make them my enemy."

"You know what they say," Donna injected. "You can't fight city hall."

Janie forced another smile. "Yes, although sometimes it's my job to do just that. However, this is a small town, and most of all I want to help Caroline and her mother."

"Speaking of Caroline"—Donna's blue eyes lit up—"I can't wait to meet her. Abby tells me that she'll be moving into the bed-and-breakfast this week."

"That's right." Janie nodded. "Did I hear that you're going to rent a room there as well?"

"I suppose so." Donna's smile faded, and she turned a pouty face toward Victor. "It seems my roommate is awfully eager to get rid of me."

Victor cleared his throat. "We're not exactly *roommates*, Donna."

She laughed. "Oh, that's okay. Janie knows what I mean."

Janie glanced at her watch. "It's been nice visiting with you two, but I promised to meet up with Caroline and tell her about my conversation with the detective." This wasn't entirely true, but it was close enough, not to mention all she had to work with at the moment. Certainly it was better than pouring the lukewarm remains of her latte over Donna's pretty blonde head. Janie stood and told them both good-bye, then hurried back around the corner to her car.

Although she felt irritated with Donna, she also felt a renewed sense of hope in regard to Victor. Perhaps she had been reading him all wrong. It seemed he'd been doing the same thing with her. Maybe their relationship wasn't really over with after all. Of course, if that was indeed the case, it might be a challenge to convince Donna of this.

As Janie drove to the hospital, she thought about Victor. Had he really been stewing all week over the possibility that she was involved with Steve Fuller? It sounded slightly unbelievable, but Victor seemed quite certain that she and Steve had been involved in some kind of romantic interlude that day. She tried to recall her lunch with Steve. The purpose had been to talk about her father, and Steve had opened her eyes to some of the harsh realities of the battlefield. His words hadn't been easy to hear, but they helped her to understand her father better.

As she parked her car, she suddenly remembered how she had begun to cry as she imagined her father's horrifying experience on the battlefield, watching his buddies dying right in front of him. That was why Steve reached across the table to put his hand over hers. It must've been at that moment that Victor, Ben, and Donna had spotted them. Of course, they had been sitting right by the front window, right in plain sight of everyone! Poor Victor.

It was starting to rain as Janie hurried toward the hospital with her head down to avoid the raindrops. She nearly ran smack into Caroline, who was coming out. "Oh!" Janie stopped herself.

"Oh, Janie!" Caroline burst into tears and fell into Janie's arms.

"What's wrong?" Janie asked as she led Caroline back inside the shelter of the hospital foyer.

"She ... she's dead!"

Janie walked Caroline over to some chairs by the doors, easing her down. "What happened?"

Caroline pulled a tissue out of her jacket pocket and blotted her eyes. "She just died. Just like that."

"No one stopped the machines?" Janie felt worried. She knew how frustrated and desperate Caroline had been feeling about this artificial means of keeping her mother alive, but surely Caroline wouldn't have unplugged anything.

Caroline blew her nose, then looked evenly at Janie. "The machines were still running, but my mom.... Well, her heart just finally stopped beating."

Janie sighed. "I know it's hard, Caroline. But you do know it's for the best, don't you?"

Caroline nodded, but tears continued to pour. "I ... I ... know that. But it's still hard, Janie. It was still hard to see her there, completely gone ... gone, gone ... gone." She began to cry again.

Janie put an arm around her shoulders. "Go ahead and cry, Caroline, as much as you need to. It's okay."

As Caroline continued to cry, Janie sat next to her. With an arm around Caroline's shoulders, she waited for her friend's grief to ebb. Really, isn't that what friends were meant to do? Janie remembered how hard it had been on her when Phil died. Like Caroline, she was expecting it, but still it had been hard. His cancer had taken him down quickly, but she'd been well aware when the end was near. It was inevitable, and yet she was crushed when it actually happened. She still hurt just thinking about his death. It would've been a bit easier to endure if she'd had her friends—the Lindas—around to comfort her. Well, at least she could do that for Caroline now.

=Chapter 14=

ABBY

Plain, hard work had always been like a tonic to Abby. Whether she was cooking, gardening, cleaning, redecorating, sewing, or whatever, she had always thrived on doing an ordinary task and doing it well. For some reason, though—and she hated to think it might possibly be her age—work was starting to feel more like just that: plain, hard work.

She sat down on the edge of the bed she had just made up and took in a slow, deep breath. Was it possible that the effort of simply making a bed had winded her? To be fair, she'd started by removing the king-sized pillow-top mattress, which was no small chore, so that she could put on a dust ruffle. When she replaced the mattress, she noticed the dust ruffle was badly wrinkled. That meant removing the mattress for a second time, pulling off the dust ruffle, and running down to the laundry room for the iron. Instead of simply ironing the dust ruffle, though, she had decided to drag the ironing board and iron up the stairs, because the other new bed linens, thanks to tight packaging, would be in need of pressing too.

On it went, putting on the mattress pad, pressing the edges of the top sheet and pillow cases, pressing the entire duvet cover, inserting the fluffy down comforter into the freshly ironed duvet without messing it up, then pressing the pillow shams, and finally completing the bed with some decorative pillows and a neatly folded chenille throw. She was exhausted.

Worse than that, she was worried. How was she possibly going to run an inn if the process of making one bed exhausted her? The simple answer was to hire a housekeeper, but she knew from her conversations with fellow innkeeper Jackie Day that until Abby's business got up and running, it might be foolhardy to hire extra help.

"Just pace yourself," Paul had told Abby that morning. She'd been complaining to him over breakfast that in one week's time she'd managed to paint only one bedroom and one bath. Of course, she'd also done a fair amount of shopping, which was both time consuming and tiring, not to mention more costly than she'd originally budgeted for. The main reason she'd been complaining to Paul was because she hoped he would offer to help or to send over one of his workers. He didn't. When it came to the bed-and-breakfast, it seemed quite clear that Abby was on her own.

"I am Little Red Hen," she told herself as she huffed to her feet, then turned around to fluff the wrinkled duvet cover back into shape, the same one she'd worked so hard to get wrinkle-free. Of course, the upside of the Little Red Hen story was that she would eventually get to enjoy the fruits of her labors. At least that's what Abby was hoping for. As far as what those fruits would be exactly, Abby wasn't completely sure.

She bent down to gather up the packaging from the bedding materials and stuffed it all into a trash bag, then turned to look at the master suite and smiled. It actually looked nice, especially considering how little time she'd had to make the transformation. In fact, thanks to the removal of the old floral wallpaper, followed by two coats of pale aqua-blue paint, it looked far better than when she and Paul had occupied this space. In some ways she liked this room better than her luxurious master suite at home. Well, except that it was missing the ocean view.

Because this was the master suite, which would be the deluxe room of the inn, and because she had what she hoped would be her first official guest, Abby had splurged a bit on the furnishings. The Shaker-style headboard and matching bedside tables were painted in a creamy antique white, a nice combination with the pale-blue-and-white-striped duvet cover and shams. Crisp, clean, and coastal. She'd also found a nice pine bench for the end of the bed, a pair of white canvas slip-covered easy chairs and ottoman, and an oversized knotty-pine TV armoire. The walls were decorated with seaside prints of lighthouses and sun-bleached beach scenes. Freshly pressed white muslin curtains, hand-sewn by Abby, graced the bay window, and on the hardwood floor rested a large braided carpet in aquatic shades of blue. All in all, the room was perfect. Abby would happily live here herself. In fact she entertained the idea of sneaking over here on those occasional nights when she and Paul were embroiled in a fight—though not, of course, while the room was occupied. Abby hoped that Donna would appreciate her efforts.

The master bath was done in a similar theme with pale blue walls, white fixtures, white linens, a pretty collection of seashells, and blue and green glass floats along the windowsill. Everything looked fresh and clean, and in Abby's opinion, inviting. All that was left to make this space livable would be to add a few hospitality items, like French-milled guest soaps, luxurious shampoos, and such. Until Abby's own online order arrived, Jackie Day had promised to let Abby purchase some of these items from her.

"Hello in the house," called what sounded like Janie's voice. She'd been in and out quite a bit these last few days. From what Abby could tell, Janie's law office was nearly ready for occupancy.

"Up here," Abby called. "In the master suite."

"Wow." Janie nodded with approval as she came into the room. "This looks lovely, Abby."

"Thanks." Abby reached up to wipe her brow. "I'm beat."

"You look a little tired." Janie put a hand on her shoulder. "I have kind of bad news—good and bad."

Abby took in a quick breath. "What? What is it?"

"Mrs. McCann passed away."

Abby felt guilty for feeling relieved. "Oh. How is Caroline doing?"

"She kind of fell apart," Janie explained.

"Oh dear. Poor thing. She's sure been through the wringer."

"She's at my house now, resting."

"Good for her." Abby let out a tired sigh. "Well, I guess that means I should start attacking her room now."

"So this room is for Donna then?"

Abby nodded. "Since she's actually going to pay rent, I thought I should give her the best room."

"Right." Janie walked over to the window and looked out. "You know for sure that she's taking this room?"

Abby went over to stand by her. "Not absolutely, positively sure." She frowned at Janie. "Why? Do you know something I don't?"

"No, not at all."

"I'd hate to think I went to all this trouble for nothing."

"You could always let Caroline have this room."

Abby considered this. As much as she loved Caroline, she didn't care for the idea of Caroline and her dog living in this room. Of course, she would not admit that to anyone. "I thought Caroline would like to use my old room." She chuckled. "Or what was more recently Jessie's old room. Sometimes I can't believe how long this house has been in my family. Anyway, the room faces southwest, and it gets such lovely afternoon light in the winter months."

Janie nodded. "Yes, I'm sure she'd like that."

"Of course, I'd planned to paint it first." Abby shook her head. "I just can't work as fast as I used to. I think I'm getting old."

Janie chuckled. "Aren't we all?"

"Do you want to see the other room?" Abby asked hopefully. What she really wanted was for Janie to approve of this plan. She felt greedy for denying poor Caroline what she knew was the best room.

"Sure, show me."

Abby led her down the hallway, then opened the door to the room, which actually looked pretty bad. "Of course that hot-pink paint has to go. Jessie thought it was so wonderful in high school. It makes my head hurt."

Janie chuckled. "I remember when my Lisa decided to redecorate her bedroom in our Manhattan apartment."

"What did she do?"

Janie wrinkled her nose. "She painted all the walls black."

"Black?" Abby grimaced. "That's a bit morbid."

"And then she painted the furniture blood red." Janie shook her head. "It was really ghastly. I should've known then the girl was going to have some problems."

"How is she doing these days?"

"According to her brother she's doing better, but she's still not speaking to me."

"She's in her early twenties?" Abby asked.

"Twenty-two."

"Well, remember how I told you how Laurie went through her I-hate-my-mom phase?"

"I do remember."

"She seems to be coming out of it. Paul's heart attack had something to do with it. But I also think age helped. Laurie will be twenty-eight in December."

"So maybe there's hope for Lisa."

Abby patted Janie on the shoulder. "Yes, there's always hope."

"Thanks." Janie walked around the smaller room, checking out the closet, which wasn't too large, and the view from the window. "What color do you plan to paint in here?"

"I picked out a yummy buttery yellow. I know how much Caroline likes yellow."

"That will be nice."

"The paint store guy assured me that it will cover this horrid pink in two coats. I told him that if it didn't I was going to make him put on the third coat."

"Is that the new furniture?" Janie pointed to some wooden pieces that had been stacked in the center of the room and covered with a plastic drop cloth.

"Yes, I asked the movers to put it there so I could paint without having to keep moving everything around."

"I have an idea," Janie said.

"What?"

"How about if I help you paint this room? We could put it all together and surprise Caroline."

"Really? You'd do that?" Abby felt like crying, she was so grateful.

"Sure. I think it'd be fun. I got quite good at painting during the renovation at my house. In fact I've just been itching to get my hands on a roller again."

"When do you want to get started?"

"No time like the present."

Abby frowned at Janie's nice pants and jacket. "You can't work in that."

Janie grinned. "Not a problem. I have a set of old clothes down in the basement. I keep them here so I can work whenever I want."

"I noticed your painting is all done down there. Did you do that, too?"

"No, my drywall guys gave me a bid for the whole thing, and I just let them go for it. But I did feel a bit left out for not getting to help."

"Well, you don't need to feel left out anymore."

Having Janie's offer of help was like wind in Abby's sails. She immediately went to work masking off the windows and baseboard and floors. In no time she and Janie got right down to work. It was nice having the company, and Abby had to admit that Janie was pretty good at painting, probably even better than Abby. After a while Janie had gotten far enough along with the walls that Abby was able to focus painting the trim a clean milky white. Covering up the splotches where Jessie slopped hot-pink paint drips so many years ago was itself a huge improvement.

"I assume you don't want to paint the closet," Janie said as she closed the door.

"No, it's best to leave that cedar alone," Abby told her, "although at some point I might hire someone to come give it a good sanding to bring out the aroma again."

It was a little past five when they finished, and Abby was so happy she hugged Janie. "Thank you so much! I never could've done this without you!"

"You're welcome." Janie smiled as she looked around the sunny room. "You're right, Abby, this is really a sweet room. The light coming in just now is lovely. I'm sure Caroline will love it." Janie set her roller down. "Speaking of Caroline, I should probably go and check on her."

"Yes," Abby said eagerly. "Please go see how she's doing, and I'll finish cleaning up in here. I'm so grateful for your help." She placed her forefinger over her lips. "Don't tell Caroline yet. It would be fun to surprise her. Okay?"

"Mum's the word."

After Janie left, Abby called Paul. When he didn't answer the home phone, she grew concerned, so she tried his cell. "Where are you?" she demanded as soon as he answered.

"On my way home," he said in a slightly gruff tone. "Where are you?"

She explained she was running late. "Can you just warm up some of that soup from yesterday for dinner?"

"Leftover soup?" The grouch in his voice was unmistakable.

"Leftover *homemade* soup," she reminded him. "And with some of that whole-grain bread and some fresh fruit, you'll be—"

"Yeah, yeah," he said quickly. "I better hang up before I get a ticket."

"I'll be home in a couple of hours." It sounded like he'd already hung up. He was right, though. He shouldn't be talking on his cell phone and driving. Oprah had been saying as much for years now, and the local law enforcement had really been cracking down on it lately.

As she puttered around, cleaning up the painting things, then moving the furnishings into place, Abby started to obsess over her husband. His attitude about her "little business venture," as he liked to call it, had been negative from the get-go, but she had hoped his heart attack would soften him up some. The more he recovered, however, the more he acted like his old grumpy self. It was getting on her nerves!

Thanks to some things their counselor had pointed out, Abby knew that Paul's bad behavior was partially her fault. Not that he didn't need to take responsibility for his own actions; he most certainly did. In a way, though, Abby had started training Paul to mistreat her right from the beginning. Back in the seventies when they'd married (too young), Abby had rejected the whole idea of women's lib. She thought it was silly to want a career. She had no need to get a degree, and she figured the reason her other friends were going to school was simply to find a husband. Abby already had found hers.

Really, none of that independent-woman nonsense had ever appealed to her in the least. She was the little girl who grew up playing with dolls. One of her favorite toys was her Easy-Bake Oven. All she ever wanted to do was to play the happy little housewife. She was so devoted to her man that she literally brought him his slippers—early on. She had wanted to have children, lots of them (well, until she had three). She wanted to cook and clean and garden and make her home a haven. And hadn't she done a knock-up job of it? But really, who had ever cared much? Her girls always wanted to go their own way. Even now they rarely came to visit. And her husband, well, he figured Abby had what she wanted, didn't he?

It seemed her sole reward for all her hard work was a man used to being waited on. King of his castle (or so he thought), Paul liked coming home to a hot meal. He expected his bed to be neatly made with fresh-smelling linens. If his socks weren't neatly folded in his sock drawer (with no static cling), he was quick to complain. If she didn't pick up after him, toss out his messy newspapers, or put his smelly tennis shoes away (complete with Odor-Eaters), he would most definitely mention it. Abby had conditioned her husband to expect a certain kind of lifestyle. He wanted perfection, on his terms. In other words Abby had created a monster. This seemed especially true now—now that Abby had other interests, now that she had things to do besides catering to him.

As Abby set her toolbox on the floor, she wondered if it was unfair to pursue her own dreams. After all, the children were grown and their oceanside home was fairly low maintenance on the inside. Plus it was time Paul learned to do a few things for himself. He could clean his own whiskers out of the bathroom sink and replace the roll of toilet paper when it was empty. Was that too much to ask?

He could also learn to help her when she needed it. Like right now—Abby was trying to insert the sides of the metal bed frame into the slots on the wooden headboard—she could really use another set of hands. But was Paul willing to give up his comfy chair and *Monday Night Football?* Of course not. Right now he was probably calling out to her (forgetting she was not there), asking her to bring him in one of those new light beers or some of that Orville Redenbacher low-fat popcorn. Ah, yes, even now she was still training him. Maybe what Abby needed was someone to retrain her!

It was past nine o'clock by the time Abby got the furniture and the bedroom fully assembled. It was as if her anger at Paul had propelled her to keep going and finish this task. Well, that and a desire to see the room completed for Caroline's sake. Now it was done, and she was utterly exhausted. She was a bit surprised that Paul hadn't called to check on her. Maybe he didn't care.

As she was driving home, she started to worry about her husband. She felt guilty for the dark thoughts she'd been harboring against him. What if the reason Paul hadn't called to check on her was because he needed help right now? What if he had suffered another heart attack? Perhaps he'd gotten into the hot tub, which he'd been warned to be careful about—but since when did he listen? Perhaps while in the hot tub, his heart had given him a problem and he had struggled ... and drowned. *Oh, horror!* What if he was still there? The image of her dead husband floating in the hot tub—the hot tub she had once named Diamond Lil—made her step on the gas. Speeding was risky this time of night, because the police had been trying to make their quota. She didn't care.

Abby suppressed her urge to use her cell phone. Two traffic violations at once would be pushing it. But she was desperate. She decided that if a cop did pull her over, she would explain that her husband was dying and ask them to escort her home. If Paul really was dead, she would be devastated. She would be guilt ridden, and she would forever blame herself. Her selfish pursuit of her selfish desires would be the cause of her husband's demise.

She pulled into the driveway, and, without even parking her car in the garage, she breathlessly ran through the front entrance and straight into the great room. With a pounding heart she discovered Paul's unconscious body stretched out in his leather recliner. The TV remote dangled in his hand. He was snoring loudly. Not dead, just sleeping.

She knew she should've been relieved, but she felt furious. She had no idea why she was so angry, but it took all her self-control not to pick up that remote and whack him over the head with it. Instead she went to bed.

Chapter 15

CAROLINE

If not for Chuck, Caroline felt certain she would've slept until the late afternoon, or maybe even into the next day. She was that tired—deep down, bone-weary tired. As she pulled herself out of Janie's comfortable guest-room bed, she knew some of her exhaustion was just plain emotional. Even so, all she wanted to do was sleep. But Chuck needed to go out, and it was her job to take him.

"Hang on, old boy," she whispered to him. "Let me get dressed." She pulled on some sweats and shoved her feet into her slip-on tennis shoes, then grabbed his leash. Not that he really needed a leash, but as a responsible pet owner, she knew she needed two things when she walked him—the leash and a couple of plastic bags stuffed in her pocket just in case.

It was just a little past seven when she slipped out the front door. The air was damp with fog, and the neighborhood was quiet as she walked toward the nearby park where she would let Chuck off his leash to run and do his business, which she would pick up and deposit in the big metal trash can by the entrance. She remembered the old days when dogs were allowed to relieve themselves where they liked. She also remembered the time she'd been wearing a brand-new pair of Keds, purchased from babysitting money she'd earned watching the bratty Snyder twins next door for twenty-five cents an hour while their mom "put her feet up." It had taken weeks to save up that money. Then, as she'd been running through this very park on her way to Abby's house, she'd stepped right into a big smelly pile of dog poop. Those Keds were never the same after that.

After Chuck was satisfied with a little run and potty break, she considered returning to Janie's house, slipping back into bed, and going to sleep again. The problem was that she was wide awake now, and so she walked on over to her mom's house—what had been her mom's house. Despite the fire the house looked fairly unaffected on the outside. It was as dismal and neglected as always, even more so in the gloomy fog. Of course, the charred roof and broken bedroom window, which the firemen had covered with plastic and tape, didn't help. Really, the best thing for this house might be to knock it down.

Caroline went up to the front door to see if the key she kept hidden (for those times when her mom occasionally locked her out) was still there. She reached up to the door frame and felt around. Sure enough, it was there. Instead of going in, she went around back and let Chuck into the backyard. She had to smile to see the backyard. The work her friends had invested in that small space was still evident. It would be what she would miss most about this place. She filled Chuck's stainless-steel bowl with water, then told him to be good.

She returned to the front of the house and let herself in. The place seemed extremely quiet, almost as if it, too, knew that her mom had died. And it stank. The acrid smell of smoke was everywhere. Holding her breath, she went to every room except for her mom's bedroom and opened the windows wide. Then, finding the master key that she kept hidden in a teacup in a high kitchen cupboard, she unlocked all the double-dead-bolt doors and opened them. Her bedroom looked slightly ransacked, but Caroline knew that was because Janie had come by and removed a lot of Caroline's clothes and personal items. Caroline couldn't blame Janie for doing this task quickly. Even with the windows open, the smell in this house was really sickening.

Caroline got down on her knees and pulled a metal box out from under her bed. It was an old fireproof file box that her dad had purchased when Caroline was a girl. Though Caroline hadn't gone through everything it contained, she had stored a lot of her mom's important papers in it, including social security records, insurance policies, and even the key to her safe-deposit box. Now she took it out into the backyard and sat down to look through it.

To her relief she found a homeowner's insurance policy. As Caroline examined it, she remembered that, several years ago, she'd helped her mom arrange for the bill to be paid biannually directly from her bank account. It wouldn't be hard to check the bank records to ascertain whether the insurance policy was still in effect. That was a comfort.

She flipped through the other papers but wasn't surprised that her mom's life-insurance policy wasn't there. Caroline vaguely remembered a conversation about this with her mom. It took place about five years ago, back when Caroline thought that her mom's memory problems had more to do with aging than Alzheimer's. Just the same, Caroline had been helping to put her mom's finances in order, setting up direct deposit payments and such in the hopes it would simplify her mother's life.

"Your brother has taken all he's going to get from me," her mom had told her.

Caroline had been relieved to hear this. She was well aware that her older brother, Michael, had been using their parents for most of his adult life. An unemployed alcoholic with an anger problem, Michael had the people skills of a steamroller on steroids. In fact Michael was one reason that Caroline had always been reluctant to come home for visits during those years. She resented the way he'd taken it upon himself to "tend" to his parents' affairs. When Caroline finally did get involved after their dad's death, she realized that Michael hadn't been just helping with his parents' finances, he'd been helping himself as well.

"I deserve to be paid for my services," he had informed Caroline.

"You're their son," she had pointed out.

They'd gotten into a heated argument, which led Caroline to expose her brother's sticky fingers to their mom. At first her mom didn't believe it, but when the bank manager agreed to meet with her, and when bank records were set out in front of her with questionable withdrawals highlighted in yellow, her mom finally accepted the truth.

After that Michael basically disappeared, although Caroline suspected he hit their mom up for "loans" and other financial handouts over the next few years. Not that her mom had much. Thanks to Michael, their father's insurance money dwindled much faster than it should've. The life-insurance policies had been a benefit of her dad's job, but they weren't really worth that much, and Caroline suspected her dad had more than paid for their value over the years. She also suspected he'd hoped to benefit from his wife's policy himself—after all, she'd always suffered poor health. It stood to reason that he would outlive her. Or, for all Caroline knew, her dad might've rationalized that his own policy, in the event of his death, might somehow compensate for all the sadness and abuse his wife had suffered during his lifetime. Caroline just shook her head as she closed the box. There was so much she would never understand.

All she knew for sure was that her family's history seemed to repeat itself. Like father like son, as soon as their dad was in his grave, Michael had picked up where his dad laid off, taking advantage of their mother. Despite Caroline's personal feelings toward her brother, she realized that it was her responsibility to notify Michael of their mother's death. She was not eager to do this and even felt a tinge of guilt for not having done it sooner. But really, how could it have helped if her bullheaded big brother stepped into the picture? She could just imagine him strong-arming the police, or unplugging their mother's life support, or picking fights with Caroline. No, keeping Michael at arm's length had been about survival and sanity, and she was not going to feel guilty about it now.

To the best of her knowledge, she had only one phone number with his name attached to it, and she didn't know if that was even current. She really hoped that it wasn't. That wasn't very sisterly of her, and it was possible that Michael had changed over the years. Sometimes people went to rehab or anger management, and sometimes they turned over a new leaf. For her brother's sake she wished it was so. But history and experience warned her not to get her hopes up.

Leaving the house windows open, Caroline locked the doors, gathered up the fireproof box as well as her dog, then headed back toward Janie's. As she walked she felt an odd sense of disconnectedness, almost as if she weren't really here, as if she were just floating through. As much as Caroline had complained about the burden of caring for her mom, that purpose had shaped her days. Now, with that need stripped away, Caroline felt adrift.

She remembered the time as a child when she'd gotten a big pink helium balloon at a grand opening of a new supermarket. Her mom tied the end of the string to Caroline's wrist, but Caroline had fiddled with the knot and the loop and suddenly it came untied. Caroline had stood in front of her house, crying hopelessly as she watched the pink balloon getting smaller and smaller in the sky until it was the size of a pinhead. That's how she felt right now. Maybe she needed therapy.

"There you are," Janie said as Caroline and Chuck came into the house. "I was getting worried."

"Sorry." Caroline held up the fireproof box. "We went for a walk and then I stopped by Mom's to get this."

"How's the smell over there?"

Caroline wrinkled up her nose. "Still nasty. But the good news is that I'm pretty sure her homeowner's insurance was paid up. I'll get to work on it today." Caroline took Chuck out to the backyard, and when she returned, Janie was already pouring her a cup of coffee. "Thanks." She sniffed the fresh brew and sighed. "You've been a great host, Janie. But today I'll start doing whatever I can to get my mom's house habitable again so I can get out of your hair."

Janie looked disappointed. "So you've changed your mind about staying at Abby's B and B?"

Caroline shrugged. "I don't want to put her out either. I think I should just try to get back on my own two feet. My room has the least amount of smoke damage and—"

"You'll need to get contractor in there first, Caroline. Someone has to make sure it's safe. There could be structural damage. And what about the electrical? None of the lights worked when I was in the house."

"I think they shut off the electricity."

"Yes." Janie nodded. "Probably because it's damaged."

Caroline sighed. "Yeah. I guess it might take longer than I imagined. I suppose I should take Abby up on her offer."

"Speaking of Abby, she just called to see if we were wanted to meet her and Marley in town for brunch."

Caroline brightened a bit. "Hey, I could actually do that, couldn't I?"

Janie chuckled. "You could, girlfriend. You are free as a bird now."

"It's just so weird. I feel more like a bird who's been in a cage so long that someone has opened the door and I don't know what to do."

"Here's to stretching your wings!" Janie held up her coffee cup like a toast.

"My wings." Caroline clinked her cup against Janie's. "What a thought."

"I'll call Abby and let her know we're on." Janie pointed to Caroline. "Do you want to change or anything?"

Caroline looked down at her old sweats and nodded. "Yes. I could use a shower, too."

"How about if I tell her ten thirty?"

Caroline looked at the clock and sighed to see that it was only a little past nine. "That sounds luxuriously good. I've gotten so used to five-minute showers and dressing in even less time. This is a whole new world."

"Take your time. Enjoy!"

Caroline did take her time, and by ten fifteen she was starting to feel almost normal, or what she imagined normal must feel like. It was good to sit with her friends without looking at her watch, feeling rushed, or worrying that her mom might need her. And yet she was sad, too. In a way it had felt good to be needed.

"You okay?" Abby asked Caroline as they were finishing up.

Caroline swallowed against the lump in her throat. "Yeah, I just feel a little blue."

"That's understandable," Marley told her. "I think that no matter how old you are, it's hard to lose your mother."

Caroline set her napkin by her plate. "The weird thing is I feel like I lost a little piece of myself, too."

Marley nodded. "I felt kind of like that when my mom died too. Like a part of me was still connected to her, a part of me that I could never get back."

"Maybe we should look at it differently," Janie began. "Maybe our mothers leave a part of themselves here with us. Don't you think that parts of our mothers are still inside us? How could they not be?"

Abby shrugged. "Well, since my mom's still around, I'm not really sure what you're talking about."

"Plus you have daughters and a granddaughter," Marley pointed out. "I think that might change things. That link among women in your family is strong, something for you to hold on to. I only have a son, so sometimes I feel disconnected."

"That's it," Caroline said with enthusiasm. "That's how I felt this morning. Disconnected."

Abby grabbed one of Caroline's hands, Janie grabbed the other, and Marley closed the circle by clasping hands with Abby and Janie. "See," Abby told Caroline. "You're not really disconnected." She turned to Marley. "And neither are you. We are all connected to each other. We are sisters."

"That's right," Janie agreed.

"The sisterhood of the Lindas," Marley proclaimed, and they all laughed.

"Now I'm inviting the sisterhood of the Lindas to stop by my B and B on our way home," Abby said. "I have something I'd like your opinions on."

Before long Abby and Janie were traipsing up the stairs in Abby's old house. "Back here," Abby called down the hallway.

"I think she's in her old bedroom," Janie said.

Caroline chuckled. "I just had a flashback to Abby's old bedroom. Remember how we used to tease her for having so many ruffles and frills—all that Pepto-Bismol pink and that princess canopy bed?"

"And the pink princess phone!" Janie chortled. "I do remember. We gave her such a bad time. But the truth is I think I was actually jealous."

"Me, too," Caroline admitted.

"Remember when she got rid of the ruffles and everything," Janie said quietly as they came to the closed door, "and she put up posters and love beads?"

Caroline nodded. "I actually missed the pink princess room."

"Then there was the color Jessie painted the room—she took pink to a whole new level. I think Abby called it headache pink." Janie knocked on the door now. "Anyone home?"

"Come on in." Abby opened the door to a room that looked nothing like her old bedroom.

"This is nice," Caroline said as she went into the room. "I love this shade of yellow, Abby. Very warm and buttery." She admired the neat furnishings and comfy-looking bedding. "Really, it's lovely. What do you need our opinions on? Is Donna going to stay here?"

"Actually I wondered if you'd want to stay here," Abby said in a cautious tone, like she was worried that Caroline might not appreciate the room.

"Seriously?" Caroline frowned. "It's not for Donna?"

Abby just shook her head. "I fixed it up for you, Caroline. Actually Janie helped. She's a great painter. Anyway, you can move in whenever you like. If you want to, that is."

Caroline grinned. "I'd love to have this room." She turned to Janie. "I'm sure you won't miss Chuck and me at your house."

"You guys have been wonderful guests, but I probably won't miss Chuck drinking out of my toilet." Janie smirked.

"Sorry about that." Caroline made a sheepish smile. "That's a little habit he learned from his previous home."

"Speaking of bathrooms," Abby injected, "I haven't had a chance to do much with the bath up here, but it's in pretty good shape anyway."

"Hey, you'll hear no complaints from me," Caroline assured her. "After living in my mom's house, everything else is an improvement."

She sighed to think of her mom. "That reminds me, I've got some funeral arrangements and things to do today. So I'd better get going." Abby told her to move in whenever she liked, and Caroline hugged her three friends and went on her way.

The Lindas really did lift her spirits, but when she got back to her mom's house, it was hard not to feel that sadness returning. The place was so depressing, and the open windows hadn't done much to improve the stale acrid smell of smoke. Every place she looked seemed hopelessly dismal and sad. As horrible as the truth sounded, it might've been better if this house had burned to the ground.

Caroline didn't have time for a pity party. She searched out her mom's worn address book, where she thought she'd seen Michael's old phone number. She found it in a kitchen drawer.

Clutching the book, she walked back to her mom's bedroom. Caroline had no idea what to expect and wasn't even sure if the space was safe, but she knew her mom had an old Bible from her girlhood days. Caroline had noticed it tucked into the top drawer of her bedside table, almost like her mom kept it there as a good-luck charm. Perhaps she had actually read it at times. For a spell Caroline's mom had returned to church, but then the Alzheimer's had set in and her routines were lost.

Anyway, if the Bible was still in one piece, Caroline planned to take it with her. She wasn't even sure what she would to do with it. Bury it with her mother? Save it as a keepsake? Caroline took in a big breath, then she pulled up the neck of her turtleneck to cover her mouth and nose. Bracing herself, she opened the door to the room.

Blackened and broken and still soggy in places, the bedroom looked like a set from a horror movie. The only thing missing was the dead body.

She hurried past the partially burnt bed, alongside the melted carpet, and, trying not to rub against the smoke-darkened walls, she jerked open the drawer, extracted the black Bible, and ran from the room, gasping. She hoped it wasn't too dangerous to breathe that foul air.

With the Bible and address book in hand, Caroline couldn't get out of the house fast enough. If she had her way, she would never go back inside there again. It was too horrible. Too hopeless. Except for the backyard, she would be happy if the house was condemned and knocked down. Probably everyone in the neighborhood would be too.

At Janie's house she went straight to work calling the insurance company for the house, as well as the life-insurance company. She called the funeral home to make an appointment to discuss final arrangements, and finally she opened her mom's old address book and called the last phone number listed for her brother. She waited as the phone rang, hoping she was about to be informed she had the wrong number. To her shock her brother's voice answered on the other end.

"Michael," she said in surprise. "This is Caroline."

"Caroline who?"

"Your sister," she said in a flat tone.

"Oh."

Without going into all the details, she explained about their mom's death, then waited for him to express his sadness, which actually sounded fairly sincere. She told him she was making arrangements for the funeral. "It's the same mortuary that did Dad's service," she told him. "They got one of those packages back in the eighties. Mostly I just need to set the date and make a few decisions. I thought I'd see if you had any preferences. For the date I mean." She had no intention of asking him to be involved in any other decision.

"I could be there by tomorrow if necessary," he told her.

"Oh. Well, okay. How about if I find out what dates work for the funeral home and get back to you?" She gave him her cell phone number and hung up. She could hardly believe she'd just been talking to her brother. The reconnection was not only surreal but slightly creepy. It wasn't that she hated Michael, but almost all her memories of him were bitter. For the most part she tried not to think about him at all. Years of therapy had helped her to get beyond the pain he'd inflicted on the family, but now it was like he was standing right in front of her. In fact that might be happening for real very soon. Caroline wasn't sure she was ready.

Chapter 16

JANIE

As the measuring tape snapped back into its case, Janie heard someone calling her name. Thinking it was probably the floor guys here to start installing the carpet and wood floors as planned, she yelled back up the stairs, "I'm down here."

She stepped back to study the wall she'd been measuring, trying to decide if that was really the best spot for her bookshelves, when she observed Victor walking toward her. Recovering from her shock, she pushed a strand of hair away from her face and smiled. "Hey, you're not the floor guys."

"I … uh … well, I noticed your car out front and figured you must be here." His tone was uncertain and apologetic. "I hope you don't mind me dropping in on you like this."

"No, of course not." She set the tape measure on a sawhorse. "I was just trying to make some decisions about furniture placement, basically killing time until the installers arrived. They were supposed to get started on the floor this afternoon." She glanced at her watch. "Apparently they're running late."

"Well, I'm sure you're busy, but I just hoped we could talk a bit ... finish up our conversation from yesterday."

She waved her hand around the basement. "As you can see, I can't invite you to sit down. But Abby's started placing some of the furnishings upstairs. Do you want to go up there? As far as I know, no one else is in the house right now."

"Sure." He waited for her to lead the way.

"Abby's been working really hard to get some things ready," she told him as they went up. "Donna's room—or what Abby hopes will be Donna's room—is all set, and it looks really great." She knew she was jabbering on, but she couldn't stop herself. She told him about Caroline's mom passing, and how Caroline would be moving in here too. He followed her into the dining room, where a table and chairs were set up, and Janie kept on talking. "Abby got this set a few days ago. I think it goes nicely in here. And she's getting some chairs for the parlor." More nervous blathering, but she didn't know what else to say.

They sat down on opposite sides of the rustic pine plank table, looking at each other for a long, quiet moment. Not wanting to start rambling on again and hoping to get her bearings, Janie pressed her lips together and waited, hoping Victor would take the hint and begin this conversation. After all, he was the one who'd initiated it.

"So ..." He took in a deep breath. "As I mentioned yesterday, Ben and I observed you with Steve Fuller at Barney's. We saw you two holding hands, gazing into each others' eyes. It seemed rather obvious—and as I said, Ben jumped to the same conclusion—we both assumed that you and Steve were, well, involved. Or getting involved."

Janie slowly nodded. "That was a natural assumption, Victor. I gave this some thought yesterday, and I understand how you might jump to a conclusion like that. But the truth is, when you described the scene to me, I almost thought you were imagining things. I honestly couldn't even remember the incident."

"You couldn't remember having lunch, holding hands, having a moment with Steve Fuller?" Victor looked skeptical. "Like it was nothing out of the ordinary?"

"No. I did remember having lunch. But the holding hands part, well, to be honest, I felt blindsided when you said that, Victor. Not that I thought you were making it up, but I had to think really hard to recall what you'd witnessed." She paused, watching his reaction, which was hard to read. "So if you'll let me explain …"

He nodded. "That's why I'm here."

She told him about volunteering to help with the VFW float, where she'd met Steve's absentminded mother. She explained how Steve had shown up and how they'd started discussing the effect of war and battles on veterans. "Our conversation was just getting interesting when the parade ended. He suggested lunch, and I wanted to hear more." Then she told Victor how Steve had helped her to understand what her dad may have gone through so long ago. "Steve's perspective really brought it home for me. I began to comprehend how my dad had probably witnessed his friends dying. I understood how a Medal of Honor might've been a harsh reminder of things my father wanted to bury. And, well, I suppose I got a little emotional." She swallowed hard as she recalled her sympathy for her father's suffering. "At that moment I think Steve reached out and put his hand over mine. That was all it was, Victor. A friendly gesture, a friend reaching out to a friend. Nothing more. I swear."

Victor's serious expression seemed to crumble. "I feel pretty ridiculous now, Janie. I just never thought of it being like that. What a fool I was."

She reached over and put her hand on his, the same way Steve had done to her, the same she would so often do for her friends. "You're not the only fool here," she assured him.

"What do you mean?" He looked earnestly at her.

She kind of shrugged, uncertain as to how much she wanted to say before she fully understood what was going on between him and Donna. "Well, I may have jumped to some conclusions of my own."

"You mean regarding me?" Now his fingers entwined around hers, warming hers with his touch.

She nodded as she looked down at their hands clasped together in the center of the table. They seemed to fit together perfectly.

"This thing with Donna is complicated," he began slowly. "I mean, I'd like to say she's just a nutty woman on a crazy mission— and part of me believes just that—but the truth is, she was once my wife. She's the mother of my two sons. At one point in my life I believed our vows would never be broken."

"I know." Janie wanted to pull her hand away but stopped herself. She needed to hear him out without reacting. To steady herself, she continued to gaze down at their clasped hands.

"Donna broke my heart a lot of years ago. You know as well as anyone that I've never tried to act like I was innocent in regard to my failed marriage. I realized too late that I was more married to my job than to my wife. Donna certainly wasn't perfect, but I couldn't really blame her for finding someone else."

"I know," she said again. Her voice sounded a bit hoarse, like tears were close to the surface. Was this the end of her and Victor?

"But I got over her, Janie." He squeezed her hand, and she looked into his eyes. "I moved on with my life. I got healthy again. I figured out what really matters. And then I met you, and life was better than ever."

She felt warmth running through her now, like an early spring breeze thawing the winter's snow.

"But Donna is forcing me to consider some pretty conflicted things." He slowly shook his head. "And the truth is, I get a little confused."

She squeezed his fingers. "I feel confused too, Victor, but I'm trying to understand. I just want you to know I won't pressure you. I mean, if you need time to figure this whole thing out, it's okay. I know it can't be easy for you. I can wait."

His eyes brightened. "Really?"

She nodded. What she really wanted to ask him—it was right on the tip of her tongue—was *Do you still love Donna?* He hadn't said that he did, but he hadn't said that he didn't either. And yet she couldn't force those words from her mouth.

"Hello?" called a woman's voice. "Yoo-hoo, anybody home?"

Victor released Janie's hand. "That's Donna."

They both stood now, and for no explainable reason Janie felt as guilty as a schoolgirl who'd just been making out with her boyfriend out behind the gym.

"In here," Victor called with no enthusiasm.

"I saw your car in front," Donna told him. "I'd tried your phone, but you didn't answer."

"It's in the car," he told her. "I thought I wasn't supposed to pick you up until two."

She grinned at Janie now. "Vic dropped me at the bike shop to look for a bike. I guess he's tired of dragging me around all the time."

"Did you find one?" Janie asked.

"I did." Donna smiled proudly. "A really nice street bike. I was just taking it for a test ride and then I saw Vic's car and decided to see what was up. What are you doing *here*, anyway?"

"I noticed Janie's car, and I wanted to stop in and talk to her."

Donna's eyes expressed suspicion. "Don't tell me you're in need of legal advice?"

Victor laughed a bit uneasily. "Maybe so."

"So are you still moving in here?" Janie asked quickly, eager to change the subject. "Because my friend Caroline is getting ready to move in too. Maybe even by this evening."

Donna's mouth twisted to one side. "Well, I suppose if Vic has his way, I'll be moving in here ASAP too."

"With your new bike you'll be able to get around town nicely," Janie suggested.

"Unless it's raining."

"Well, if you and Caroline become friends, maybe she'll give you a ride sometimes." Janie had no idea what Caroline's opinion of Donna was, but it seemed a reasonable possibility.

Donna gave Victor a pitiful look. "So you're really going to throw me out of your house?"

Victor exchanged a quick glance with Janie. "I'm not throwing you out, Donna. It's just that, like I already told you, I need my space."

Donna winked at Janie. "He doesn't like how I leave my things all over his clever little bachelor pad. You know he has the sweetest place, right on the beach. Very swanky really."

Janie just nodded, using an expression that she hoped would not convey that she'd seen it, that she'd been there plenty of times, that she could imagine how it might look with Donna's things strewn about, that the sloppiness would aggravate her as much as it did Victor. Instead she wore her attorney smile and feigned sympathy.

"You need your space too, Donna," Victor continued. "Really, it's for the best."

"I think Caroline would appreciate the company too," Janie assured her. "Her mother just died, and I know she's feeling a little down."

"If you like, we can get you moved over here this afternoon," Victor offered hopefully. "Just leave your bike here and we'll get the rest of your things and come back."

Donna smiled in a catty sort of way. "Yes, I suppose that's what we should do. Perhaps my absence will make your heart grow fonder." She reached over and gently patted his cheek now. "Have it your way, dear. If I have to wait for you, I will wait. Because I know that in due time God is going to turn your heart around. God has promised to restore what the worm has eaten, and God will replace what the moth has destroyed. I'm relying on those promises, Victor, because God has shown me that he plans to keep them."

Janie felt like she'd just been socked in the stomach. "Well, if you'll both excuse me," she said abruptly, "I need to do some measuring downstairs before the floor guys arrive." She turned and hurried away. Was she a coward? Yes, but how could she refute a claim that God planned to reunite Donna and Victor? Really, who was Janie to stand in the way of God?

* * *

By the time Janie got home, she was resolved to do as she had promised, to wait. Of course, it had irked her to hear Donna promise Victor that she was willing to wait too. So they would all play the waiting game. Janie was a patient person. She'd already experienced many life lessons in the art of waiting.

"How's it going?" Janie asked Caroline, who was sitting at the breakfast bar with her phone and a bunch of official-looking papers.

Caroline looked up with a slightly haggard expression. "Ugh. I had no idea all the paperwork that's involved when someone dies."

Janie nodded as she opened the fridge. "Yes, it's a bit of a quagmire. Want some water or soda or something?"

"I'm fine." Caroline sighed as she began to stack the papers. "I'll get out of your way."

"No, it's okay." Janie opened a water bottle and took a swig. "In fact, if you need any help with anything, I'm happy—"

"Seriously?" Caroline looked at her with wide blue eyes. "I would love some help. I mean, I'm trying to figure it out myself. But some of this stuff, well, it just doesn't make sense."

"Why don't we go over it piece by piece together?" Janie suggested.

"You're sure you don't mind? I hate to take advantage of—"

"The truth is I'd love to help. I need something like this to distract me right now."

Caroline frowned. "Distract you?"

Janie nodded as she picked up a paper. "Yes, when we get finished with this, I'll tell you the whole story, okay?"

"All right!" Caroline grinned. "Let's get 'er done."

* * *

It was nearly seven by the time they finished the last piece of paper-work. "It's a small way to say thank you," Caroline said as she put the paperwork back into the folder, "but I insist on taking you out for a nice dinner to show my appreciation."

"It's a date," Janie agreed. "I'm starved."

At dinner Janie told Caroline about her encounter with Victor and Donna's interruption, as well as Donna's statement in regard to waiting for Victor. To Janie's surprised relief Caroline seemed scandalized by the whole thing. "What nerve!" Caroline exclaimed. "Who on earth does she think she is anyway?"

"Victor's wife?"

"*Ex-wife*. And for her to speak for God like that, well, that just irks me." Caroline frowned. "I'm not sure I want to share a house with a woman like that." Then she smiled. "But don't worry, I do plan to move in there. Who knows, maybe Chuck and I will make her want to move out. Maybe she'll decide to go home to Chicago."

Janie laughed. "Well, if you can do that, I'll owe you one."

Caroline's expression turned serious.

"Still feeling sad about your mom?"

She closed her eyes and sighed.

"It'll get better," Janie assured her.

"Oh, it's not just my mom." Caroline frowned. "It's my brother, too."

"Your brother?"

"Remember Michael? Well, he's coming to Clifden for the funeral."

Suddenly Janie did remember. Michael had been kind of a creep back when the girls were young. He had a bad temper, a foul mouth, and some greasy-looking friends. Janie never trusted him, and sometimes she'd actually been afraid of him. Like Caroline she was relieved when Michael was drafted. "How old is Michael now?"

"He's six and half years older than me, so that makes him makes him more than sixty."

"Wow, that's hard to believe." Janie shook her head. "I still remember him as a mouthy teenager with a chip on his shoulder." She forced a laugh. "I'm sure he's nothing like that now."

"Don't be too sure." Caroline took a sip of her cabernet. She had insisted on ordering them a rather expensive bottle of wine. She held the glass up to the candle and squinted at it. "You know I spent about ten years and a lot of money in therapy trying to get over that brother of mine."

"Seriously?" Janie frowned at her.

"Oh yeah." Caroline nodded. "Michael is a real piece of work." Caroline proceeded to tell Janie about some of the horrible things her brother had done to her while she was growing up. "I wouldn't go so far as to call it sexual molestation," she finally confessed, "but it was close."

Janie just shook her head. "I knew he was bad, Caroline, but I never knew he was that bad. Why didn't you confide in us?"

Caroline sighed. "I was probably too scared. Michael threatened me all the time, and I'd seen him do some really cruel things to animals. I never doubted that he'd do similar things to me. Don't you remember some of the bruises I had?"

"We all thought you were just clumsy," Janie admitted. "You got better."

"Yeah, because Michael was gone." Caroline looked close to tears. "Do you know that I actually hoped he'd get killed over there?"

Janie didn't know how to respond.

"I felt so guilty about that. Then I thought maybe the war would change him. In some ways it did, but in some ways it only made him meaner."

"Was he ever arrested?" Janie asked quietly. "Does he have a court record or criminal history?"

"I don't know for sure, but I wouldn't be surprised." Caroline talked about how he'd stolen money from her mom. "I'm sure charges could've been pressed. But my mom never would've done that. She was always trying to protect him—don't ask me why. Probably because my dad was so hard on him. He was hard on all of us, although he did favor me in a warped sort of way. My therapist said Dad's favoritism might've had a lot to do with Michael hating me so much. To be fair, my dad was extremely cruel to Michael. In a lot of ways Michael became like my dad."

"So what are you going to do when he gets here, Caroline?"

She shrugged. "Act civilized and avoid him as much as possible."

"Where will he stay?" Suddenly and unexplainably, Janie envisioned Michael assuming he should stay at her house too, although she knew Caroline would probably be moved out by then. Still, the idea of it was horrific.

"I have no idea. That's his problem."

Janie nodded with relief. "Yes. You're right. He's a grown man. Let him find his own place to stay."

Caroline chuckled. "He's welcome to my mom's smoked-out house."

Janie laughed. "That might keep his visit short."

"Anyway, I'll be at the B and B by then. I plan to move my stuff tomorrow. And I'll make sure that Abby understands Michael isn't welcome there."

"Abby's not ready for any more guests anyway."

"Maybe he's grown up by now," Caroline said wistfully. "I mean, he's in his sixties. It could happen, couldn't it?"

Janie forced a smile. "Sure. Why not?" But the truth was, she doubted it. Short of a miracle, Michael was probably still an older version of his mean self. For Caroline's sake Janie hoped she was wrong.

===*Chapter 17*===

MARLEY

Wednesday afternoons had taken on new meaning for Marley because of her midweek dates with Hunter. Maybe her maternal instincts were enjoying one last chance to mother a child. Or perhaps she was simply ready for grandmother-hood. Whatever the case, Marley loved Wednesdays.

She and Hunter put the finishing touches on their sculpting-clay Christmas ornaments. While these were baking, Marley got out some fabric scraps and, due to a desperate need in Barbie's wardrobe, gave Hunter her first sewing lesson. Hunter's enthusiasm over seeing Barbie's new skirt and top was contagious, and before long Marley was ready to take on a big sewing project herself.

"Can we make Barbie a coat, too?" Hunter asked as they sorted through the fabric scraps that Marley had been collecting for years. At one time she thought she'd get into fabric collage, and later on she considered quilting, but mostly she had collected her pieces based on color and texture. Occasionally she did small sewing projects, like the pillows and curtains she'd created for her beach bungalow.

"Sure." Marley picked up a piece of garnet-colored velvet. "This would be pretty."

"Yeah!" Hunter nodded eagerly. "A Christmas coat!"

Marley had just finished drawing out the lines for Hunter to cut when the phone rang. "You get started while I get that," she told Hunter as she answered the phone.

"Mom?"

"Hey, Ashton," she said happily. "How are you doing?"

"I'm okay." But something about the way he said this made her think just the opposite.

"And Leo?"

Ashton groaned. "Don't ask."

"Oh?"

"So what are you up to these days, Mom?"

Marley gave him a quick lowdown, then explained she had Hunter with her. "We're making Barbie clothes."

"Why?"

"Because she was naked." Marley chuckled. "And because it's fun."

"So Hunter is Jack's kid?"

"She's his granddaughter."

"But she's staying with you?"

"Not staying with me, Ashton." She told him about their arrangement for Wednesdays.

"Oh, that must be nice for her."

"And for me."

"Right, so she's your pseudo-grandchild? Or that daughter you never had?"

"Not exactly." Marley detected a trace of jealousy in her son's voice, which made no sense. Neither did this conversation. "Are you *really* okay, Ashton?"

"Yeah, I'm fine."

"You don't sound like yourself."

He didn't say anything.

"Really, Ashton, is something wrong?"

"Marley?" called Hunter. "I need some help."

"Just a minute, honey."

"What?" Ashton sounded confused.

"Oh, not you, Ashton. I was talking to Hunter."

"Yeah, well, sorry to bother you, Mom. I know you're busy."

"I'm not busy, Ashton. I'm talking to you."

"I won't take any more or your time."

"But Ashton—"

"Later, Mom." He hung up.

"Marley," called Hunter, "I think I accidentally cut off Barbie's sleeve."

"That's okay, honey, we can fix it." As she went over to see how to remedy the miscut fabric, she was thinking about Ashton. What on earth was going on with him? Usually Ashton was so grounded, so calm, so together. In fact Marley often went to him when she was in crisis. Also, he didn't usually call her just to chat, especially not during business hours. She was certain that something was wrong with her only child. Later tonight, after she'd taken Hunter back to Jack's gallery, she would call Ashton and gently attempt to get to the bottom of it.

"We'll just redesign this garment," Marley explained to Hunter as she cut off the other sleeve. "That's the beauty of sewing, it's usually easy to fix a mistake." As she reworked the coat into a rather pretty vest and matching skirt, she prayed that whatever was going wrong in Ashton's life wouldn't be too difficult to fix.

"I wish I could live with you," Hunter said to Marley as they loaded Hunter's things into the car.

Marley smiled at her. "Oh, you'd get tired of me after a while. I can be pretty grumpy in the morning. Sometimes I get so busy with my painting that I forget to do things like cook dinner."

"My mommy forgets to cook too."

Marley wished she hadn't said that. She knew that Hunter's mom, Jasmine, wasn't about to win Mother of the Year anytime soon. But Marley didn't want to get Hunter's thoughts going the wrong direction. "It's not always easy being a mommy," she told Hunter as they got into the car. "But your mommy is lucky to have you. I'll bet you help her a lot in your apartment."

Hunter shrugged and buckled her seat belt.

"I know how much your mommy loves you," Marley said as she drove through the fog toward town. "She would be really lonely if you lived somewhere else."

"Even if I lived with Grandpa?"

Marley didn't know what to say. "Why would you live with your grandpa?"

"Because he's Mommy's daddy."

"Oh yeah." Of course, this didn't really explain much.

"Mommy could live with him too."

"Is your mommy thinking about moving to your grandpa's house?" Marley hadn't heard mention of this yet, but it could be possible.

"I don't know. But Grandpa said we could live with him if we wanted to."

"Oh." Marley nodded. In some ways it wouldn't surprise her if Jack encouraged Jasmine and Hunter to move in with him. Jack didn't approve of Jasmine's lifestyle or of how she sometimes left Hunter home alone. For that matter Marley didn't approve either.

"Then, if you married Grandpa, I could live with you, too," Hunter declared.

Marley just laughed.

"Why are you laughing?" Hunter sounded wounded.

"I just think it's funny how you've got this thing all worked out. But don't you remember that I told you I wasn't planning on marrying your grandpa, Hunter?"

"Because of his wooden leg?" Hunter harrumphed. "I knew I shouldn't have told you about that."

Marley laughed even louder. "No, it has nothing to do with his leg, Hunter."

"Then why?"

Marley almost said because Jack hadn't asked her but realized that would open a whole different can of worms. Hunter would probably go tell Jack that Marley was waiting for him to get down on his knees, which might be tricky with a wooden leg. "Getting married to someone is kind of personal, Hunter."

"Why?"

"Because it just is. And remember I told you that if I decide to get married, I will definitely let you know?"

"I know. I just don't like to wait."

"How about you, Hunter?"

"Huh?"

"Do you plan to get married?"

Hunter giggled. "I'm only seven and a half. I'm too little to get married, Marley."

"I know. But do you have a boyfriend?"

Well, that did the trick. Because for the rest of the ride into town, Hunter told Marley all about Addison Lexington and how she liked to chase him at recess, but when she caught him, he told everyone that he hated her and that hurt her feelings. The day after, though, he wanted to sit by her at lunch, but when she offered to share her fish sticks with him, he got mad.

"Boys are like that," Marley confided to Hunter as they walked across the street to the gallery. "The good news is that if Addison *didn't* like you, he probably would just ignore you altogether. So try to be patient with him."

"You try to be patient with my grandpa, too," Hunter said as Marley opened the door. Naturally Marley had no response to that.

"Hey, there are two of my favorite girls," Jack called out. "Did you have a good afternoon?"

Hunter immediately began to relay everything that they'd done, from working on the Christmas decorations to Barbie's new wardrobe.

"Here's the proof," Marley said as she handed Jack the grocery bag she'd filled with Hunter's treasures.

He smiled as he looked into her eyes. "Thank you, Marley. You are truly a gift."

She felt her cheeks warming. "Well, Hunter is a gift too."

"Your mom's not here," he told Hunter. "So you're going home with me."

"I need to get going too," Marley said quickly. She didn't want to linger long enough for Hunter to start discussing the possibilities of them all happily living together. "I'll see you guys later." She noticed the questioning look in Jack's eyes but simply made a little finger wave and hurried on out. Yes, she knew she was acting slightly juvenile. But with Hunter around, well, she never knew what was going to come out of that little girl's mouth.

Besides, she wanted to get back home and call Ashton. The more she'd thought about his strange phone call, the more worried she'd become. As she drove, she remembered the last time she'd heard a tone like that in his voice. It was a night she didn't like to remember. But as she drove through the darkened streets, it came back at her like a flash.

It hadn't been easy for Ashton to tell his parents about his sexual orientation. For that matter it hadn't been easy for his parents to hear about it. But Marley had tried to be understanding. She'd read and heard enough to know that their acceptance was imperative to his emotional well-being. Unfortunately John hadn't read or heard the same information. Despite the fact that Ashton was nearly nineteen, John had treated him like a naughty child, acting as if Ashton should've known better.

It was as if John took the whole thing personally, as if he thought Ashton's homosexuality was nothing more than a bad reflection on John as a father. The truth was, John hadn't been a very good father. Not that it had anything to do with Ashton's sexual preference. But John was narcissistic. Everything was about him.

As a result Marley had been caught in the middle. Like a frustrated umpire, she tried to make father and son understand each other. Later, when she discovered that John was still cheating on her, she gave up on the marriage completely. But she never gave up on Ashton. She never would.

Her thoughts in regard to homosexuality, however, had gotten a bit murky in the last month or so. As a result of her surrendering her life to God, she'd begun to attend Abby's mother's weekly Bible study group. It hadn't troubled Marley that Doris and her friends were all at least twenty years her senior. When they asked her to tell them about herself, among other things, she had mentioned her divorce and that her thirty-year-old son was an artist, a successful entrepreneur, and gay. "He's in a committed relationship," she'd said quickly when a couple of them looked shocked by her admission. "And I'm okay with it. Really."

"You're *okay* with it?" Louise questioned her.

"Sure." Marley had smiled. "He's my son. I love him no matter what."

Suddenly the ladies got into a somewhat heated discussion over whether homosexuality was wrong. Marley had tried not to show it at the time, but some of their comments had hurt her deeply.

"I don't know," Fran had finally said. She was the quietest member of the group and for the most part had simply been sitting there listening as the others spouted their contrasting opinions, though most seemed to believe that God frowned on homosexuality. "Maybe God makes people different from each other," Fran continued slowly. "Maybe we don't understand everything. Don't forget that Scripture in 1 Corinthians 13: 'For now we see in the mirror dimly, but then we'll see face to face … for now we know in part, but then we will understand fully, even as we have been fully understood.' I know that's not exactly verbatim, but it's close."

"What are you saying?" Louise had demanded. "That God made homosexuals on purpose?"

"I'm not sure." Fran had gotten a thoughtful expression then. "But I do believe God *loves* homosexuals on purpose. I believe that's what we should do too."

Of course, that wasn't the end of the debate. Marley almost wished she'd never mentioned a word about Ashton to any of them. As much as some of their words stung, they had also made her wonder. Fran's gracious response had been a bit more encouraging, but what was Marley, as a new believer in God, supposed to believe about all this?

Finally she had metaphorically thrown up her hands, asking God to help her to come to grips with the gay thing. Even if God himself had shown up and declared that homosexuality was wrong, wrong, wrong, she wasn't sure how she'd react. She was a mother, and there was no way she would ever stop loving her son. That would be as easy as stopping the surf that pounded outside her bungalow around the clock. She suspected that God's position wasn't as black and white as people like Louise tried to make it seem. Finally Marley had decided that God was big enough to handle the issue and wise enough to help her to understand it in time.

As soon as she got into the house, she called Ashton's cell phone. When he didn't answer, she left a message. "I really want to talk to you. I can tell that something is bothering you, and I'd like to hear what's going on. I'm sorry I was busy when you called. I'm not busy now." She looked at the calendar on her refrigerator. "By the way, it's Thanksgiving next week. Maybe you and Leo would like to come over and spend it with me at the beach." She could think of nothing more to say. "Please call me, Ashton. I love you. Bye."

She hung up the phone and began to pace around her small bungalow. Instead of obsessing and worrying like she used to do, however, Marley simply prayed. She begged God to watch over her son, to protect him from whatever was troubling him, to bring him peace, to have him call her, to bless him in his business, and to bless his partner Leo. "And teach Ashton to call out to you, God," Marley said finally. "Show him that you are real and that you love him and that you have all the answers he's looking for. Amen."

Chapter 18

CAROLINE

"Good news," Janie announced on Thursday afternoon.

"What's that?" Caroline had just returned from her mom's house, where she'd spent a couple hours cleaning things up. It wasn't easy being over there, but Janie had told her that insurance companies appreciated it when homeowners took this kind of initiative.

"Joan Wilson is back in town."

"Seriously?" Caroline took Chuck through the kitchen, letting him go out into the backyard.

"She had the audacity to show up at the nursing care agency and ask for her paycheck."

"You're kidding." Caroline went over to the sink to wash.

"Apparently Joan assumed everything would've blown over by now."

"How did you hear about this?" Caroline dried her hands.

"Detective Alberts called. Fortunately someone at the agency had the good sense to call the police. So Joan Wilson was picked up and taken in for questioning."

"And?"

"She confessed that she was a smoker and that those were her cigarettes."

"I knew it!"

"But she said that the cigarettes had been securely zipped in a pocket of her purse, and that she forgot they were there. She thinks your mom must've gotten into her purse and sneaked them out and then taken them to her room."

"I guess that's believable. But it seems that Joan should've been paying better attention to her patient."

"Exactly. The agency claims that their caregivers know they are not to have certain things in their possession while caring for patients. The list includes obvious items like firearms, knives, and pharmaceuticals, but it also includes cigarette lighters and matches."

"So can I assume there are will be some consequences for Joan?"

"To begin with, Joan was fired from the agency." Janie's brow creased. "But it's possible the DA will pursue this further. You could push for her to be charged for wrongful death or—"

"I don't want to do that!" Caroline cringed at the thought of being pulled back into this mess, being expected to make more statements to the police, or even going to court. "I just want this to be all over with, Janie. I want to get on with my life. Is that wrong?"

"No, I can understand why you'd want to do that."

"It's not like it would help my mom to drag this out. Of course, I'm angry that Joan brought something dangerous into my mom's house, but I don't think she intended to hurt my mom."

"No. But she was negligent."

"And she'll have to carry that with her forever—knowing that her negligence killed my mom. She's lost her job, and I suspect she won't be hired as a health-care provider again." Caroline sighed. "It's not that I want to seem like a coward, but I just don't see how any good would come of me going after Joan now. Most of all I just want to move on. Is that selfish?"

"No, I don't think so."

"Oh, Janie, I'm so relieved this part of the nightmare is over."

"And now you are free and clear," Janie said happily.

"Thank you!" Caroline hugged her. "And now you'll be free of me and Chuck."

"Why?" Janie looked surprised.

"I'm moving into the B and B tonight."

It didn't take long to pack up her few belongings. By that evening, Caroline and Chuck were somewhat settled into the inn. Although the sunny yellow room was thoughtfully decorated, and despite being cleared with the police, Caroline still felt out of place and out of sorts. Almost like a refugee or displaced person. So much of her life felt unsettled and unresolved. It wasn't that she was eager to have her mother buried and gone, but due to two other deaths in town, her mother's funeral was delayed until next Monday, just a few days before Thanksgiving. Thinking of the upcoming holiday reminded her that perhaps she should simply be thankful that her name had been cleared and she had some downtime now.

By Friday, Caroline was finally feeling more together. She'd had a chance to finalize most of the funeral arrangements, tend to her mother's business, and basically catch her breath. She had only one more unpleasant chore to attend to, and she knew she couldn't put it off any longer. It was high time to call her brother and inform him about their mother's funeral details.

"I'm already on my way up there," he said after she'd relayed the information.

"Really?" Caroline hypnotically watched her lunch, a bowl of soup, rotating around and around in the microwave in the inn's big kitchen. "Uh … so where are you coming from anyway?"

"I've been living in Phoenix the past couple years."

"Oh. I didn't know that. Are you flying into—"

"I'm driving."

Caroline felt relieved. Driving here from Phoenix should take a couple of days. "When do you expect to arrive?"

"Well, I'm just outside of Weed now."

"Oh?" Caroline looked at the clock on the microwave. "Weed, California?"

"You know about another Weed?" He chuckled like this was funny.

"No, but that's only about four or five hours away, right?"

"Sounds about right. I should make it to Clifden early this evening."

"Okay. Then drive safely, Michael."

"Are you staying at Mom's house?"

Suddenly Caroline wasn't sure if she'd given Michael all the details. Hadn't she mentioned the fire? Or maybe she'd said that while the connection was breaking up. "Hey, are you driving while talking on the phone?" she asked.

"Yeah. But it's okay. I'm on the freeway."

"No, it's not okay. It's against the law and it's dangerous. I refuse to talk to you unless you pull over."

Michael let loose with a couple of expletives, which transported Caroline straight back to her childhood. Then he hung up.

She pocketed her phone and removed her bowl of soup from the microwave.

"Mmm, that smells good." Donna sniffed the air as she came into the kitchen.

"It's just minestrone." Caroline held up the empty can of soup to show her the label before she tossed it into the trash compactor. "Sorry, I don't have any more to offer. But I've got some black bean if you're interested."

"No, thanks, I just had lunch in town." Donna followed Caroline to the dining room, pulling out a chair on the other side of the table as Caroline sat down. "So are you all settled in?"

Caroline nodded as she took a bite of the hot soup. She had met Donna briefly this morning while hauling an armful of clothes up the stairs. Although Donna was attractive and cheerful and chatty, Caroline had taken an instant dislike to the woman. To be fair, she'd taken a dislike to her right after Janie had told her about what Donna had said about waiting for Victor to have a change of heart.

"How long do you think you'll be staying here?" Donna asked.

"I'm not sure." Caroline stirred her soup to cool it down a bit.

"Did I hear your mom's house burnt down and that she died?" Donna made a sad face. "I'm sorry for your loss, Caroline. That must be terrible."

"It's been a rough couple of weeks. But I'm starting to feel a little better." She was—until she'd learned that her nasty brother would be here in a few hours. Not that she intended to tell Donna about any of that.

"So did Victor tell me that you grew up in Clifden too?"

"I did. Abby, Janie, Marley, and me—we all grew up here."

"Yes." Donna nodded. "I haven't met Marley yet. But I believe Victor mentioned her name. You're all in some kind of club?"

"Well, it's not exactly a club." She blew on a spoonful of steaming soup. "I mean, we started it as a club when we were girls." She paused for a cautious bite. "But we got back together last summer." Caroline quickly explained the concept of the Four Lindas.

"How interesting. Four girls named Linda in the same classroom. How very unusual."

"Well, Linda was a pretty common name for girls back in the fifties. Anyway, we all started using our middle names after that, and thus began the Four Lindas club."

Donna made a disappointed face. "I suppose that I won't be invited to join the club, then."

Caroline made a half smile, then took another bite of soup.

"So you're really good friends with Janie, right?"

Something about the tone of Donna's voice put Caroline on her guard. "Sure. Janie and I are friends."

"I understand that Janie and Victor used to date a bit, right?"

Caroline wished her soup would cool faster. She didn't like the sound of where this could be going.

"But it sounds like Janie has a new man in her life." Donna seemed to be watching Caroline closely.

Caroline tried to hide her surprise at this announcement. Since when was Janie seeing someone else? Was this some kind of a setup to extract information from Caroline? "Seeing someone else?" Caroline shrugged. "What makes you think that?"

Donna's eyes lit up. "My son told me he saw Caroline with another man last week, and that it looked like a date."

Caroline frowned but didn't respond. To her relief her phone rang again. Thankful for good timing, she reached for it, but upon seeing it was Michael, she had to disguise her disappointment. "Please excuse me, I need to take this," she said in a forced cheery tone. "It's my brother." Then with her soup in one hand and phone in the other, she answered the phone and hurried upstairs to her room, quickly closing the door.

"Okay, Caroline. I'm not driving now. I can talk."

"Good. You wouldn't want to get a ticket or get in a wreck."

"Thanks for your concern." His voice had an edge to it. "Now back to my question, baby sister. Are you staying at Mom's house or not?"

"No, I'm staying with a friend." Now that wasn't exactly a lie. This house did belong to her friend Abby.

"So I can stay at Mom's then?"

"Well, I suppose you could, if you really wanted to." She quickly filled him in on the fire.

"What?" This news was followed by more expletives. "So you're telling me that our family home has burned to the ground?"

"No, it's not that bad. But Mom's bedroom is pretty much totaled. The smoke damage is extensive and—"

"How did the fire get started anyway? Wasn't someone there taking care of mom? Where were you anyway?"

Caroline attempted to explain this but was cut off again.

"So let's cut to the chase. If you're saying the biggest problem is the smoke damage, why haven't you had someone in there to clean it up yet?"

"The insurance adjuster is coming by this afternoon. After that I'll see about getting someone in to clean it, or whatever."

"What do you mean *whatever?*"

"Well, I don't know. Maybe it would be best to tear it down."

"Tear the whole house down?" Michael spewed more off-color language. "You said Mom's room was the only part that burned, Caroline. And now you're talking about bulldozing the place?"

"There might be electrical problems or structural damage. It's not like the house was in good shape before the fire. And now it's—"

"Well, don't think you can tear down Mom and Dad's house, Caroline. For your information I'm part of the McCann family too. I have some say in what happens to that house, and everything else for that matter. I'm warning you, baby sister, don't get any crazy ideas that you're going to make off with anything before I even get there."

Like a freight train barreling down the tracks straight at her, the truth that Michael was going to make everything difficult became clear to Caroline. "Don't worry," she assured him in a calm voice. "There's nothing of any real value in the house anyway."

Even as she said this, she wondered. What if there were things that she didn't know about? Perhaps some mementos from her grandparents. What about her grandfather's old stamp and coin collection that she used to help him organize? She recalled some of the old boxes she'd shifted to clear a path through the garage. They were so heavy she assumed they contained old newspapers, but what if they held rare books or even old magazines that were collectible? Did she really want Michael to waltz in there and just take everything? If he did, he would only take what he could sell.

"So if there's nothing of any value"—his voice took on that old slippery quality—"then why not let me sort it all out for you?"

"You'd want to sort through all the garbage and take it all to the dump?" she questioned. "You know how Mom never threw anything away. The house is really a mess."

"I've got a pickup. I can take care of what needs to be thrown out." Suddenly it seemed he was trying to sound like a responsible human being, and this worried her. "I can handle the business end of things too, Caroline. I'm sure you don't want to bother your pretty little head with all legal stuff that anyway."

That just made her mad. "Actually I have an attorney helping me to sort through—"

"What're you doing wasting Mom's money on a lawyer for?" he growled.

"I'm not wasting any—"

He cut her off by hanging up again. Caroline closed her phone and picked up her soup, which was now lukewarm. She considered going back down to renuke it in the microwave, but she didn't want to risk another conversation with that nosy Donna. As she finished her tepid soup, Caroline revamped her afternoon plan. She would go directly back to her mom's house, where she'd left Chuck, and she'd start sorting through things while she waiting for the insurance man to show up.

As she drove, Caroline estimated that Michael would arrive in Clifden around six or seven that night. By that time she hoped to have removed anything and everything that she did not want her selfish brother to take or perhaps destroy. She remembered how destructive he could be when he'd been drinking. No doubt he'd go straight for things like the old sterling silverware that her mom never used because she preferred the convenience of stainless. The silver might not be worth much, but it was one of their few family heirlooms, a fact that would be completely lost on Michael. More than likely he'd pawn it even before he left town.

Perhaps he'd want her mom's old china teacup collection, too. Caroline had loved this set. As a child she'd enjoyed tea parties with Grandma Moore. Worried they'd get broken by her absentminded mother, Caroline had safely stowed the fragile cups and saucers on a high kitchen shelf. What if her six-foot-two brother spotted them there and began chucking them into the fireplace just for the heck of it? She wouldn't put it past him.

Caroline stopped by the grocery store to scrounge up a bunch of cardboard produce boxes. By two o'clock, looking like an outlaw with her bandana scarf tied over her mouth and nose, she was carefully packing up anything of her mom's that she felt should belong to her. According to Janie, who had gone over the will and other legal documents, it all belonged to Caroline anyway. Convincing her brother of this would be a major challenge, and with a few days until the funeral, there was no telling what Michael might do to rock Caroline's boat.

At three o'clock, just as she was loading her third box into the back of her car, the insurance adjuster showed up. She walked him through the house, answered some more questions, and he promised to get back to her early the following week.

"Is it okay if I get someone in here to start cleaning things up and to deal with the smoke damage?" she asked as she walked him outside.

"Of course. Just save your receipts. Same thing for any repair work. You'll probably want to get estimates from several contractors." He handed her an insurance booklet. "This has some good suggestions and guidelines." They talked a bit longer, and then he left and she returned to work. She wanted to be well out of the house before five thirty, just in case Michael was closer than she'd estimated. When she finished, she would lock the place up as usual. She had no doubts that Michael would find his own way inside.

Unfortunately it was nearly five forty-five by the time Caroline was putting her last load, along with Chuck, into the back of the SUV. She'd had no idea there would be so much to salvage from the heaps of trash in the garage and elsewhere. But the more she looked, the more she found. After getting Abby's permission to temporarily stow her finds in the garage of the bed-and-breakfast, she'd worked as hard and fast as she could, taking trip after trip. Now, worried that she might actually get caught red-handed by her hot-headed brother, her heart pounded wildly as she watched for strange vehicles coming down the street. "We gotta get outta here, boy," she said to Chuck as she started her engine and practically peeled out of the driveway.

She had driven only one block when she saw a big black pickup rumbling toward her. For some reason—maybe it was instinctive—she knew it was her big, bad brother. Fortunately it was already getting dark, and she was fairly sure that the tinted windshield in her vehicle made it impossible for him to see her. Just the same, she grabbed her sunglasses and put them on. Feeling slightly ridiculous, but with eyes straight ahead, she slowly continued on past him.

Sure enough, in her rearview mirror she observed the black pickup turning into the driveway of her childhood home. Heaven help her and the rest of Clifden. Michael McCann was back in town.

* * *

Caroline heard her phone ringing as she drove toward the bed-and-breakfast. She felt certain it was Michael but had no intention of answering it. For one thing it was against the law, but besides that, she had no desire to speak to him. She pulled into the driveway at the bed-and-breakfast and, with a box in hand and Chuck at her heels, she hurried up the walk, unlocked the front door, and went inside. Since the place wasn't officially an inn yet, Abby had understood that Caroline and Donna would need to keep the place locked like a regular home. She'd given them both exterior-door keys.

Caroline was extremely thankful for this as she closed and locked the door behind her. It wasn't that she expected Michael to actually do anything to hurt her, but it would not be beneath her brother to track her down, come storming over here, and make a lot of noise, particularly if he got some beer under his belt.

"You're back." Donna came out from the kitchen now. "Any plans for dinner?"

To Caroline's dismay she felt relieved to see Donna. The woman's happy face welcomed her like a port in a storm. "No plans." Caroline set the box she was carrying at the foot of the stairs and sighed. "I just figured I'd warm up some more soup."

Donna frowned. "Woman does not live by soup alone, Caroline."

Caroline chuckled. "Really? What did you have in mind?"

"I rode my bike to the grocery store and got a lovely salmon filet and some salad things. How about if I fix us both a nice little dinner?"

"That actually sounds wonderful. I'm famished."

Donna smiled. "You go ahead and finish up whatever it is you're doing."

"I've just got to unload a few more things from my car."

"I know you've been moving stuff from your mom's place." Donna wrinkled her nose. "Maybe you could go take a shower or fumigate your clothes or something when you're done. No offense, Caroline, but you smell horrible."

"Sorry." Caroline chuckled at Donna's candor. "It's from the smoke, and I know it's really stinky. I promise to clean up before dinner."

"Good. I think dinner will be ready in about forty minutes."

"Perfect."

Caroline felt an unexpected twinge of guilt as she went out to the garage. Okay, so maybe she *was* a traitor, or maybe she was blowing the Janie versus Donna face-off out of proportion. After all, she was simply sharing a meal with Donna, not swearing to become bosom buddies until the end of time. Under the circumstances Janie should understand. Besides, Caroline remembered as she carried a box of old books into the garage, back before Donna came to town, Janie had encouraged her friends to be nice to Victor's ex. As long as Donna was being nice too, why shouldn't Caroline reciprocate? Besides, Caroline was starving. Really, Janie would get this.

Caroline finally unloaded the last of the boxes, closed and locked the garage, and was just heading in to shower when her cell phone rang for about the fifth time. Of course, it was Michael again. She knew she should answer it—he'd only get more and more angry if she didn't—but all she wanted right now was to feel that good hot water and her new moisturizing shower gel washing away all the grit and grime and smoke from the day. Sorry, but her brother would have to wait!

Chapter 19

ABBY

"How is it possible to have three daughters but not one who can come home for Thanksgiving?" Abby complained to her mother on the Saturday before the holiday.

"Because they have their own lives?" her mother replied somewhat predictably.

"Yes, I understand that. But what about my life? What about Paul? And you? Wouldn't they want to take some time out of their busy lives to be with family?" Abby set a bag down on her mom's butcher-block table with a thud.

"What on earth is *that?*" Her mom leaned over to peer into the grocery sack.

"Your aebleskiver maker."

"What?" Her mom pulled the cast-iron pan out of the bag and looked curiously at Abby. "Why are you bringing this back to me now?"

Abby shrugged. "I borrowed it."

"Yes, about twenty years ago."

"So." Abby went over to the window that looked out over the ocean and sighed loudly.

"So why are you bringing it back to me now, Abby?"

"I thought you might need it."

Abby felt her mother's hand on her shoulder, turning her around. Abby looked into her mother's face. That sweet, old, wrinkled, age-spotted face. "What is going on here, Linda Abigail?"

"Oh, Mom." Abby threw her arms around her mom and started to cry. "I just wanted to tell you, you know, that I … I … I really love you."

Without speaking they embraced for a long moment, and then her mom released Abby, holding her at arm's length as she peered into Abby's eyes. "What is going on here?"

"Can't a daughter tell her mother she loves her?" Abby sniffed.

"Certainly, if that's all there is to it. But I sense there's something else." Her mom's expression changed to worry. "Is it your health? I know you went to the doctor last week. Was there something wrong—"

"No, Mom. Thank God, I'm healthy as a horse." Abby grabbed a paper towel to blow her nose. "Although my doctor says I should take off a few pounds. But thanks to changing my eating habits for Paul's sake, it seems my cholesterol has improved and my blood pressure is down."

"Is it Paul then?"

"No, Mom. Paul is fine too." Abby frowned. "Well, as far as I know."

"Then what is it? Why this unexpected display of emotion? Or should I say *affection?*"

Abby threw the used paper towel into the trash and gave her mom a sheepish grin. "I guess I just realized how I sometimes forget to show my appreciation for you."

"Oh, Abby, I don't expect you to—"

"I know. We're not a very demonstrative family, but, well, seeing Caroline losing her mother last week, and then hearing Janie and Marley talking about how it felt to lose their mothers, well, I realized that I should be more expressive to you while I have the ..." Abby pressed her lips together.

"While you have the chance?" Her mom chuckled. "Well, don't be worried, dear, I'm not planning on kicking the bucket anytime soon."

Abby hugged her again. "Good to know, Mom."

"But it's nice to be appreciated."

Abby frowned to think of her own daughters. "Yes, I can only imagine."

"Come sit down," her mom said. "I'll pour you a cup of coffee, and you can pour your woes out to me."

So, over coffee, Abby lamented the fact that Jessie, Brandon, and Lucy had already decided to spend Thanksgiving with his folks. "Brandon said it was his turn this year. And Laurie had promised to try to come, but now she says that she has to work on Friday and it's too much traveling to come for just one day."

"At least she called and told you that," her mom pointed out. "That wouldn't have happened last year."

Abby sniffed. "Yes, I suppose you're right."

"And Nicole is still in France," her mom finished for her. "Or so I assume. I just got a letter from her yesterday saying that she's not coming home until Christmas."

"Nicole wrote *you* a letter?" Abby tried not to feel jealous. Nicole never wrote Abby letters. All Abby got was an occasional email or a rather expensive phone call.

"To thank me for sending her a check."

"Oh." Abby nodded.

"See, you raised her right."

"Thanks." Abby took another sip of her mother's strong coffee.

"It might help you to recall that sometimes you and Paul took the girls to his parents for Thanksgiving or Christmas. Remember?"

"I'm so sorry, Mom." Again Abby felt badly for not being more appreciative of her mom. "I kind of forgot."

"My point is that your dad and I managed to get along just fine, Abby. In fact we were often surprised at the fun we could have even when our kids couldn't be home for the holidays."

"Right." Abby shook her head. "I guess you've always been a more well-adjusted person than I can ever hope to be."

Her mom laughed. "It's never too late."

"Honestly the idea of sitting home alone with Paul and eating turkey is just not that appealing. I know you'll be in Tucson with Marjorie by then. So we can't even have you over."

"Why don't you do something with your friends on Thanksgiving?"

"My friends?" Abby looked blankly at her mom.

"The Lindas. I'll bet they're feeling lonely with the holidays approaching too." Her mom pointed in the direction of Marley's house. "If fact Marley is going through a very hard time with her son right now."

"Really?"

"Yes, she's worried about Ashton. She came over here last night and asked me to pray for him. He's extremely depressed about something."

"Oh, poor Marley. And poor Ashton. Did she say what?"

Her mom shook her head.

Abby thought for a moment. "You know, Mom, you're probably right. I hadn't even considered that. Caroline just lost her mom. Janie and Victor are facing some challenges. And now this thing with Marley and her son."

"I'm sure they'd all love to have someone like you offer them a place to gather on Thanksgiving, Abby."

Abby set her coffee mug in the sink, then hugged her mom again. "What would I do without you, Mom?"

"Oh, you'd probably just grow up a bit more." Her mom patted Abby's cheeks with both hands like she used to do when Abby was little. "That's what happens when a girl loses her mother. She has to grow up and be even more of a mother than she was before."

"Really?" Abby blinked. "I'm not sure I'd even know how to do that."

"Oh, if the time comes, you will."

Abby gave her mom a serious look now. "Just don't hurry that time along any, Mom. You and Marjorie better be careful as you travel. Don't forget to get up and move around the plane and—"

"It's a short flight, Abby."

"I know." Abby nodded. "But drink plenty of fluids and make sure you get the low-sodium meal and—"

"Yes, yes—and if you start acting too motherly, well, you never know."

Abby laughed. "Okay, I get it. Just have fun in Tucson."

Before Abby left, her mom handed her the aebleskiver pan. "Here, you might need this more than I do."

"Huh?" Abby was confused.

"Good grief, Abby, don't you ever make aebleskivers with Lucy?"

Abby chuckled. "Good point."

"I know you were just using it as an excuse to stop by." Her mom smiled. "But you never need an excuse to come see me, Abby. You know that."

She nodded. "Yes, you're right."

"I'm sure Marley won't mind if you pop in on her, too."

"I think I'll do that. Thanks, Mom."

Abby did knock on Marley's door, and when Marley answered, Abby could tell she was upset. "Mom told me that something's up with Ashton," Abby told her. "Is there anything I can do?"

"I don't know." Marley led Abby inside and immediately went to pacing, wringing her hands as she walked back and forth in the small space. "I spoke to him late last night, Abby, and he did not sound good."

"What's wrong?" Abby set her aebleskiver pan on the coffee table and waited.

"He wouldn't go into any details."

"Is it his business? I know a lot of small businesses are hurting right now."

"Maybe. But he sounded so depressed, almost despondent. When I asked if I could talk to Leo—I told Ashton I only wanted to say hello, although I really planned to question Leo about Ashton's emotional well-being—Ashton actually hung up on me."

"Oh?" Abby sat down on the sofa.

"That is so not like him. At first I assumed it was because his cell phone got out of range or something."

"Did you call him back?"

"Yes, several times for the next hour. He must've turned his phone off. I tried his business number, too, but I just got voice mail. I was so worried I went next door and asked Doris to pray for him. I know I'm probably overreacting, but suddenly I'm recalling all these things I read when Ashton was younger. Homosexuals have a suicide rate that's much higher than the general population. I think about one in three suicides are estimated to be homosexuals, and if you figure that per capita, well, it's just very frightening."

"Don't you think those statistics are focused on adolescents?" Abby suggested.

"Maybe, but still ... Ashton sounded so sad, so down."

"And this morning? Did you try to call?"

"Same thing. I'm sure his phone is off."

"What about Leo? Doesn't he have a cell phone?"

Marley frowned. "Yes, of course. But I don't have his number. I have the business number and Ashton's cell. That was always enough."

"You tried the business?"

"Voice mail." Marley shook her head. "The drum shop is always open on weekends. So I don't get this."

"Why don't you drive over and see what's up?" Abby said.

"Yes." Marley nodded. "That's what I'm about to do. I thought maybe I was just overreacting. But now that you said it, that's what I'm going to do."

"Do you want me to come with you?" Abby offered. "I was going to work at the bed-and-breakfast today, but there's nothing there that can't wait. I'd be happy to go."

Marley seemed to consider this but finally shook her head. "No. I can do this on my own, but I appreciate the offer."

Abby was actually relieved to hear this. She was perfectly willing to go with Marley, to be supportive of her friend, but she felt in over her head. Not only had Abby never parented a son, she could not imagine parenting a homosexual son. Although she tried to act tolerant for Marley's sake, she still wasn't even used to the idea that Ashton was gay. The truth was, it made Abby uncomfortable.

"Well, you call me if you need anything," Abby told Marley. "I'll be praying for you and Ashton." She forced a smile. "Hopefully you're just overreacting a little, like a mom. I know how that is. I've done it lots of times."

"Yes." Marley was putting on her coat now. "I'm sure that will be the situation. But I don't mind. It's only a one-hour drive. Maybe I'll do some shopping while I'm over there."

"By the way," Abby said as they went out together. "I'm going to invite everyone to have Thanksgiving with us. The girls aren't coming home, so it's just Paul and me."

"That sounds nice." Marley was already unlocking her car, and Abby could tell her friend's troubled mind wasn't ready to talk about pumpkin pies and turkey. "I'll get back to you on that, okay?"

Abby waved as Marley got into her small car and drove away. "God, go with her," Abby said aloud. As she drove to town, she continued to pray for Marley and Ashton, and for a good outcome to whatever was going on. Even as Abby said amen, though, she felt doubtful. Something about this whole thing felt wrong. She pulled up to the bed-and-breakfast feeling seriously worried for Marley's emotional well-being. What if all was not well? What if Ashton really had done something regrettable?

This thought made Abby feel guilty. Why hadn't she simply dropped everything and gone with Marley? What would it have hurt? Really, what kind of friend was Abby anyway?

===Chapter 20===

JANIE

"You've got to see what just arrived at the shop," Bonnie Boxwell exclaimed over the phone. "Remember I told you about the new company with the great nautical line?"

"Nautical line?" In her new law office Janie paused from unpacking a box of books. She'd come over early this morning to work. Her goal was to have the space open for business by Monday.

"For Victor's boat. Aren't you still working on that for him?"

"Oh. Yes. Of course." She slid a heavy volume onto a low shelf, then stood back up, stretching her spine.

"Well, you've simply got to get in here and see these things, Janie. There's this small set of dishes that's to die for. They were featured in *Coastal Living* a month or so ago, and trust me—they'll be absolutely perfect for the boat."

As Bonnie continued to describe the various pieces she felt certain that Janie would want, Janie grew confused. Still unsure as to the status of her relationship with Victor, she wondered if, for the time being, she should step down from her promise to outfit his sailboat. The idea of doing that made her feel inexplicably sad. She always had difficulty not finishing something she'd started. Plus it was because of this project that Bonnie had ordered a lot of the items that she was so enthused about now. It seemed wrong for Janie to let Bonnie down.

"I thought your shop open didn't open until ten on Saturdays." Janie glanced at her watch.

"I'll let you in early," Bonnie said enticingly. "Come around the back door, and I'll give you a private showing."

"That's an offer I can't resist. I'll be there in about five minutes."

As Janie drove, she rationalized that helping Victor as a designer didn't necessarily fall into the category of being "seriously involved" with him. After all, Victor wanted her assistance because he admired her sense of style. She was simply playing the role of an interior decorator. No big deal.

Janie parked in back of the design shop, and before long she and Bonnie were oohing and ahhing over the interesting pieces. "Tell you what," Bonnie said, "I'll give you a ten percent discount for anything you purchase today."

"What if these plates are too big for the cabinets?" Janie asked. "I don't have the measurements with me."

"Take them over and try them out," Bonnie told her. "If they don't work, you can bring them back."

"All right." Janie nodded. Tempted by her one-day-only discount, Janie picked out a lot of things. As Bonnie rang up the purchase, Janie loaded the items back into some of the packing boxes. She held up one of the pale blue tumblers, admiring the light through the bubble glass. "You don't think these might get broken on the boat? I mean if the ocean is rough."

"Not if you pack them carefully in the cabinet." Bonnie held up a set of blue-and-white striped cloth napkins. "Tuck these around them and they'll be fine." She pointed to the unbreakable set of acrylic cups with yachting flags. "Use those on bumpy seas."

"Yes, that makes sense."

"Trust me, you don't want to be stuck eating out of plastic all the time." She grinned as she held up one of the matching bubble-glass goblets. "And for those romantic sunset dinners, you'll want these."

Janie almost admitted that she wasn't sure there'd ever be another "romantic sunset dinner" but figured that wasn't something Bonnie needed to know. "Thanks for calling me," she told Bonnie as they loaded the boxes into the trunk of her car.

"Let me know how everything looks."

"Hopefully I won't have to bring anything back." Janie closed the trunk.

"Have fun!" Bonnie waved as she went back into her store.

Janie intended to have fun. She'd been focused on setting up her law office lately, mostly to divert her attention from Victor and Donna, but other than Caroline she didn't have any real clients yet. This sudden change of direction—getting to play house on Victor's sailboat—was a welcome distraction.

She parked near the wharf. Taking one box at a time, Janie carried them down the dock and set them on the deck of Victor's boat. Finally she boarded, unlocked the cabin, and began to open and sort through the boxes. It felt like Christmas. To add to her merriment, she put a jazz CD into the Bose player. After seeing that the plates did indeed fit in the rather compact cabinets, she decided to give the insides a thorough cleaning first. Once that was done, she decided to go ahead and wash the dishes, too. That way they'd be ready to use.

Of course, as she washed, dried, and started to put away the dishes, she daydreamed about when she and Victor might set out on a sailboat trip, perhaps something more than just looping up and down the river and bay. Maybe someday—if things went as she secretly hoped—they would do long trips, overnight trips, perhaps even sail up to the San Juans like Victor had been dreaming of.

"What are you doing here?"

Janie nearly dropped the goblet in her hand. She turned to see Donna halfway down the ladder into the galley. With a suspicious scowl Donna slowly continued down the steps, finally standing before Janie with an accusing expression. "Answer me! What are you doing here?"

Janie set the goblet back into the sudsy water. "I'm just cleaning up and putting things away."

"But *why* are you here?" Donna demanded.

"I found some things at—"

"Just stop!" Donna pointed at the door that led to the bedroom now. "Is Victor here with you now? Is he hiding in there?"

"No, of course not."

Donna stormed over to the bedroom door, throwing it open as if she expected to find her ex-husband in some sort of compromising position. Of course, he wasn't there. She turned back to face Janie. "Then *why* are you here?"

"I'd tell you if you were willing to listen."

"What are you doing with those things?" Donna pointed to the half-full boxes.

"I was cleaning them to—"

"Are you *stealing* Victor's things?" Donna stood closer to Janie now, looking up at her with narrowed eyes.

"No." Janie stepped away from Donna.

"Then *why* are you here?"

Janie quickly explained about Bonnie's morning phone call, going to the décor shop, and finding these things, but Donna was still not satisfied.

"That does not answer my question," she said stubbornly. "*Why are you here?* Why are you acting like Victor's boat is yours? And why are you filling his cupboards with your things?"

"These aren't my things. I bought them for Victor and—"

"Why are you buying things for my husband?" Donna's voice was shrill. "What right do you have to interfere like this?" Janie was tempted to point out that Victor was Donna's ex-husband and that he had invited Janie to do this, but she suspected that would not help the situation.

"A while ago," Janie began carefully. "Victor asked me to help him to outfit the new sailboat. He … uh … he wasn't quite sure where to begin, and he thought I could help him with it. That's what I'm doing, I'm helping him."

"Don't you mean you're *helping yourself to him?*"

Janie took in a deep breath, then slowly let it out. "Listen, Donna, I don't really understand what's going on between you and Victor. I'm simply trying to do what I'd agreed to do. Think of me as an interior decorator."

"Are you an interior decorator?"

"No, not really. I mean, I—"

"I thought you were a lawyer, but perhaps I was misled about that as well."

"No, I am an attorney."

"Then you should stick to what you know—practicing law!"

"Donna," Janie began gently. "I know that you must still love Victor, and this is all rather awkward, but I—"

"What's awkward is finding you trespassing onto—"

"I am *not* trespassing." Janie fished the key to the boat out of her pocket now, holding it up as evidence.

Donna reached out and snatched it from her. "I'll take that."

"That's mine—"

"And I will thank you to vacate this boat immediately." Donna glared at Janie.

"I need to finish—"

"The only thing you need to do is leave right now." Donna held up her phone. "Before I call the police and have you arrested for trespassing and burglary and God only knows what else—husband stealing, although I'm sure you think that's perfectly legal, and being that you're a lawyer, you'd find some way to slip out of it."

"You're all wrong about everything," Janie tried again. "I have every right to be here, and even if you call the—"

Donna looked at the table where kitchen things were haphazardly sitting. Seeing a shell-handled butter knife, she picked it up, wielding it like a weapon. "I am warning you," she said. "Get out of here. Now!"

Janie glanced at the mess she was leaving behind, the half-full boxes, dishes still in the small galley sink. She had wanted to leave the place looking like perfection, as a surprise for Victor.

"Fine." She picked up her bag and stepped away from Donna, inching toward the ladder at a safe distance. Not that she was afraid of a butter knife, but the look in that woman's eyes was a little intimidating. "I'm leaving."

"In the future," Donna called as Janie scaled the ladder, "I would appreciate it if you would keep your hands off my husband!"

Again Janie was tempted to yell, "Ex-husband!" but she did not. She simply got off of the boat, and, feeling confused and a bit like a whipped puppy, she hurried back to her car.

Instead of returning to the inn to finish her work on her office, Janie drove directly home. By the time she pulled into her driveway, she was furious. What right did Donna have to act like that? What was the basis for all those accusations? Throwing Janie off of Victor's boat? Taking away her key? It was all so wrong.

Janie picked up her phone and was about to dial Victor's number, but she stopped herself. Really, what was she going to tell him? That Donna had been mean to her? Threatened her with a butter knife? Would Janie whine and complain and say she'd simply been trying to outfit his boat, but his crazy ex-wife had taken her key and thrown her out? How childish did that all sound? Really, did Victor need more stress about this from Janie? Wasn't it bad enough he had Donna to put up with?

She had promised Victor she would be patient. If Donna was really the wicked witch that Janie had seen on the sailboat, wouldn't Victor be painfully aware of this already? If he wasn't aware, perhaps it was better to let Donna show her ex-husband her true colors in due time. But what if Donna was too smart to do that? What if Donna somehow twisted their strange encounter on the sailboat, making it seem that Janie was the one at fault? Wasn't it in Janie's best interests to stand up for herself? Or would it seem strange or even territorial for Janie to take this up with Victor?

She felt like a dog chasing his own tail.

Confused and angry, Janie got back into her car and drove over to the inn. Her plan was twofold now. She would work on her office as well as try to figure out what exactly was going on with Donna. Maybe she'd bump into Caroline or Abby and ask them for advice. Really, that Donna was infuriating!

As Janie arrived at Abby's B and B, she noticed a black pickup pulling in behind her. "Hey there," called the driver. "Have you seen Caroline McCann around?"

Janie frowned over at him, trying to figure out why he seemed familiar. He stepped out of the truck. "Are you Caroline's brother?" she finally ventured.

He smiled to reveal yellowed teeth, then stuck out his hand. "That I am. Michael McCann, at your service."

She cautiously accepted his hand, trying not to grimace as she shook it. "I'm Janie Sorenson. I used to be Janie Andrews. Caroline and I were friends in—"

"Not the same skinny Janie Andrews with braces?" he said in a teasing tone.

She forced a smile. "Same one."

He grinned in a sleazy sort of way. "Well, my, my, my … but you have *changed*."

She didn't know whether to thank him or slap him, and so she did neither.

"So have you seen my sister around? One of her friends used to live in this house, and she said she was staying with a friend."

"This was where Abby lived when we were girls," Janie said carefully. No reason to divulge everything to this guy. "And now I have a law office here."

"So where might I find my sister?" He folded his arms across his chest and waited.

"I'm not really sure. I haven't seen her—" Janie stopped just as the garage door opened to reveal Caroline's small SUV coming out.

Michael followed her look, then nodded. "Well, I'll be. There's my baby sister right now." He tossed a dark look to Janie. "You probably knew she was here all along."

Janie watched as Michael went over and blocked Caroline's car, loudly thumping on the roof to get her attention. Poor Caroline looked so startled that Janie was surprised she didn't run right over her brother.

Caroline got out of the car. "What are you doing here?"

"Looking for you!" He stepped toward her in a way that appeared threatening.

"Well"—Caroline glanced over at Janie—"here I am."

"Why are you hiding from me?" he demanded.

"I'm not. I just—"

"And not answering your phone?"

"I've been really busy, Michael."

He grabbed Caroline by the forearm, and Janie could see the fear in her friend's eyes. "I know what you've been doing, baby sister, and I plan to—"

"Excuse me." Janie stepped up to Michael, looking him in the eye. "You need to let go of Caroline's arm."

"Don't tell me what I need to—"

"You let go of Caroline's arm, or I'm calling the police." Janie didn't miss the irony that she was using the same words Donna had said to her about an hour ago. Janie reached into her bag and pulled out her phone, holding it up like a weapon. "I mean it. I'm Caroline's attorney, and I'm well aware of what's going on here."

Michael released Caroline's arm, then pointed his finger right in Caroline's face. "You're going to need a lawyer by the time I get done with you." Then he turned, glared at Janie, and stomped away.

"Oh my." Caroline grabbed onto Janie. "I'm so thankful you were here."

"Looks like your big brother hasn't changed much." Janie shook her head as the pickup roared away from them. "Besides putting on a few pounds."

"And getting uglier." Caroline let out a big sigh. "What am I going to do?"

"First of all, tell me why he's so angry."

So Caroline explained how she'd gone into her mom's house and removed everything that she wanted to keep.

"That's completely within your legal rights, Caroline."

"Not according to Michael." Caroline frowned. "He's left me all these messages—really angry messages. Who knows what he might do now?"

"Maybe we should file a restraining order."

"I don't know." Caroline pushed a strand of hair away from her face. "I actually feel a little bad. I mean I should probably be more generous to him. He is their son."

"He already swindled your parents out of a lot of money," Janie reminded her. "Wasn't that why your mom took him out of her will?"

Caroline nodded sadly.

"Legally you don't owe him a thing."

"Maybe not legally."

Janie sighed. "Well, it's up to you how you handle this, Caroline. I just don't want to see you get hurt. I'm sorry, but your brother looks like he could hurt someone if he wanted to. In fact I'm quite serious about filing that restraining order. Do you still have your phone messages—the threatening ones?" Caroline nodded. "And I just witnessed him being rough with you, and you said he may already have a criminal record. I'm sure we'd have no problem getting a restraining order."

"I'm afraid that will just make him madder."

Janie nodded. "That's possible."

"For now I'd like to see if I can resolve this in a peaceful way."

Janie put her hand on Caroline's shoulder. "I can appreciate that. But don't try to resolve it on your own, okay? If you're going to have a conversation with that man, I think you need someone else with you, like a witness or a referee. I'm more than willing to do that."

"Thanks." Then, as Janie watched Caroline leave, she thought about how she could have used a witness on the boat today. How great it would've been to have had someone besides Janie to report Donna's bad behavior to Victor. Maybe the next time it happened—if there was a next time—Janie would have her pocket recorder along for proof. Of course, it would appear strange if she tried to use a secret recording against Donna. There had to be a better way to expose that woman for who she really was.

══Chapter 21══

MARLEY

It was only an hour-long drive to Ashton's house, but Marley felt like it took her days to arrive. At first Marley tried to listen to her Judy Collins CD as a distraction, but as soon as "Cat's in the Cradle" started, Marley had to turn it off. She didn't like to think about what a poor excuse for a father John had been. John Phelps hadn't been only a lousy husband, but a loser of a dad as well. Marley had often blamed herself for the family's troubles. What if she hadn't gotten pregnant in college? What if she hadn't married John simply because he was the father?

She'd been too young and idealistic to realize that John didn't have what it took to be faithful to either her or her child. Instead of figuring this out before it was too late, she'd allowed him to convince her otherwise. She'd taken the risk, and for more than twenty-five years she'd paid the price. Despite her divorce several years ago, she still felt like she was paying for her poor choices. It seemed that Ashton was still paying too.

She knew it was probably unfair to blame all of Ashton's troubles on his father, but John had left some deep wounds on his only child—well, "only child" as far as Marley knew. For all the times her pilot husband had cheated on her, John might have a child at every international airport.

"No, no, no," she told herself. "This is no good." Taking this forlorn trip down memory lane wasn't only depressing, it was counterproductive. Instead Marley decided to pray. For most of the drive, she prayed for Ashton, and for Leo, and for herself. When she ran out of things to pray about for the three of them, she prayed for the other Lindas, and then she prayed for little Hunter and Jack and Jasmine. Finally she was pulling into the parking lot at Ashton and Leo's apartment complex.

The stucco apartments were old but nice. Built in the fifties, they had been completely restored about ten years ago, and located in the heart of downtown, they were on prime real estate. Marley parked in the visitor section then tried Ashton's number once more on her cell phone. Still no answer. This was deeply troubling. She spotted Ashton's little car, a red MINI Cooper, in his numbered parking space. Unless he was on his bike or on foot, he was probably home. She slowly climbed the wrought-iron stairs and knocked on the heavy wooden door. Bracing herself, she waited. When there was no answer, she knocked again, louder this time.

"Ashton," she called out, "it's your mother. Please open up!" Still there was no answer. She pounded on the window, continuing to call loudly.

"Something wrong?" asked a young woman with a small dog.

"I'm worried about my son," Marley confessed. "I've been trying to reach Ashton for days, and he's just not—"

"Ashton is your son?"

Marley nodded eagerly. "Do you know him?"

"Yes. He's really bummed about Leo."

"What happened to Leo?" Marley asked.

"Oh, you haven't heard?"

"What?" demanded Marley.

"Leo left Ashton for someone else."

"Oh dear." Marley turned back to the door, pounding even more loudly now. "Ashton! Open the door!"

"Ashton's really taking it hard," the girl continued. "Yesterday I invited him to come over for dinner with some friends and he refused."

Marley turned back to the girl. "So you saw him yesterday?"

She nodded with a grim expression. "He didn't seem like himself, though."

Marley pounded once more. "Ashton Phelps, you come and open this door, or I'll get the manager to let me in!"

"Want me to call the manager for you?" the girl offered.

"Yes," Marley said firmly. "I would appreciate that."

The girl got on her phone, but before she reached the manager, Marley heard the dead bolt click, and the door cracked open. "Ashton!" Marley exclaimed as she pushed her way into the dim apartment. She threw her arms around him and held him tight. "You're okay!" Tears of relief filled her eyes.

"Actually I'm not okay," he admitted when she finally let him go.

She reached up and touched his cheek. It looked like he hadn't shaved in days. "Oh, Ashton," she said gently. "I'm so sorry to hear about you and Leo. Why didn't you tell me?"

"I wanted to tell you." He turned and walked away from her. "But you were busy making Barbie clothes."

She followed him into the kitchen, surprised to see dirty dishes piled up in the sink and a saucepan containing something brown and smelly sitting on the stove. The whole apartment seemed to be a mess. The only times she had been here before, all had been tidy and pristine. "I'm never too busy to talk to you, Ashton. You know that." She put her hand on his shoulder. "I can tell you're hurting. Do you want to talk about it?"

With his back still to her, he shrugged like he used to do as a boy. "I don't know. Not much to talk about."

"How about if you clean up a bit and we'll go get a bite to eat?" she suggested.

He looked down at his stained T-shirt and wrinkled pajama bottoms and frowned. "Yeah, I guess I could do that."

While he showered and changed clothes, Marley attacked the kitchen with vigor. She rinsed the dishes, loaded the dishwasher, dumped what appeared to be some kind of Asian sauce into the garbage disposal, and wiped down all the surfaces.

"Oh, Mom." Ashton frowned. "You didn't need to do that."

"I know, but I guess that's just how some moms work." She made a weak smile. "You look like you're ready to go."

He shrugged again. "I guess so."

"Well, I'm starving." She linked her arm in his. "How about if we walk to that little deli around the corner?"

He didn't argue, so she simply took the lead, and before long they were seated at the deli. As they waited for their soup and sandwiches to arrive, she gently prodded him to tell her about what had happened between him and Leo. Gay or straight didn't matter, apparently—it was the same old worn-out story. Someone falls out of love with one person and into love with another, and the one left behind suffers the agony of a broken heart.

"I know you might find this hard to believe right now," she said gently, "but it will get better in time."

He groaned as he ran a hand through his wavy brown hair.

"It really will."

"Man, when I think of all the times Dad hurt you, and the way you put up with it … it used to kind of blow my mind."

She frowned. "Yeah, me, too."

"Except that now I think I'm starting to get it."

"How so?"

He shook his head. "If Leo came back and apologized, I'd probably take him back."

"Oh."

"Kind of how you'd do with Dad."

"The reason I put up with your dad was for you, Ashton. I had this crazy idea that a boy needed his father, but the truth is, if I could do it all over again, I'd do it differently."

"Really?"

"Absolutely." She nodded vigorously. "It wouldn't have been easy. Divorce is always hard on kids. But knowing what I know now, I would've ended it with your father a whole lot sooner."

For a while they both ate quietly. Marley was relieved that Ashton was actually eating. He admitted that he hadn't eaten in days, and he looked gaunt and pale, with dark shadows beneath his eyes.

"It's just such a mess, Mom," he said as he pushed his soup bowl away.

"What do you mean?"

"Life. I mean *my* life."

"How is it a mess?"

"Well, for one thing, you know that Leo and I were business partners. And there's the apartment lease. And, well, it's just such a mess trying to figure it all out." He rubbed his temples. "It literally makes my head hurt."

"You don't have to figure it all out at once, do you?"

He shrugged.

"What you need to do is take care of yourself. You need to get up every morning, take a shower, eat a good breakfast, then put one foot in front of the other."

"Easier said than done."

"I know." She nodded. "There's something else you need too, Ashton."

He looked slightly curious. "What?"

"You need God in your life."

He rolled his eyes. "Yeah right."

"I'm serious."

He faked a laugh. "Get real, Mom."

"I am getting real." She told him she had started praying to God, and God was making a difference in her life. "It's hard to explain, but it is very real, Ashton. I feel more complete, more centered, more on track now than I have ever felt in my life. Even my art seems to be working."

"That's great. For you."

"It would be great for you, too, Ashton."

His expression grew hard. "Maybe you haven't heard yet, Mom, but God hates homosexuals."

"Oh, that's not—"

"Hey, we hear it all the time. We gays are disgusting, repulsive, an aberration, a blight on this fine country, and God would rather strike us dead than—"

"That is not true, Ashton."

"Says who?"

"Says me. And other Christian people too." Okay, she could actually only think of one other person—Fran. But Doris was coming around, and maybe the other Lindas. Surely they would love Ashton too.

"Nice try, Mom, but I'm not buying."

"Look, Ashton, I'm sorry for what you might've heard—that God hates homosexuals—but I know that's not true. That's just some narrow-minded, judgmental people trying to speak for God. I'm sure God does not appreciate it. And it seems unfair that you would listen to some mean-spirited person's take on God rather than allowing God to speak for himself."

He sighed. "Yeah, I might be overstating it a bit."

"I might not exactly be an expert on all of this, but I just started reading the Bible, and one of my favorite Scriptures says that God loved the whole world, meaning every single person in the world. He loved us so much that he sent his son so that everyone could have a chance to believe."

Ashton nodded, and Marley could tell he was losing interest.

"Okay, my sermon is over." She wiped her mouth with her napkin and thought for a moment. "I have an idea."

"What?"

"Why don't you come home with me for a few days? It's Thanksgiving this week, and I was hoping you and—well, that you could come. You haven't seen my little beach bungalow yet."

"I don't know."

She stood now, tugging him up to his feet. "Don't you try to use work for an excuse, Ashton. Since no one's been answering the phone in the drum shop, my guess is that no one's been going in to work either. Right?"

Again with the shrug. "It's just a mess. My life is one great big mess."

"So why not come spend the week with me? It certainly can't mess things up any worse, can it?"

"What am I going to do at your house, Mom?"

"I don't know. Walk the beach, eat some homemade food, meet my friends."

His dark brows knitted together, forming the expression he wore as a little boy when trying to figure out something much too difficult for him to understand.

"Come on," she urged him as they walked back to the apartment. "Just throw some things in a bag and we'll be on our way."

"But what if ..."

"What?" She turned to peer into his face.

His mouth twisted to one side. "What if Leo comes back to the apartment, you know, looking for me?"

She held up her hands. "So? What if he did?"

"He might be worried, you know, to find me gone."

She smiled. "So let him worry."

Ashton nodded. "Yeah. Why not?"

As Marley drove them back toward the coast, Ashton slept. Or at least he appeared to be sleeping. It was possible he was simply trying to avoid having a conversation with her, but Marley didn't mind. Something about her boy—yes, a grown man—riding quietly next to her was strangely comforting. Once again, as she drove, she prayed. This time it was not the frantic, desperate kind of praying she'd done on her way to Ashton's apartment. Now her prayer was simple and concise: *God, please help Ashton to find himself, and help him to find you. Amen.*

Chapter 22

CAROLINE

"I'm going to try to make it for the funeral," Mitch assured Caroline for about the third time.

"I'll understand if you don't," she told him.

"I *want* to be there for you."

"I know." She sighed as she glanced out the window overlooking the street. Michael hadn't made an appearance since yesterday, but she would be surprised if he didn't. He wasn't one to give up easily.

"How are you holding up?"

"I'm okay." She let the curtains fall closed again. Mitch didn't know anything about Michael. As badly as she wanted Mitch to make it in time for the funeral, she was not eager to have him meet her volatile brother. She was getting seriously worried that Michael might say or do something at the service tomorrow, something that would embarrass them all. For her mother's sake she hoped she was wrong.

Caroline had spent most of Saturday night going through the boxes of things she'd salvaged from her parents' home. Her goal was to gather some items she thought Michael might actually appreciate, if that was possible. Janie had said she was wasting her time, but Caroline's conscience had been nagging her. She was determined to do all she could to mend her bridges with her brother—for her mother's sake. When Michael and Caroline were kids, their mom had blatantly favored Michael, and their dad had made no secret over preferring Caroline. As dysfunctional as their family was, the division of favor had worked for a while.

When Michael turned into a rebellious teen, he severely tested their mother's affections, and their father sometimes acted like he wanted to kill his surly son. However, when Michael was drafted and sent to Vietnam, things changed. Their father started drinking more and staying out later. Meanwhile their mother became obsessed over Michael's welfare. Constantly writing letters and sending care packages, she watched the nightly news with fear and trembling. When Michael returned home in one piece, she had nearly suffocated him with her attention. Her reward for this was simply more bad behavior and disappearing acts. Michael would come and go, never accounting for himself. When he came, he needed money. When he left, something from the house was always missing.

"You said that Michael already got all of your dad's guns and sporting goods," Janie had reminded Caroline, "not to mention all the insurance money he managed to swindle from your mother. I don't see why you think you owe him anything now."

"It's complicated," Caroline had told her. And it was.

"As your attorney I would recommend that we freeze all assets for now," Janie had advised. "Let some time pass. If Michael is as determined as you think, let him get his own legal counsel and have at it, not that it will do him any good. I've looked over everything and don't see that Michael can contest anything. But perhaps things will cool off in time."

Caroline had a hard time imagining Michael ever cooling off. For her mother's sake Caroline wanted to do all she could to smooth this thing over *now*. If she was a fool for her efforts, so be it.

She made dozens of photocopies of old family photos, mostly snapshots her mother had taken on holidays or birthdays. Caroline arranged them chronologically as best she could and placed them in a nice photo album. Besides that, she boxed up some old things of her father's—a few family items that she wasn't emotionally attached to—and packed them in her father's old army trunk. It wasn't much, but other than the house and her mother's small insurance policy, it was all they had. Their family had never had much. It was what it was.

While going through these old things, Caroline brought out her mother's old Bible, the one she'd fetched from the charred bedroom. To her surprised delight she had found little notes penciled in on the margins of some of the pages. It seemed that before Alzheimer's set in, her mother had taken her Bible quite seriously. As much as Caroline wanted to keep this Bible, she felt her mother would prefer it go to Michael. It was the final item Caroline placed in the trunk. She hoped Michael would appreciate it. If not, well, Caroline did not want to know.

The big question now was how and when to get this trunk to Michael without creating an even bigger problem. She suspected that he was staying at the house in spite of its condition. How he could stand the stench of smoke was beyond her, but she and her friends had seen his truck parked there at all hours.

"Let me deal with Michael," Janie had told Caroline last night.

"I will explain to him in legal terms that the house belongs to you. If he has any questions, he can direct them to me."

"Good luck with that." Caroline hated to imagine how Michael would respond to that piece of information.

"I don't mind being the fall guy," Janie had assured her, and Caroline hadn't argued. In fact, as she closed the army trunk, she was halfway tempted to ask Janie to deliver this to Michael as well. Was she being a chicken? Well, yes. But, as they used to say as kids, better to be a smart chicken than a dead duck.

Caroline picked up her phone and called Janie. "Hey, are you terribly busy?" she asked cheerfully.

"Not really." But Janie's voice had a hard edge on it, like maybe she really didn't want to be bothered.

"Are you okay?"

"Depends on how you define *okay*."

Caroline was getting worried. "What's going on?"

Janie let out a long, exasperated-sounding sigh. "I wish I knew."

"What do you mean?"

"Oh, Caroline, I feel like I'm going crazy."

"Huh?"

"I know, it sounds silly." Janie explained how she'd gotten a bunch of things for Victor's boat. Donna had confronted her there and used some harsh words. "Now all the things I thought I'd left on his boat are gone."

"What?" Caroline was trying to wrap her head around this. "How could they be gone?"

"Precisely what I'm wondering. But after I called Victor, explaining about the showdown and how Donna snatched my key, he went down there to check on the boat, to make sure it was locked up and all."

"And he said the things were gone?"

"Yes. He called me from the boat and said that everything looked perfectly normal, except that none of the things I'd told him about were there. Honestly, for a moment I wondered if I was losing it. So I told him about getting those things at Bonnie's shop, and how they weren't cheap, and that it was upsetting to hear they were missing."

"Do you think Donna took them?" Even as Caroline said this, it sounded preposterous. As far as Caroline could see, Donna was a nice, rational, thoughtful person. Why would she steal anything from anyone?

"I just don't know. I mean she was there. We had that weird conversation. And now, according to Victor, everything I put on his boat is not there." Janie sighed. "It sounds crazy."

"Maybe someone broke onto Victor's boat," Caroline suggested. "There are some shady characters around the wharf at night sometimes."

"No locks were broken. And everything else—including his flat-screen TV and DVD player and stereo—is intact."

"Oh."

"I know it's not that big of a deal—although it's a big waste of money. Still, it's only money, not someone's life. And even though Donna was there, it doesn't mean she's guilty. I'll feel silly if I end up making it into something it's not, but it's really aggravating. Where could all that stuff have gone to?"

Caroline lowered her voice. "So you really think Donna might've taken it?"

"I honestly don't know how. I mean, she's only got a bike to ride. And I carried several boxes of items to the boat. It took a few trips."

"And you're sure you put them on Victor's boat?"

Janie let out a loud groan.

"Sorry. I'm sure you know what you did, Janie."

"Anyway, I probably just need to let it go. I mean, it's a mystery for sure, but not one I'll ever get to the bottom of. In light of other things, like your mom's funeral tomorrow, and your brother's behavior, and even Marley's son—"

"What's up with Ashton?"

Janie explained that he was staying with Marley after getting his heart broken. "Abby said Marley was actually worried he might be suicidal."

"Poor girl."

"So, compared to all that, some disappearing dishes seem pretty inconsequential."

As Janie rambled on about the possibility of losing her mind, Caroline tiptoed out of her room and down the hallway. The door to Donna's room was ajar, and Caroline used her toe to push it open, quickly glancing around to see that the suite appeared to be unoccupied. "Donna?" Caroline called out just to be sure.

"What? Are you with Donna right now?" Janie sounded worried.

"I'm in her room," Caroline explained. "She doesn't appear to be here. Oh, Donna," she called out again, more melodically this time. "Oh, Donna … Oh, Donna." She was singing the old Ritchie Valens song now. "Where could you be?"

"What on earth are you doing?" hissed Janie.

Caroline kept singing the "Donna" song as she poked around the master suite. Finding nothing suspicious, she quickly retreated to her own room and relayed her findings, or lack of them, to Janie. "Sorry."

"I can't believe you just did that, Caroline." Even as Janie scolded, Caroline could hear the laughter in her voice. "That's like breaking and entering. Trespassing."

"Yeah, yeah. I was just seeing if she was home," Caroline said casually.

"Well, thanks for trying. I owe you one."

"No, I'm the one who owes you." Caroline grew more serious as she explained that she wanted to deliver the trunk to her brother. "I'm a little afraid to face him on my own, and I just talked to Mitch. He might not even make it here by tomorrow."

"Do you want me to take it over for you?"

"No, but if you wouldn't mind accompanying me, I would really appreciate it." Caroline frowned at the olive-green trunk. "It's kind of heavy. Maybe you could help me get it down the stairs and stuff. I was hoping to get it to him this evening. Maybe he'll go through these mementos and remember some of the good times...." She laughed. "Who am I fooling? There weren't many of those. Anyway, I hoped it might soften him up for the funeral tomorrow. I know there won't be many people there, but for my mom's sake I just don't want him spewing his venom."

"I'd be happy to help." Caroline offered to buy Janie dinner, and Janie promised to come by the inn around six. Together they would "deliver the goods." In the meantime Caroline decided to write her brother a heartfelt letter. What could it hurt?

* * *

When they got to Caroline's mom's house, Michael's black pickup was nowhere in sight. Caroline backed up into the driveway, and then she and Janie lugged the chest up to the front porch. Caroline set the envelope containing her note on top, securing it with a rock. Then, curious as to whether Michael was actually cleaning up as promised or if perhaps he'd changed the locks, she tried her key in the front door. To her relief it opened. But her relief was cut short when she peeked inside the house.

"Omigosh!" Caroline gasped as she pushed her way past the piles of debris and junk that littered the small entryway. Her mom's house had never been tidy, but for safety's sake, Caroline worked hard to declutter it while she'd lived there. Now it looked like a hurricane had swept through. As she picked her way toward the kitchen, she was thankful the insurance appraiser had already been here.

"What on earth is going on?" Janie demanded as she followed Caroline past the living room.

"I have no idea." Caroline looked around in horror. "I think my brother may have lost his mind."

Janie's brow creased as she glanced back toward the still open door. "Maybe we should get out of here—"

"—before Michael returns." Caroline finished for her as she grabbed Janie's hand. "Hurry!" They stumbled through the mess, emerging outside, where Caroline thankfully gasped in a breath of fresh air. "I wish we'd brought Chuck along for protection."

"Let's get out of here."

Once they were safely back in the car, Caroline just shook her head. "I just don't understand him."

"You said he'd offered to clean up. Do you think he was just trying to clear some things out?" Janie asked. Caroline could hear the doubt in her voice.

"Maybe."

"Or he might've been looking for something specific? Something of value?"

Caroline nodded as she turned at the corner. "Yeah, that sounds more like it."

"Do you think we should call the police?"

Caroline swallowed hard. She so didn't want to do this. "I don't know. I mean, at least not yet, Janie. Maybe he was just clearing things out. I just want to get through the funeral, okay?"

"Okay. But it might be that we'll need to take some legal action, Caroline."

"Let's not rush things." All Caroline wanted was to keep a lid on things. At least until the funeral was over.

"It's your call, Caroline. I don't want to pressure you. I just want you to be safe, that's all."

"I know." Caroline knew Janie was probably right, but she was still hoping that her goodwill offering and her letter might soften her brother up. There was no denying Michael was a jerk, but Caroline hoped there was a bit of goodness somewhere inside of him. When she'd been making copies of the old photos, she'd studied some shots of him as a boy. Seeing that innocence and sweet smile, she'd wondered how he could've turned into such a mean person. She'd told herself that meanness might simply be a protective exterior, something he'd constructed over the years to protect a tender heart, but she suspected that Janie wouldn't understand this. Also, it was possible that Caroline was totally wrong. Maybe Michael was just plain mean—bad to the bone!

***

Caroline woke Monday morning to the sound of her phone ringing. In her blurry state and without her reading glasses, she could only detect the capital letter M on her caller ID. Thinking it was Michael calling to tear into her again, she answered with hesitant caution, then was pleasantly surprised to hear Mitch's voice.

"I couldn't get an earlier flight out of Tokyo," he said sadly. "I'm sorry."

"It's okay."

"No, it's not. I should've tried to rearrange my schedule last week instead of waiting for the last minute like I did. Really, I'm sorry."

"It's okay." She forced some cheer into her voice. "You'll make it home for Thanksgiving, right?"

"Absolutely."

"Because Abby is planning a big shindig, and I told her I thought you'd be able to come."

"Mmm. Turkey and dressing sounds so good to me. I'm tired of sushi and weird food. It's like these guys get a kick out of shocking me every time we sit down to eat." He described his latest meal, and Caroline actually lost her appetite.

"Poor Mitch," she said with real empathy. "So how do you feel about pie? Pumpkin, pecan, or apple?"

"Oh, babe, you're killing me. I love all three. And pie sounds heavenly."

"Well, I just happen to be a pretty good pie maker. So maybe I'll go ahead and make all of them. Abby has this fantastic kitchen at the B and B, and so far all I've used is the microwave."

"So is the inn up and running now?"

"Not exactly." Caroline filled him in a bit.

"So I wouldn't be able to rent a room then?"

Caroline considered this. "Let me check with Abby."

"Or I can just make a reservation at my regular spot."

"I'll get back to you on it," she promised, "after the funeral."

"Speaking of the funeral, I should let you go."

Caroline glanced at the clock by her bed and was surprised to see it was past eight. "Yes, I've got a lot to get done."

"I know it's not much, but I did wire some flowers," he said sadly. "I really do wish I could be there."

"Me, too," she told him as she slipped her feet into her slippers. "But I've got my Lindas."

"As much as I hate to admit it, I sometimes feel jealous of those Lindas." He chuckled. "But for the most part I'm very thankful you have them, Caroline."

They said good-bye, and as she showered, Caroline felt thankful for her Lindas too. Abby had coordinated everything for a small buffet lunch following the funeral. Caroline had no idea if anyone would come, but it was nice of Abby to be prepared just in case. Marley had put her artistic talents to work by arranging the extra copies of old family photos on a picture board that would be displayed at the service. And Janie, well, she'd been Caroline's rock through everything, including managing Michael.

It wasn't that Caroline didn't appreciate Mitch, or didn't wish he could be by her side and, if necessary, defend her against her brother, but it felt good to be standing on her own two feet. As it turned out, she was strong enough to handle these things without being rescued by a man. And it was good to know she had such loyal friends.

Chapter 23

ABBY

"You always take on too much," Paul complained as Abby picked out a tie for him to wear to Ruby McCann's funeral.

"Too much according to who?"

He frowned. "According to your husband."

"All I did was offer to cater the luncheon today."

"The luncheon today, a major Thanksgiving dinner on Thursday, and on top of that you seem obsessed with getting the B and B going before Christmas."

"I'm not obsessed." She stuck her feet into her black pumps. "I'm excited. Jackie Day's B and B is overbooked, and she's depending on me to handle her overflow. Not every innkeeper has guaranteed guests before they officially open their doors."

"You already have two guests," Paul reminded her.

"Yes, well …" Abby shrugged and went into the bathroom to do something with her hair. She hadn't told Paul that she wasn't charging Caroline yet. It wasn't his business particularly, but she did prefer for him to think that she was already bringing in money. Besides, why was he acting like this? Just recently he'd been nagging her to do something besides babysit him. And now here she was doing other things, and he was griping about it. Men! Sometimes it seemed that nothing made them happy!

Did Paul appreciate that she was hosting the post-funeral gathering at the inn rather than at their home? She didn't want him to feel responsible to play host to strangers, and he could come home and rest. Did he care that it had been more work for her to get that other kitchen all set up, or to do her food preparations over there? Apparently not. She set down the curling iron and frowned at her frowzy hair. Really, it was useless. Her friends were right. She did need a makeover. She studied the dull color—dishwater blonde tinged with gray—and considered how her friends had been urging her to do something about it. Well, maybe she would go ahead and book a weave or whatever it was they were doing to hair nowadays. Maybe she'd get herself some new clothes, too. She wondered what Paul would think of that. Probably not much.

"Are you ever going to be done in there?" he called from the other side of the door. "Or maybe you'd like me to go unshaven to the funeral."

She pushed open the door and frowned at him. "It's all yours."

"Are we still taking separate cars?" he asked as he pushed past her.

"Yes. I'm leaving now to take care of some things for the luncheon. I'll just meet you at the funeral home. If you get there first, save me a seat."

He laughed. "You think it'll be crowded?"

She punched him in the arm. "Be nice!"

"I'm just saying. Poor old Ruby McCann probably didn't have many friends."

"If my mom were here, I'm sure she'd go."

"Well, the only reason I'm going is for you, and Caroline, too. But as soon as it's over I plan to go to the health club."

She wanted to question this, but she was burning daylight. "Just remember to save me a place," she called as she grabbed her coat.

As Abby drove toward town, she still felt irked at Paul. Really, that man could be so insensitive sometimes. Ruby McCann hadn't been Abby's favorite person, but that day on the boat when the Lindas helped Caroline rescue her, Abby had felt real compassion for the old woman. It wasn't Ruby's fault she'd gotten Alzheimer's. If younger folks like Paul couldn't show a bit of empathy for the challenges the elderly faced, how would someone like him feel when the tables turned and *he* was the one running around town buck naked? She chuckled to imagine this. Then she shuddered. Really, if she thought about it hard, it was not that humorous.

Balancing a Crock-Pot on her hip, Abby unlocked the front door and let herself into the house. As usual she loved the feeling of coming in here, loved the idea that this place belonged to her. Well, to her and Janie. And the bank. Even so, the smell of old wood, the whispers of old memories ... they never failed to comfort her.

"Hey, Abby," said Donna as she came down the stairs. "How's it going?"

"Okay." Abby dropped her bag on the table in the foyer. She wished she'd thought to get some fresh flowers to set there. That's what she planned to do once the inn was really up and running.

"Looks like you've got lots of good things to eat in the kitchen. I controlled myself from sneaking one of those deviled eggs."

Abby laughed as she made a beeline to the kitchen. "Oh, you can sneak one if you want. I really doubt there will be many people here for lunch anyway."

"Caroline said her mom didn't have too many friends." Donna trailed Abby into the kitchen, watching as Abby bustled about.

"Are you going to the funeral?" Abby placed meatballs into the Crock-Pot.

"I don't know. I didn't know Caroline's mom. I expect Victor might be going, since he's friends with Caroline." Donna made a sad expression. "It's hard not to envy all of you, the way you grew up together in this town, the way your friendships remained strong over the years, and how close you are."

"I'm sure you must have some good old friends too, Donna."

Donna just shook her head. "The way Caroline's friends will gather around her today, showing their love and support—I suppose I'll never have anything like that. Even if I live in Clifden for twenty years, I'll probably never really fit in."

Abby felt sorry for Donna, and wondered if she was fishing for an invitation to the funeral service. Was it Abby's place to extend this to her?

"There you are," Caroline said as she joined them in the kitchen. "Thank you so much for doing this, Abby." She came over and gave Abby a sideways hug. "I wish I could stick around and help you, but I need to get over to the funeral home to take—"

"Don't you worry about a thing," Abby assured her. "It's all under control. You just run along, and I'll catch up with you later."

"Thanks so much!"

"You're so lucky to have so many good friends," Donna said to Caroline.

Caroline smiled. "Yes, I feel very blessed."

"On a day like today it must be a comfort." Donna sighed.

"Very much so," Caroline assured her. "I don't suppose you'll want to come to the funeral—although you're welcome, of course— but I do hope you'll join us for lunch if you'd like."

Donna put a hand on Caroline's shoulder. "You are the most gracious person, Caroline. It's your mother's funeral, and here you are being nice to me—practically a stranger. You make me feel like I'm really your friend."

Caroline looked slightly stumped by this. "Of course you're my friend, Donna."

"Thank you. That means so much to me."

"I'll see you both later," Caroline called as she hurried on her way.

"Well, I can't very well refuse that invitation," Donna told Abby. "I better run upstairs and change. Do you think I could get a ride with you?" She laughed. "Or else I could ride my bike, although that might be tricky in a dress with heels."

"Of course you can ride with me," Abby said as she turned on the Crock-Pot. "I'll be leaving about a quarter to ten."

"Perfect!"

Abby wasn't sure why it bothered her that Donna was coming to the funeral, but for some reason it did. Of course, she wouldn't let on about this to anyone. She felt slightly bad for Janie's sake, which reminded her that she hadn't talked to Janie specifically about Donna lately. Tomorrow morning Abby and the other Lindas would meet for coffee and, hopefully, updates. At the moment, Abby had no clue as to what was going on in the Victor love triangle. She was curious.

"I hope I'm not overdressed," Donna said when she returned to the kitchen.

Abby studied the elegant black dress and shrugged. It looked more like a cocktail dress than funeral-wear, but Abby had no intention of saying this. "You look very pretty, Donna." She glanced down at the woman's black high heels. "As my daughter Nicole would say, those shoes are killer."

Donna laughed. "If I wear them too long, they kill my feet, too."

Abby put the salad she'd just tossed back into the fridge, quickly washed her hands, then looked at the kitchen clock. "I guess that's it for now."

As Abby drove to the funeral home, Donna reminisced about Victor's mother's funeral several years ago. "Even though Vic and I were divorced, I stayed close to his mom. She was such a dear woman, and of course, she was the grandmother of my sons. I couldn't have stayed away even if I'd wanted to."

"I suppose divorce does complicate things like funerals and weddings. I can't imagine how I'd handle holidays and such under those circumstances. Goodness, it's challenge enough just getting the grown children together, and sometimes they're not getting along."

"Speaking of holidays, I am so thrilled that both of my boys are coming to Clifden for Thanksgiving," Donna exclaimed. "It will be the first time in years that we've all been together. I can hardly wait."

Abby felt her brows lifting. "So you'll all celebrate together then? At Victor's house?"

"Yes. I think that's the plan."

"Victor is cooking?"

Donna laughed. "Good grief, I hope not. No, I'm sure he'll let me handle the cuisine. I seriously doubt that man's ever cooked a turkey in his life."

Abby suspected Donna was right about this. Now more than ever, Abby wanted to hear Janie's thoughts on the subject. "Here we are." She parked across the street from the funeral home. "It looks like there are quite a few people here." She spotted Paul's pickup as they got out of the car. "I hope my husband saved a place."

As it turned out, Paul was sitting by himself in the back. "Come on," Abby urged him, "we need to sit up there near Caroline and Janie."

"That's for family," he insisted.

"We are her family." She grabbed his hand and pulled him up. "Come on, Donna, you can sit with us too."

As they sat down behind Caroline, Abby estimated there were as many as thirty people at the funeral. Thankful she'd made what she'd assumed was too much food, she wondered how many of them would come to the luncheon. Most were friends of Caroline's. A few of the old timers must've been acquaintances of Mrs. McCann. It didn't escape Abby's notice that Caroline's brother was sitting on the opposite side of the room by himself. With his arms folded tightly across his chest, Abby suspected he was eager to get this over with.

Just before the service began, Marley and a young man whom Abby assumed was Ashton slipped into their row and sat down.

The service was actually quite nice. Abby was surprised by the eulogy, which had been written by Caroline. It seemed that Ruby

McCann had done some interesting things in her life, including winning a local beauty contest, serving in the Philippines as a member of the Women's Army Corps, and working briefly in advertisement sales for the newspaper. Unfortunately it seemed that Mrs. McCann's life shrank considerably after her marriage. Not surprisingly, very little was said about Mr. McCann.

When people were invited to share memories about Ruby McCann, several people went forward, including old Doc Richards, who spoke so fondly of the deceased woman that Abby wondered if they might've been romantically involved at some time. Then white-haired Vera Dewberry, leaning on her cane, slowly made her way to the podium and shared some interesting memories about beach bathing and USO dances and the night they took a wild ride with three sailors.

After Vera made her way back to her seat and the laughter subsided, and it seemed no one else cared to speak, Caroline went up. "First I want to thank everyone for coming today. I know my mother—whom I thankfully believe is in her right mind again—would appreciate you being here." Caroline spoke briefly about Alzheimer's and the toll it had taken on her mother. "She didn't have a real easy life even before that," Caroline admitted. "In fact one of the things that most impressed me about my mother was that through everything, she kept her spark of humor. I hope that I can keep that part of her alive with me."

Caroline opened her Bible. "When I was cleaning up my mom's house, I found her Bible. To be honest, I was kind of surprised by how well worn it was, and how she'd made notes by some of the passages. This particular section was underlined in red ink. It's from the gospel of John, verses one through four of the fourteenth chapter."

She cleared her throat to read. "'Do not let your hearts be troubled. Trust in God; trust also in me. In my Father's house are many rooms; if it were not so, I would have told you. I am going there to prepare a place for you. And if I go and prepare a place for you, I will come back and take you to be with me that you also may be where I am.'"

Caroline was crying as she finished the last verse. "I can't tell you how much that comforts me, the idea that my mother knew what Jesus had prepared for her … that she knew what was waiting for her. As many of you know, her earthly life had its challenges. So she is truly in a better place now."

After "Amazing Grace" was played and a final prayer said, the pastor extended the invitation to the final interment, followed by a luncheon and further fellowship at Abby's house in town. He even mentioned that Abby was transforming her old family home into a bed-and-breakfast that would be opening soon. This remark was probably made at Caroline's suggestion, but it was sweet and much appreciated by Abby just the same.

"I'm not going to the interment," Abby told Donna as she stood. "I want to go home and get the luncheon set up."

Donna frowned as if this was greatly disappointing. She pointed to where Victor was sitting. "I'll ask Vic to give me a ride then." Just like that she was on her way. Abby felt guilty for Janie's sake now. Perhaps she should've insisted that Donna ride home with her. Truthfully Abby wouldn't have minded if Donna had offered to lend a hand getting the food set up, but it was too late now. And really, it wasn't Abby's problem.

As they went to the back of the room, Marley introduced Abby to Ashton. "He's staying with me until Thanksgiving," she explained.

"That must be cozy."

Marley just smiled.

"Hey, I'll bet my mom wouldn't mind if you used her place, Ashton," Abby said. "I mean if it's too crowded in your mom's little bungalow."

Ashton seemed to brighten just a bit. "Really?"

"Sure. I'll give her a call and see if it's okay. I have a key."

"That might be nice," Marley admitted. "I didn't realize just how small my house was until I had a guest." She linked her arm with Ashton's. "Not that I mind. It's been really nice. I think Ashton's been enjoying the beach."

Ashton nodded. "Yeah, it's a nice beach."

Abby wanted to say something else, something that might comfort the sad-looking guy, but her mind was blank.

"I'm outta here," Paul whispered to her as they were making their way to the door.

"Feel free to stop by the inn if you're hungry," Abby offered. Maybe it was the funeral service, or maybe it was the sight of Paul in his good suit, but her heart toward him had softened some.

"If I don't stop by, feel free to bring home leftovers." He winked, then pecked her on the cheek. "Later, doll."

Abby waved at Caroline and Janie, mouthing that she'd see them later. Caroline smiled and waved back, but Janie wore a troubled expression. She must've spotted Donna and Victor together. As Abby headed back to her car, she wondered if Janie was aware of the pair's Thanksgiving plans yet. Maybe Abby should give her a gentle heads-up today. Poor Janie.

===Chapter 24===

JANIE

She'd never played the role of bodyguard before, but Janie felt that was the perfect description for what she was doing today. She was determined to stay by Caroline's side until they were safely out of harm's way, or at least a few blocks away from Michael McCann. Despite Caroline's optimism that her brother might be softening, Janie was seriously doubtful. Seeing him glowering on the other side of the room during the funeral service had only driven this home.

She was actually surprised when he didn't make a showing at the cemetery. She wasn't sure whether she should be relieved or worried. On one hand he might have realized that his attempts to terrorize his sister in order to obtain financial gain were not working. Or he might be plotting even more devious plans. Either way Janie would keep her eyes wide open. It was a good distraction from obsessing over Victor and Donna.

She couldn't believe that Donna had come, not only to the funeral but the graveside service as well. Really, that took some nerve. After that scene on the sailboat, Janie knew that although

Donna might be missing some marbles, the woman did not lack nerve. Janie still hadn't gotten to the bottom of the disappearing dishes, but it was eating her far more than she cared to admit. It wasn't just the wasted money that bothered her, although the things she'd gotten from Bonnie were not cheap. Donna's bizarre behavior and nasty attitude toward Janie had been worse. She acted as if Janie were at fault, trying to make her feel as if she were the "other woman" or some cheap kind of home breaker. Really, it was insane.

"I'm so thankful it didn't rain like the weatherman predicted," Caroline said as Janie drove them back to the inn. "It was a nice service, wasn't it?"

"It was really nice." Janie nodded. "I didn't tell you, but I loved what you said, and those Bible verses."

"Thanks." Caroline sighed. "That was really a God thing."

"Did you, uh … did you notice that Michael didn't go to the cemetery?"

Caroline didn't say anything.

"Do you think he might've gone home?"

"To Phoenix?" Caroline sounded doubtful.

"I guess I was just hoping."

"Somehow I don't think Michael will give up that easily."

"Do you think he'll come to the inn for lunch?"

"Oh, I doubt it." Caroline sadly shook her head. "My guess is that he's at Blue Anchor, tying a few on."

Janie suspected Caroline was right. To change the subject, she mentioned Donna. "I was a bit surprised that she came to the funeral," she admitted.

"That was probably my fault. I kind of invited her. I mean, I didn't really know what to say. She mentioned it this morning at the inn, and she sounded so lonely. It seemed unfriendly not to invite her." Caroline held up her hands. "I honestly didn't think she'd come. I mean an old woman's funeral, someone she'd never even met ... who'd'a thought?"

"She certainly dressed up for it."

Caroline started to giggle. "I'll say. I hate to sound catty, but it did appear she wanted to turn someone's head. Didn't it seem a bit desperate?"

"That Donna is a hard one to figure."

"So have you talked to Victor? I mean since the disappearing dishes and all that?"

"Not really. I think he's got his hands full just now."

"Because it really is mysterious, Janie. I was thinking about that this morning when I was talking to her. I honestly wanted to ask her, 'What did you do with Janie's dishes?' But I controlled myself."

"Thanks. I appreciate it."

Caroline started to laugh harder. "Still, I keep imagining Donna carting away those heavy boxes of dishes on her bike."

Janie couldn't help but giggle. "I know. I've had the same thoughts."

"So how did she do it?"

"I'm clueless. At one point I thought maybe I'd dreamed the whole thing. You know how you sometimes have a dream that seems so real, you almost think it happened?"

"Yeah, I've had those."

"But I still have the receipt from Bonnie's shop. So I know I didn't dream it."

"Crazy."

"You got that right. That woman is crazy." Janie pulled in front of the inn.

"Speak of the devil." Caroline pointed toward Victor's car, which was just parking on the other side of the street.

"This is so awkward." Janie took her keys out of the ignition and just sat there. "What am I supposed to do? Just be polite and act like nothing happened?"

Caroline didn't answer.

"Oh, I'm sorry," Janie said. "I'm being so selfish. Today is about your mom, not me and my silly troubles."

"No, that's okay." Caroline smiled at her. "I was actually kind of enjoying the drama. I don't know what to tell you, I mean how you should act. That's a tough one, Janie."

"Well, I know how to act." Janie dropped her keys in her bag. "I'll simply put on my lawyer face and mind my manners. No biggie."

"Oh, darn." Caroline made a disappointed face. "Just when I was looking forward to a showdown."

"Not today." Janie got out of her car, holding her head high. "Not from my end anyway."

Victor called out a hello to them, and Janie and Caroline waited for the couple at the front of the inn. "That was a nice service, Caroline," he said politely. "I'm sure your mother would've appreciated it."

"I loved that old woman," Donna chimed in. "Vera Somebody."

"Vera Dewberry," Janie supplied.

"Yes." Donna's voice grew a bit frosty. Then she turned to Caroline with a bright smile. "She was such a hoot. She and your mother must've really been something back in their day."

Caroline turned surprisingly friendly toward Donna, actually taking her aside to tell her that what she said was "an even funnier story, but not suitable for men's ears." Victor and Janie stood there alone, and Janie suspected Caroline had done this intentionally.

"Want to go inside?" Victor said quietly.

"Sure." Janie nodded and began going up the steps, trying to think of some way to get him to herself for a few minutes.

He smiled as he opened the door for her. "I'd love to see how your office is coming, Janie."

"Really?" She looked into his eyes and was surprised by the warm rush that ran through her. "Sure," she said quickly. "Come on down."

Soon they were downstairs, where she quickly showed him around and led him into the private room where she hoped to one day do her legal consultations. She closed the door behind him. She was tempted to lock it but feared that might be pushing things a bit.

"It's very nice," he said.

"Care to sit?" she nodded to a leather club chair.

"Thank you."

She took the chair opposite him and crossed her legs, waiting.

"Is this a good time to talk?" he asked.

"It is for me." She glanced at the closed door. "I'm not so sure about your, uh, your date."

He frowned. "She is not my date."

Janie smiled. "Sorry. Appearances can sometimes be deceiving."

"A lot of things can be deceiving, especially when you're not pay-ing close attention."

Janie wondered if he was talking about her. Had she deceived him in some way?

"So, first of all, how are you doing?" he asked with what seemed genuine concern.

"I'm okay, I guess." She wasn't sure how to answer. Did he mean in regard to him? To life in general? "Mostly I've been trying to stick close to Caroline these past few days. Her brother is, well, an odd character."

Victor nodded. "I know."

"You know?"

"I remember him from when we were kids. He seemed like a tough guy then, and I wouldn't say it to Caroline, but he doesn't seem to have changed much."

"I have to agree. Poor Caroline keeps hoping for the best. She's trying so hard. I appreciate her optimism, but I'm afraid she's going to get hurt. In fact I should probably go up and stick with her now, just in case he shows up." She made a half smile. "I'm pretending to be her bodyguard."

Victor chuckled. "You don't strike me as very threatening."

"Maybe not. But I can talk tough."

"I'm surprised Mitch isn't here. I think he'd make a good bodyguard."

"He's stuck in Tokyo." Janie glanced nervously at the mantel clock in the center of her bookcase. "You know I probably should go up there. Just in case." She stood and placed her hand on the doorknob.

"What would you do if Michael did come and make trouble?" Victor studied her.

"I'd speak some fancy legalese to him and hopefully convince him to act civilized, but explain the consequences if he doesn't."

"How about if we just leave this door open? Wouldn't we hear if something was erupting up there?"

She considered this. She really did want to talk to Victor now, and his suggestion did seem reasonable. If that loudmouth beast showed up, he'd make some noise. "Okay." She opened the door and sat back down.

"My boys are coming for Thanksgiving," he said without much enthusiasm.

"That's wonderful, Victor. Both of them?"

He nodded. "Yes. I haven't seen Marcus since last summer. He's bringing his fiancée."

"He's engaged?"

"Didn't I tell you? Well, it's a recent development. Her name's Katie, and they've been going together for about six months, but I guess I didn't realize it was that serious."

"How nice for you to meet her."

He frowned. "Except that Donna is insisting we must celebrate Thanksgiving together."

Janie considered her response. "Well, that seems reasonable. I mean, Ben and Marcus are her sons, and she must be eager to meet her future daughter-in-law."

"I suppose." He brightened. "How about your kids? Will they be coming for Thanksgiving?"

She sighed and looked down at her hands, fingers tightly folded together like she would to do as a child when her father questioned her. "Matthew is in the midst of fall term and plans to spend the holiday weekend snowboarding with a buddy up in Vermont. And Lisa, well, you know how it is with her. At least she's talking to Matthew now. That's something. It's a long shot, but I'm hoping I can get them both to come out here for Christmas."

"Right." He exhaled loudly. "Janie, I don't really know what to say. I'm embarrassed and so sorry about Donna, the way she treated you on the boat last week, all that weirdness. I feel so badly."

She looked eagerly at him. "So you do believe me then?"

He blinked. "Of course."

Relief washed over her. For some reason she feared he thought she manufactured the strange story. She was about to say something when she heard raised voices upstairs. "That sounds like Michael!" she exclaimed. "He's here!"

"Let's go!" Victor was out the door ahead of her, bolting up the stairs two at a time. Meanwhile Janie followed, grabbing her cell phone, ready to call 9-1-1 if necessary.

"This is family stuff, jus' between me and my sister!" Michael bellowed in a slurred voice. "Everyone elz can jus' butt out!"

"We are Caroline's family," Abby said, planting herself between Michael and Caroline.

"That's right," Victor said as he stepped forward.

Janie said, "If you don't leave this house immediately, the police will be here in five minutes." She stepped next to Victor, locking eyes with Michael.

"Not until my sister answers to me!" Michael pushed Abby aside and grabbed Caroline. "She's got some explaining to do."

"What do you mean?" Caroline cried out as he jerked her toward the front door with him.

"I mean what'd you do with the money?" he demanded.

"What money?" Caroline's eyes were full of fear.

"Our parents' money—and all the stuff—where is it, Caroline?"

"There isn't any—"

"You took it all, Caroline! I know you took everything. Before I got here, you took it all!" He opened the door.

"I'm Caroline's attorney," Janie announced loudly, for the sake of everyone in the room, as she shoved her cell phone at Marley. "I already hit speed dial for 9-1-1," she said quickly. "Tell them what's going on while we take this outside." Then she took off after Michael and Caroline, with Victor by her side and Abby and Marley trailing behind.

"Let Caroline go," Victor warned Michael as he chased after them. "Do not put her in that pickup with you!"

"That's right," Janie yelled. "You will be charged with kidnapping, Michael. That's a felony punishable by a lot of prison time in most jurisdictions. You better stop right there unless you—"

"The police are on their way," Marley called out.

Michael pinned Caroline against the truck with one hand as he opened the driver's door with the other. "Get in!" he yelled. "This is *not* kidnapping. This is big brother taking little sister for a ride so we can talk in private. Now get in." He shoved her, but she resisted.

"Do *not* get in the truck!" Janie looked directly Caroline. The fear in her eyes made Janie realize they needed to act quickly.

"Don't listen to them," Michael yelled into Caroline's face. He reached into his pocket and pulled out a large pocketknife, flipping it open with one hand. "I don't want to hurt you. I just want to talk to you! I want you to give me what's mine. Now get in!"

Victor spoke in a calm but firm voice. "Michael, you need to let Caroline go before this gets out of hand. Just let her go. Okay?" He was only a few feet away from Michael now, but he looked ready to lunge if necessary. Janie hoped it wouldn't be. That blade looked lethal.

"Come on, Michael," Janie said quietly as she moved to stand next to Victor. "You don't want to spend the night in jail, do you? Just let Caroline go. I promise you that we will all sit down and discuss this later."

"I'm sick of your lawyer talk!" He shook his knife toward her. "You're just messing everything up. We're family—me and Caroline. We can sort this out ourselves. She can give me what's mine. Just leave us alone."

Janie held up her hands as she took a step closer to him. "I know you can sort this out, Michael. But not like this. This will only get you into some serious trouble. You don't want trouble, do you?" She heard sirens. "See, Michael, the police are already on their way—"

"Please, Michael," Caroline pleaded with tears streaming down her cheeks. "Just let me go, okay? It doesn't have to be like this."

The sirens were louder now, and Michael looked uneasy. "I wasn't going to hurt you, Caroline."

"I know," she said quietly.

He closed his knife and let her go. "I just wanted what was mine."

"I know," she said again, but she was backing away. Janie went to her, gathering her into her arms as Michael got into his pickup.

"Hey, man," Victor said gently. "Don't drive in your condition. The cops will pull you over for sure, and then you'll be stuck with a DUI."

"He's right," Caroline called out. "Don't go, Michael."

Michael leaped into his cab and tore off down the street just seconds before the police arrived. While Janie and Marley took Caroline back into the house, Victor and Abby spoke to the police.

"I can't believe he did that," Caroline said through her tears as they walked her up the stairs to her room. "What did he think he'd accomplish?"

"It was desperation," Janie told her. "Drunken desperation."

"The cops have probably got him by now," Marley said as they sat Caroline down on her bed. "You're safe."

"I know." Caroline sniffed. "But Michael's not."

"There's nothing you can do about that," Janie told her. "Like my mom used to say, he's made his own bed, and he'll have to lie in it now."

"Hello?" The three of them looked over to see Ashton standing in the doorway.

Marley went over to him. "What is it?"

"The police want to speak to Caroline," he said.

"I'll go down." Caroline stood, taking in a deep breath.

"I'll go with you," Janie told her.

Ashton looked bewildered. "Is it always this interesting in Clifden?"

Marley let out a chuckle. "It can get a little crazy," she told him, "especially when your friends are all named Linda."

He just shook his head. "I guess."

Janie went down with Caroline, and together they answered the policeman's questions. "I really don't want to press charges," Caroline said. "I mean, he is my brother, and I honestly don't think he was going to hurt me."

Janie had to bite her tongue.

"I'm sorry," the officer told her. "Even if you don't press charges, your brother has broken some laws, and he will be held accountable for those."

"Oh." Caroline nodded sadly.

After the police finally left, Janie assured Caroline that she would do whatever she legally could to help Michael. Of course, even as she promised this, she suspected that Michael would not appreciate her generosity. Furthermore he might not even accept it. Really, some jail or prison time would probably not be such a bad thing for Michael McCann.

Chapter 25

MARLEY

Abby's idea to let Ashton use Doris's beach house turned out to be brilliant. Both Marley and Ashton appreciated the extra space, and Ashton even repaired Doris's dripping bathroom faucet as well as a loose floorboard. Best of all, by Thanksgiving morning, Marley felt pretty certain that her boy had turned a corner. He showed up at her door with beach-blown hair and his old smile.

"Whatever happened with Caroline's brother?" He asked her as they shared coffee and the newspaper in Marley's tiny sun-filled kitchen.

"Caroline told me that they're letting him out of jail today."

"Do you think that's safe?"

Marley shrugged. "I don't know. Caroline doesn't seem too concerned. Apparently Janie helped him to work a deal. He agreed to surrender his truck, since he already had a suspended license in Arizona, and he promised to return to Phoenix and remain there, as well as to quit pestering Caroline for money. That last bit will probably be hardest for him. But he did all that in exchange for his freedom."

"He was okay with that?"

"I guess so." Marley flipped to the entertainment page.

"And Caroline was good with it too?"

"I'm sure she was relieved. It tore her apart to hear he was locked up."

"Even though he nearly kidnapped her at knifepoint?"

"Like my mom used to say, blood is thicker than water."

"Yeah, it's rough when families fall apart like that."

Marley put down her paper to study his face. "You mean like *your* family? Like Dad and me and you?"

His mouth twisted to one side. "And like Leo and me too. It's just really sad, you know, what we all do to each other when we're supposed to be family."

She considered this. "I know."

"I mean, you'd think the human race would improve, wouldn't you? That we'd all get better at resolving our differences, that we'd eventually learn to just get along? Sometimes it seems like everyone is degenerating, like someday there will be no such thing as family."

She forced a weak smile. "But we're family, Ashton, you and me. Right?"

His face brightened. "Sure, Mom. You and I will always be family."

"Maybe family is what you make of it. Like Caroline, Abby, and Janie—I think of them as my family too."

"You're right. I have friends like that." He let out an exasperated sigh. "But now I'll have to sort it out, you know, because some were friends with Leo, too. That'll be tough." He set his coffee mug down with a crooked grin. "Fortunately I think a lot of our friends liked me better than Leo."

"I like you better than Leo too." Marley patted his hand. "Today I'd like you to meet some of my other friends."

"That's right." He nodded. "I get to meet Jack today."

"And Hunter and Jasmine, too."

"They're all coming to Abby's Thanksgiving bash?"

She nodded. "Which reminds me, we need to start working on that sweet-potato dish. As I recall, you said you'd help."

"Only if you promise—no marshmallows."

She made a pouty face. "How about just half of—"

"Just say no to marshmallows, Mom. Seriously they are so tacky."

She laughed. "Okay. Fine. But I still get to use brown sugar and nuts, right?"

"You know," Ashton told her as they peeled and pared sweet potatoes together, "it's been pretty cool getting to visit you like this. I mean, even though the circumstances were a little rough, I'm glad you forced me to come here."

"I've loved having you here, Ashton."

"I can see why you like living on the beach. I'm going to miss it."

"Meaning?" She gave him a sideways glance.

"Meaning I have to go back, Mom. The business is suffering, orders are backed up, and with Christmas coming … well, life goes on, right?"

She nodded. "Right."

"If it's okay with you, I'd like to come back for Christmas."

"It's more than okay, Ashton. I would love it!"

* * *

Marley and Ashton arrived at the B and B early so they could help Abby get things set up. "I've never had more than a dozen people for a sit-down dinner before," Abby admitted as they squeezed two more chairs into the long line of tables that extended from the dining room into the living room. "Eighteen at one table is a record for me."

"I was surprised Victor and his family decided to come," Marley said quietly.

"To be honest, I was too. But I think Janie was pleased to hear the news."

"So what's up between Janie and Victor and the ex?" Marley glanced around to be sure that Donna wasn't lurking around a corner.

"I'm not sure." Abby was arranging the place settings now, trying to make everything fit. Marley had encouraged her to use disposable plates and things, but Abby would not hear of it. She wanted to try out the new dishes and glassware that had just arrived for the inn. A glutton for work, she'd insisted on cloth napkins, too. Marley had to admit the final effect was lovely.

"Where's Caroline?" Marley asked as they returned to the kitchen, where Ashton was starting to mash the potatoes.

"Didn't I tell you? She and Janie picked up Michael at the jail this morning."

"Is he coming here too?" Marley suddenly imagined a food fight breaking out at Abby's elegantly set table, police coming, and Hunter terrified.

"No. I told them it was okay to bring Michael, but Janie had already arranged for him to fly back to Phoenix today. They were driving him over to Eugene to catch a flight, which should be leaving"—she looked at the kitchen clock—"shortly."

Marley started working on the veggie tray. "Is Donna around?" she asked quietly, still worried that the woman might pop in.

"No, her boys picked her up this morning. They were going to do a beach walk and blow out the carbon before they stuff themselves. Not a bad idea, really."

Marley felt relieved that Donna was gone. "I'm just so curious about what's going on with them. Janie was tight-lipped when we had coffee on Tuesday, which only makes me think that she and Victor are not history yet."

"You wouldn't know that hearing Donna talk." Abby sighed and pushed a strand of hair away from her forehead as she closed the oven door.

"Hey, I just realized you did something different with your hair." Marley looked more closely at Abby. "It's a little shorter and lighter, too. I like it."

"Thanks." Abby smiled.

"Reminds me of when you were younger."

"Paul didn't even notice."

"Oh, you know how men can be."

"I know how Paul can be." Abby frowned.

"You're still doing your marriage counseling, aren't you?"

"We missed our last session. And we'll miss this week, too."

"Oh."

"Hey there!" called Caroline as she entered the kitchen. "It smells absolutely yummy in here!" She went over and gave Ashton a squeeze. "Hey, good-looking, what you got cooking?"

Ashton chuckled. He and Caroline had seemed to hit it off right from the start. Marley couldn't even put into words how great this made her feel. Abby and Janie liked Ashton as well, but Ashton seemed to brighten up when Caroline was around.

"Spuds," he told her. "But I'm spiking them with some pretty heavy cream and butter."

"Don't tell Abby," Caroline said in a hushed tone.

"Abby knows," Abby said. "I figured one serving wouldn't kill Paul."

"Did you notice Abby's hair?" Caroline asked Marley. "Doesn't it take about ten years off of her?"

Marley nodded. "It's great."

"How was your brother this morning?" Abby asked. "Everything go okay?"

Caroline's expression grew more serious. "Yeah, it went pretty well."

Janie came into the kitchen. "That's an understatement," she said. "It went incredibly well." She put her arm around Caroline, giving her sideways hug. "You guys would've been so proud of our girl here."

"Tell us!" Marley urged. "What happened?"

"Do you mind?" Janie asked Caroline.

"No, this is family."

Janie told them that Caroline and Michael had this amazing heart-to-heart conversation as Janie drove them to Eugene. "Caroline confessed to Michael how rough her childhood was. It seems that Michael thought he was the only one who had it bad, but Caroline opened up and told some pretty heart-wrenching stories. Well, let's just say there wasn't a dry eye in the car."

"Then Michael opened up a little," Caroline injected. "I mean, I knew he'd had some tough times with Dad, but I didn't know everything. Good grief, it's not even that surprising that he's been such a mess."

"I think it's amazing that *you're* not a mess," Janie told Caroline.

"Well, you weren't around me in the seventies and eighties. Trust me, it wasn't pretty."

"Anyway," Janie continued, "we talked to Michael about getting some counseling in Phoenix, maybe even some alcoholism treatment. He wasn't totally opposed to the idea."

"I'll cover the cost out of my mom's insurance money," Caroline explained. "There's nothing I'd rather spend that money on. It would make Mom happy too."

"Michael even apologized to Caroline at the airport," Janie said. "It was truly amazing!"

Caroline nodded with glistening eyes. "I have an awful lot to be thankful for this Thanksgiving."

"That reminds me," Abby said. "Mitch called here about an hour ago. I guess he tried your cell but couldn't get through."

"Is he here yet?"

"Yes. He decided he'd walk here from his hotel. I offered to call Paul to pick him up, but he said he wanted to walk."

"It's a beautiful day for it." Janie washed her hands at the sink. "Now tell me, Abby, what can we do to help?"

Marley felt happy as she and the other three Lindas, along with Ashton, worked together in the kitchen. Really, she couldn't ever remember preparing for a Thanksgiving dinner with so much joy in her heart.

"I think everything's as ready as it can be," Abby said as she looked around the kitchen.

"You know the old saying." Marley grinned. "Many hands make light work."

"I have a surprise," Caroline said as she opened the refrigerator and pulled out a bottle of chilled champagne and a carton of orange juice. "Mimosas!"

"Perfect!" Janie exclaimed.

"I'll get the glasses," Abby offered.

As the five of them clinked glasses, Marley winked at her son. "Here's to friends who are like family, and to family who are like friends," she proclaimed.

"Cheers!" they all said.

Chapter 26

JANIE

As Janie sat at the Thanksgiving table, it wasn't easy to pretend all was well. Certainly all was well as far as the challenges Caroline had faced this morning. Truly it couldn't have gone better with Michael. But when Janie saw Victor, Donna, Marcus, and Ben walking into the inn, she felt a chill run through her. She knew that Victor had opted to eat with the Lindas to avoid the appearance that he and Donna were getting back together, but as far as Janie could see, Donna was not getting this message.

"How about this great weather for your flight up here?" Janie said to Mitch as she passed him the rolls. Janie had arranged the place cards on the table, making sure to allow plenty of distance between her and Donna. As a result Janie was at one end of the table with Caroline, Mitch, Marley, Ashton, and Jack and his family. It was actually a rather comfortable grouping, and the conversation down here was flowing as smoothly as the wine that Mitch had brought with him from Napa Valley. At the other end of the table, where Victor's and Abby's families sat ... not so much. Janie felt a tad bit guilty, but she thought Abby would understand.

To make up for it, Janie decided to make herself extra useful after the meal was finished. "I'm in charge of cleanup," she announced, "and Abby is banned from the kitchen."

"I'm Janie's assistant," Caroline said quickly, "since we weren't here to help much this morning."

"Ashton and I are helping too," Marley proclaimed.

"Nope," Ashton told his mom. "I'm helping. You're staying put."

Both Marley and Abby protested, but, outvoted, they had no choice.

"How are you doing?" Caroline quietly asked Janie as they rinsed plates together.

"I'm okay." Janie forced a smile for Ashton's sake.

"Hey, you can let your guard down around me," he assured her as he set a stack of dishes by her elbow. "I know what's going on out there. You have my sympathy."

"Thanks." Janie lowered her voice. "I appreciate it. And the truth is"—Ashton and Caroline leaned in to hear—"I felt like I was about to die out there."

They both nodded in sympathy.

"It's the weirdest situation, and it's taking all my self-control not to run out of here screaming." Janie rinsed a plate and sighed.

"Poor Janie." Caroline patted her shoulder.

"That Donna is a real piece of work," Ashton whispered. "And that outfit she's wearing!" He shook his head with a frown. "It's so last year."

This made Janie and Caroline laugh loudly.

"Sounds like you're having way too much fun in there," Abby called out.

"I better go finish clearing," Ashton said.

"Yes, and spying," Janie said in a hushed tone.

He chuckled. "You got it."

"That Ashton is okay," Janie said as he left.

"He is adorable," Caroline said. "I told Marley she should encourage him to move his drum shop to Clifden. I think he would fit in well in this town."

Janie loaded another plate into the dishwasher. She was obsessing over Victor and feeling excluded from the chance to get better acquainted with his sons. She already knew and liked Ben, but today was the first time she'd met Marcus. They'd exchanged a few words and his fiancée Katie had barely said hello before Donna interrupted them. Janie couldn't help but feel Donna wanted to cut Janie off, ignore her, and push her away. Janie had no doubt that Donna wanted to paint a bad picture of her for her sons and future daughter-in-law.

With cleanup done, they started serving dessert and coffee. Janie kept herself busy playing waitress, but after a while everyone was served, and eventually the meal—the longest meal of Janie's life—was finally over. This was announced by Paul, who, seated at the end of the table next to Victor, stretched his arms back and yawned loudly. "The only thing missing here is football," he said.

Abby laughed a bit uncomfortably. "I haven't gotten a TV for the inn yet."

"Which is why I'm inviting anyone interested to come out to my house to watch the big game." Paul patted his midsection as he stood. "Any takers?"

It seemed everyone jumped up to figure out what they wanted to do with the remainder of the day. Mitch and Caroline announced they were taking Chuck to the beach. Marley and Ashton planned to head over to Jack's house to see a new painting he'd just finished and to help decorate the Christmas tree, which Hunter insisted they put up today.

"How about you, Victor?" Paul asked. "Want to bring your boys over and place some wagers on the big game?"

"Thanks for the offer, but I promised to drive the kids out to see the lighthouse this afternoon," Victor told him.

"I just got a new camera," Katie explained. "I can't wait to use it, and I absolutely adore lighthouses."

"It's such a lovely day for that too," Donna chirped, as if this was all part of her plan. "I'll just run upstairs and change into something more casual."

Victor tossed an uncomfortable glance at Janie, suggesting that perhaps Donna had just invited herself into this outing. Maybe it was fatigue, stupidity, or plain impatience, but Janie suddenly decided to join this crazy game.

"What a splendid idea," she said to Victor. Donna paused at the foot of the stairs. "I heard that the Christmas lights will be lit for the first time tonight. If you stick around long enough, they'll have carolers and cookies and everything." She made a firm nod as if she'd just decided something. "In fact I think I'll drive up there myself. Anyone care to join me?" She glanced at Abby. Everyone else was gone or had other plans.

"I'm beat," Abby admitted a bit sheepishly. "In fact falling asleep in front of a football game is surprisingly appealing."

"That's okay," Janie said in a cheerful tone. "I'm fine on my own—"

"Why don't you come with us?" Victor said eagerly.

"Oh, you wouldn't have room," she told him.

"Actually, if we could take your car, we'd have even more room. It would be more comfortable for everyone."

Janie glanced at Donna, who was still at the foot of the stairs. Although she was partially in the shadows, Janie could see a frown on her face. Common sense warned Janie this might not be such a good idea, but she just didn't care.

"Sure." Janie grinned at Victor. "I'd be happy to have someone ride with me."

Victor turned to Ben now. "You know your way to the lighthouse. Do you mind waiting for your mom to change? That way we can head out now, and Katie will get there while there's still good light for her photos."

"Sure, Dad."

Victor handed Ben the keys. "Great. Meet you up there." He turned to Janie. "Are you ready?"

She nodded. "I've got hiking shoes in my trunk."

"Then what are we waiting for?"

Janie couldn't help but notice the surprised expressions on Marcus's and Katie's faces as they hurried out the door. She tried to act calm and normal on the outside, but on the inside she felt like singing and dancing.

As they approached her car, she remembered that she'd had a bit to drink with dinner. Though it wasn't much, she was still not comfortable driving. Stopping Victor on the sidewalk, she quietly explained her dilemma. With a solemn face he held out his hand for her car keys. "In that case I must insist that I drive."

"Uh, thanks." She handed over her keys and then he chuckled, pointing to her sporty silver Mercedes parked across the street.

"All right!" He nodded victoriously to Marcus and Katie. "I've been dying to try out this little beauty, but Janie has never once invited me to drive it for her."

Without further ado Marcus and Katie got in back, and Janie sat next to Victor. Just as he pulled out, a disheveled Donna popped out the front door, holding her shoes in one hand and waving frantically, as if she expected them to stop and wait for her to pile in. Fortunately Janie seemed the only one to notice this. Although she felt a twinge of guilt, she had a strong suspicion Donna would repay Janie for this intrusion on her excursion.

Instead of worrying over this, Janie decided to play tour guide by pointing out sights of interest along the way. A couple of times she even suggested they might stop to allow Katie to take some photos, but Victor seemed intent on reaching the lighthouse. Perhaps he was as worried about Donna as Janie was.

"Easy on the curves, Dad," Marcus said. "You don't want us getting carsick on Janie's nice leather seats."

"Oh, they clean up nicely," she assured him.

"This car has great suspension," Victor told Janie, "but I guess I could slow down a bit."

Before long they were in the parking lot and emerging from the car. "We're going to head straight up the trail as fast as we can go," Marcus informed his dad, "so Katie can make the most of this late-afternoon light."

"Since we're the old folks, we'll meander on up and take our time." Victor winked at her, and just like that Victor and Janie were alone, slowly walking up one of the twisty, shadowy trails that led to the lighthouse.

"Is this the regular lighthouse trail?" Janie asked as they turned another sharp corner. "I don't recall it going this way."

He chuckled. "Actually I thought we'd stop by the blow hole first. Do you mind?"

She smiled. "Do you think we should let the others know which route you took?"

He pulled out his cell phone and, holding it up for her to see, he turned it off. "I'm sure we'll meet up with them in time. Besides, it's probably more than an hour before we have to get up on top to see the Christmas lights, right?"

"Yes, but we don't want to get lost on this trail." She paused by a mossy boulder that overlooked the ocean, turning to peer into his face.

"We don't?" Now he reached out and pulled her close to him. "Oh, Janie, I have missed you so much."

She felt a strange mix of emotions now—giddy happiness and fretful concern, not to mention curiosity. They all churned within her, almost as wildly the waves down in the inlet below. "I've missed you too."

He leaned in and kissed her, and everything about his kiss felt as solid and reassuring as it had felt before. But even as she kissed him back, she wondered: Was this right? Was it smart? Was it even safe? Janie imagined Donna bursting up here, armed with something more than a butter knife, as she forced Janie over the edge of the cliff like a scene from a Hitchcock movie.

"We need to talk." Janie pulled away and looked into his eyes.

"Those four words that nobody in love ever wants to hear."

She blinked. "In love?"

He was still holding to her hands, squeezing them warmly

between his own. "Of course. You know that I love you, Janie. Haven't I made that clear?"

She cocked her head to one side. "Clear in a foggy sort of way."

"I know, I know." He tipped his head back and let out a deep sigh. "Donna has confused and complicated and convoluted almost everything. I had hoped that she'd come to her senses by now, that she'd realize I don't love her anymore. She needs to remember that she was the one who ended our marriage in the first place. I want her to just move on and go home."

"Have you told her that?"

"I've tried."

"But have you specifically said those exact words to her, Victor?"

"She makes it difficult." He ran his hand through his hair. "It's like she has radar, Janie. Every time I'm about to make everything very plain and clear, she throws up some kind of smoke screen. She does or says something very thoughtful and sweet, or she brings up the boys or starts talking about Marcus's wedding, or else she goes all spiritual on me and starts talking about God. That's when I get really confused. Take it from me, Donna is a confusing woman."

Janie made a sad smile. "She knows how to work you, Victor. She's slowly but surely reeling you in."

"She can't reel in what she hasn't hooked."

She studied him closely. "Are you sure about that?"

"What do you mean?"

"I mean she hooked you once, Victor. Why shouldn't she be able to hook you again?"

He looked out over the ocean with a firm jaw. "Because I don't love her."

Janie believed him.

"The truth is, I feel a little guilty for *not* loving her." He turned back to look at Janie. "Especially when she starts talking about God, about the promises we made … until death do we part and all that." He shook his head. "Even though I know I don't love Donna, I still want to honor God."

Janie wanted to turn and run from him. She wanted to grab her car keys and get out of there as fast as she could, let Victor sort this mess out for himself. It was one thing for him to admit he felt no love for his wife, but once he started bringing God into it, Janie felt lost too. She had no good answers.

"I know I've frustrated you," he continued gently. "I can hardly believe how patient you've been with me."

Janie looked out over the ocean, watching as the clouds on the horizon began to turn peachy. She was in over her head.

"I can't believe how you hang in there, Janie, and you do it with such grace and dignity. Any other woman probably would've run away screaming by now."

She wanted to tell him that was exactly what she felt like doing. Instead she took in a deep breath and prayed a silent prayer, asking God for clarity, for direction, and most of all for *peace*. Then she simply smiled.

"What is it?" Victor asked hopefully. "Why are you smiling?"

"It's hard to explain."

"Please try," he urged.

"Well, when you said that thing about wanting to honor God, I could understand. Not totally, but in a way I got it. I want to honor God too."

Victor looked slightly confused.

"So I have a question for you," she said quietly.

"What?"

"Do you experience a sense of peace when you're with Donna? Do you feel centered and happy and hopeful, peaceful?"

He actually laughed. "No way. In fact just the opposite is true."

"I'm no expert, and I could be wrong, but I was under the impression that God gives us a sense of peace when we obey him. I believe that God has our best interests at heart, and when we're in his will, I believe we experience a peaceful calm, even happiness." She looked into his dark eyes. "I know that I do."

He nodded eagerly. "So do I."

"And?"

"You're absolutely right. I have none of that with Donna." He balled his hands into fists. "I swear if she were with me right now, I would be thinking about jumping off this cliff."

Janie felt alarmed. "And now?"

"Now, when I'm with you, I feel like I know who I am. I feel a calm and a peace. I know who you are too, Janie, and I feel like I know who God is."

"But with Donna? Do you know who God is?"

"No!" he exclaimed. "You have totally nailed it, Janie. When I'm with Donna I begin to see God as I saw him in my childhood—as this old white-haired man who's scowling and shaking his finger at me, despising me for my weaknesses, condemning me to hell for how bad I am. It's pathetic and depressing, but it's the truth."

"I don't believe that's God."

"No. That's not my God." Victor took in a deep breath and smiled.

"My God is loving and forgiving. He's gentle, kind, encouraging. He doesn't want to beat us down and torture us. He wants to lift us up."

"That's what I believe too."

Victor pulled Janie toward him again, holding her tight. "When I think of God like that, well, I know that I need him in my life."

"Me, too."

"I know I need you, too, Janie."

"Me, too." She sighed and rested there in his arms for a while, but finally she pulled away. "I think that's what you need to tell Donna."

He nodded. "I know."

"If you don't mind, I will drive myself back home." She held out her hand for her keys. "Don't worry, I am completely sober."

He frowned as he handed them over. "I know you're right, but I also know this isn't going to be easy."

"I have one suggestion for you."

"What?"

"Don't break your news to Donna while she's standing near any of these cliffs."

"Good advice." He chuckled, then turned serious. "You think she might push me over?"

"I just don't think she's entirely predictable."

"Tell me about it."

She patted him on the shoulder. "Good luck, Victor. I will be saying a prayer for you." She headed back down the path, got into her car, and—sorry that she'd miss the Christmas lights but not sorry to miss the fireworks—she drove away. As she saw the lighthouse in her rearview mirror, she told herself she'd have to come back up here again soon—hopefully with Victor.

Chapter 27

CAROLINE

After their beach walk Caroline and Mitch drove to the small municipal airport, where Mitch showed her his small plane. "This is so cute," she said. "I wish I could go up in it with you sometime."

"No time like the present," he said.

"Seriously?"

"Absolutely."

She looked over to where her SUV was parked. "What about Chuck?"

Mitch frowned. "Do you think he likes to fly?"

She laughed. "No, I mean do you think it's okay to leave him in the car there? I've left the windows open, and I know he's tired from the beach."

"I don't see why it wouldn't be okay."

"Really?" Caroline looked at the small plane again. "We can just do this? Get into your plane and take off? Just like that?"

He smiled. "Well, I'll do my regular flight check and clear my takeoff. All the normal stuff. But yeah, pretty much just like that."

While he did his "normal stuff," she checked on Chuck. He did seem perfectly fine. Just in case, she filled his travel water bowl and tossed him a Milk-Bone. "We'll be back in a while," she promised. Then she hurried back to the plane. Mitch was checking something on the outside.

"Everything okay?" she asked as she watched him.

"A-okay." He grinned at her. "Ready to go?"

"You're sure we can just do this?"

He threw back his head and laughed. "Yes, Caroline. Trust me, I do this all the time." He walked her around to the passenger side, opened the small door, and helped her in. Then he showed her how the seat belts worked and finally he leaned over and kissed her. "Don't worry, I know what I'm doing."

She laughed at herself as he walked around to his side. She didn't know why she was being so silly about this. Of course, it wasn't every day she climbed into a small plane and went for a ride. She watched as he flipped some switches, turned on the engine, and, while talking onto the radio, taxied over to the small tarmac runway.

For some reason she was thinking about how it was to ride with her dad when his car wasn't running right. In a grumpy voice he'd tell her to shut up so he could hear the engine and figure out the problem. If she made any noise, he'd get mad and even blame his mechanical troubles on her, as if a seven-year-old girl could be responsible for a car that wouldn't run properly. She knew her father's behavior was twisted, but still, the memory was real. As a result she sat very quietly as Mitch got the plane in position to take off.

As he revved the engine and the plane began to propel down the runway, she was holding her breath and silently counting as if she thought these were the last seconds of her life. Then, just like that, they were in the air, and the small plane was shooting over the tops of coastal pines, climbing into the sky until everything below her became small and toylike.

"You can breathe now," he told her.

She let out her breath and laughed. "How did you know I was holding my breath?"

"It was pretty obvious." He grinned. "But surely this isn't the first time you've flown."

"It's my first time in a small plane. To be honest, I haven't flown all that many times in big planes. It always makes me a little nervous."

He patted her knee. "How are you now?"

She smiled and leaned back. "I'm okay." She watched as he circled around town, flying over the river and the docks and then looping around to fly over the ocean, dipping down so low that she thought she might be able to spot a large fish. "Wow!" she exclaimed happily. "This is so amazing!"

He nodded eagerly. "It is, isn't it?"

"I feel totally free." She looked down at the ocean again, trying to absorb everything in sight—the crab boats, the Coast Guard boat just going out, pelicans flying in formation, surfers, a couple of surf-sails, people and dogs on the beach. She wanted to take it all in. "It's incredible."

He flew up the shoreline and clear to the lighthouse before he made a wide, lazy circle over the ocean and turned back. "I'm glad you like it."

"I *love* it!"

"You seemed a bit unsure at first. I was a little worried."

"You know what I think was happening?" she said as realization hit her. "It's like I've been in a cage these past few months, stuck in the house most of the time, caring for my mom. Even when I got out, it was just for short bursts of time. Suddenly I'm like a bird that's been let out, and I don't know what to do, how to feel. It's like I'm not used to having this freedom. Then you give me all this!" She waved her arms. "It's just so exhilarating!"

He laughed. "Okay, so you do like it!"

Even though she liked it, she was relieved to be safely on the ground again. In a way the flight reminded her of ice cream. It was wonderful once in a while, but she didn't think she could handle a steady diet of it.

"You seem quiet," he said as they drove back through town.

"I think I might be tired," she admitted. "It's been a long couple of weeks."

"I know. You had the funeral, and that business with your brother was stressful."

"Yeah. Hopefully life will settle down some."

"I was going to invite you to dinner, but maybe we should do that tomorrow instead."

"I'm still stuffed from eating turkey," she confessed.

"And I'm feeling jet-lagged."

They agreed to call it an early night. She dropped him at his hotel and drove back to Abby's inn. She was actually relieved that Mitch wasn't staying there. A little space and a little quiet was most welcome.

To her relief the B and B was quiet now. Remnants of their Thanksgiving feast were still here and there, but the only beings in the house seemed to be her and Chuck. She let Chuck out into the backyard, fixed herself a cup of tea, and settled down in one of the easy chairs Abby had recently placed in the parlor. Letting out a contented sigh, she kicked off her shoes, put her feet on the ottoman, leaned her head back, and closed her eyes. Ahh … peace. Lovely.

Caroline woke up to the sound of a loud door slamming. She jumped and looked around the dim parlor to see who was in the house. Suddenly she thought of Michael—they had dropped him off at the airport this morning, but there was no telling if he'd actually boarded the plane. He'd seemed so sane and sober, but what if?

With a pounding heart she tiptoed around a corner, trying to see who was stomping up the stairs. She tripped over one of her own shoes, letting out a yelp as her knee smacked onto the hardwood floor. Outside Chuck was barking wildly, and Caroline was trying to remember where she'd left her purse and her phone.

"Who's that?" yelled a female voice.

"Donna?" Caroline called weakly as she stood back up. Though not exactly thrilled by this, she was so relieved it wasn't Michael that she actually smiled when Donna clicked on the overhead light.

"What are you doing in the dark?" Donna snapped at her from the stairs. "Hiding from someone like a common criminal?"

"No." Caroline rubbed her sore knee. "I was simply having a nice little nap until someone slammed the front door and scared me half to death." She walked through the kitchen to the back door and let Chuck back into the house. Caroline didn't know what was eating that woman, but she didn't particularly care either.

Seeing that there was still some cleanup left to do, Caroline decided to unload the dishwasher and finish things up. She'd removed only a couple of plates before Donna stomped into the kitchen and slammed her purse down onto the counter in what seemed an obvious cry for attention.

Well, Donna was in a foul mood, but Caroline didn't have to be sucked into it. She said nothing and, for Abby's sake, continued working, hoping Donna would take the hint and leave.

"Well, aren't you Miss Helpful?"

Caroline blinked. "Pardon me?"

Donna frowned like she was thinking hard. "Let me see, which Linda are you anyway?"

Caroline set the plate on the counter and peered at this strange woman. "Excuse me? Have you forgotten my name? I'm Caroline."

Donna narrowed her eyes. "Yes, Caroline, I *know* your name. I was thinking more about your identity. Who are you?"

Caroline just shook her head as she bent to retrieve another plate. Donna was seriously losing it.

"I've been watching all you Lindas, the way you run your exclusive little club."

Caroline blinked. "What are you saying?"

"You push everyone else out."

"You mean everyone who's name isn't Linda?"

"All four of you are a bunch of small-town snobs."

Caroline didn't know what to say. It seemed obvious that Donna was out of sorts and possibly jealous of the friendship the Four Lindas shared. Caroline was tempted to tell Donna to go back to her own friends, but she controlled herself.

Donna made a catty smile. "Yes, I've been studying the Four Lindas since I got here. I think I know what makes you tick."

Caroline couldn't help but roll her eyes. This woman was wacko!

"Yes. And I'll start with you, Caroline. You are the ne'er-do-well Linda, the wannabe actress who flunked out of Hollywood. Very pathetic."

"What?" Caroline stared at Donna.

"Oh, I figured all of you out pretty much right from the start."

Caroline leaned back against the counter, folding her arms across her front. "What exactly did you figure out?"

"Just that you're a sorry bunch of old women trying to act like you're not. And you, Caroline, are the neediest of the bunch. You flit from man to man. You use your beauty as a trap, but age is catching up with you and your looks are fading fast. Your old age clock is ticking away like a time bomb, and you are desperate to catch a man before it's too late."

There was a time when a statement like that would've elicited one of two responses from Caroline: (1) She would get really, really angry and lash right back, or (2) she would retreat and cry in her pillow. Today she would do neither. Instead she looked evenly at Donna. "I guess that just shows you don't really know me at all."

Donna laughed, but there was such wickedness in the sound. "Oh, I know you. I know all you Lindas, and I know the way you operate."

Caroline shook her head. "I seriously doubt that."

"I suppose I should leave Abby out of it. She's the strong one."

This almost made Caroline laugh. Abby was the strong one? Since when? Caroline stopped herself from saying as much. After all, Caroline loved Abby dearly, and besides, Abby did have some strengths.

"Abby is a businesswoman. She owns this inn," Donna continued with confidence. "She's in charge of her life, she's well known
in this town, established. She's the anchor of your messed-up little
group of losers."

Caroline shrugged as she reached for another plate. Really, this
woman didn't even deserve a response.

"Then there's Marley," Donna droned on. "Like you she's on a
man hunt. She pretends to be an artist, but that's clearly a ploy to
attract Jack. Even though he's a lot older, Marley is willing to settle
for him if she can. Because, well, she has no choice. Her looks are so
far gone that she has to take what she can get."

Caroline slid a stack of plates into the cabinet. Listening to
Donna was a bit like witnessing a train wreck. It was disturbing, but
she couldn't turn away.

"And Janie—well, she's the sorriest one of the bunch. A real
pathetic little weakling. Oh, sure, she tries to hide her insecurities
beneath her lawyer persona, but we all know she doesn't have a real
practice, and I doubt she ever did. I'm sure that after her husband
died, she knew she couldn't make it without someone to replace him.
Obviously she has set her sights on my Victor."

"*Your* Victor?" Caroline couldn't control herself now. "Do you
honestly think Victor belongs to you?"

"He married me. He fathered my sons. He promised to be my
lawfully wedded husband until death parted us."

Caroline waved her hand to stop her. "Hey, wait a minute. You
didn't honor that vow, Donna. You broke the contract with Victor
when you slept with your boss, and you totally cancelled it when you
married your boss. It was over." Caroline softened a bit. "In fact I'm

wondering why you're not still with your second husband, Donna. What about the vow you made to him? Aren't you supposed to honor that?"

"He cheated on me," she snapped.

"Okay." Caroline nodded. "He cheated on you, just like you cheated on Victor. If you made the same vows with him, why aren't you forcing him to take you back? Or would that get tricky? You'd have two husbands."

Donna looked slightly stumped.

"Just for the record, Donna, you don't really know me or my friends. I think all you've done is superimposed your own neediness onto us, turned us into caricatures to feel better about yourself." Caroline shook her finger at her. "First of all, I've had plenty of men who wanted to marry me. I could've settled for any of them, but I don't want to settle. And even though I think I love Mitch, I'm not even sure I'm ready to marry him anytime soon. I happen to *like* my independence. And while Abby might've been flattered by your take on her, you were wrong about that, too. Abby's trying to get strong, and she's working to get her business going. Janie owns half of it, by the way. If Abby were here, I'm sure she'd admit she's spent a lot of years being overshadowed by Paul, and she hasn't felt very strong or secure. At least she's standing up for herself now, and she's working on her marriage, too. You were wrong about Marley as well. She is a very good artist, and she is *not* trying to trap Jack into marriage."

Caroline didn't know why she was going to this much trouble to straighten this stupid woman out. Was it even possible? In a way it felt good to set her straight. She took a step closer to Donna. It seemed the woman's jaw had dropped ever so slightly, probably because she thought Caroline was too dumb and sweet to stand up for herself or her friends.

"And now for Janie," Caroline said a bit loudly. "When she moved here, she was still grieving her husband, and she was most certainly *not* looking for another husband. *Victor* pursued *her.* As for strength, Janie has been my rock during everything I've been through with my mom and brother. I don't know what I would've done without her." Caroline pursed her lips and shook her head. "I feel sorry for you, Donna. Not only are you clueless about people, you probably don't have any real friends like these Lindas. I suspect that the reason you're in such a bad mood is because Victor has finally set you straight about your relationship with him. Right?"

Donna picked up her purse and scowled, but she didn't answer that last question. Instead she turned away and loudly clomped up the stairs. Caroline felt a bit guilty as she returned to her kitchen chores. She probably could've handled that more gently, but Donna seemed to be one of those bullheaded people who needed to have the truth beaten into them with a sledgehammer. Anyway, Caroline could apologize to her later. That is, if Donna ever spoke to her again. The truth was, Caroline didn't really care.

Chapter 28

MARLEY

It was amazing how well Jack and Ashton hit it off on Thanksgiving, both at the inn and later at Jack's house. When Marley dropped Ashton in town the following morning while she ran errands, she wasn't surprised to discover he'd spent the whole time at the One-Legged Seagull.

"I don't know what I'd have done without him," Jack told Marley. "We were busier than ever with Black Friday Christmas shoppers, and Jasmine had to run Hunter to a soccer game. I had my hands full, and then Ashton just stepped in like he worked here."

Ashton grinned. "Well, in some ways selling art's not that much different from selling drums."

"He won't even let me give him a commission." Jack shook his head.

"Hey, it was fun. It makes me want to get back home and take care of my own business." Ashton looked at Marley. "Are we ready to head out now?"

"Ready when you are."

"I was trying to talk Ashton into relocating his drum business here," Jack said lightly. "There's a building a couple blocks from here that'll be available in January. I've been wanting more space, but it's a little too big for me."

"I'm seriously considering it," Ashton admitted, "but I need to sort things out with Leo first." He frowned at his watch. "I told Leo I'd be back this afternoon."

"So we better get going." Marley dug her keys out of her old Kenya Creations handbag.

"Drive safe," Jack said, but as she was going out the door, he stopped her with a hand on her shoulder. "If you're not busy tonight, Marley, I was … uh, I was wondering if you'd like to have dinner with me? I thought I'd cook us up some halibut."

"Sounds delicious," she told him.

His face lit up. "Great. Around seven then?"

"Perfect." As Marley exited the gallery, she experienced an unexpected rush of happy apprehension. Several weeks ago, and for no particular reason, she'd begun to assume that her relationship with Jack was never going to evolve into anything more than friendship. She'd thought otherwise during the summer, but then things had slowed down, life had gotten in the way, and she'd reached that place where she'd been okay with simply having Jack for a friend. No doubt about it, he made a very good friend.

But after spending time with him yesterday, being in his art-filled home, watching him decorate the Christmas tree with Hunter, hearing him discuss jazz music with Ashton, well, she had felt more attracted to him than ever. In fact her longing had taken her quite by surprise, but she figured the emotions were hers alone. Now, realizing that perhaps Jack was having similar thoughts, Marley felt almost like a teenager looking forward to a big first date!

"What's up with you and Jack?" Ashton asked as she drove along the river. "At one time I thought you two were an item, but this week I got the impression you were disinterested. Now I'm not sure."

She let out a little giggle. "I'm not really sure either, Ashton."

"Do you really like him?"

"I like him a lot."

"He seems like a genuinely good guy, Mom. I'm not an expert when it comes to matters of love and the heart, but I can't help but get the feeling Jack is into you."

"Really?"

"Uh, yeah. I mean I saw him watching you while you and Hunter were getting out the Christmas decorations yesterday. It seemed like there was something there."

"And what would you think"—she glanced at her son—"if there was something there?"

Ashton smiled. "Cool. Very cool."

Marley sighed. "Not that I *know* there's something there, mind you, but it's nice to know you'd approve if there was."

"I think it'd be awesome for you to find a great guy. I mean you put up with so much with Dad. You deserve better. And Jack seems like a real improvement."

She laughed.

"Seeing you like this actually gives me hope," he said.

"Hope?" She wasn't sure whether to feel relieved or worried.

"Yeah. Not with Leo though. I'm pretty sure that door's been closed."

"And you're okay with that?" she asked tentatively.

"I'm getting okay." He confessed that the relationship had not been very solid from the start, admitting that he'd always suspected it would end badly. She listened, allowing him to unload on her, trying not to grieve over how much heartache Ashton had been through.

"I'm so sorry," she told him. "When I say I know how you feel, you know I'm not making it up."

"I know, Mom."

"I guess I hoped that you might've learned from me—I mean, how it doesn't pay to remain in a bad relationship."

"You'd think, wouldn't you? But I guess history sometimes repeats itself."

Marley felt a bit guilty now, like perhaps Ashton's situation was partially her fault. "Well, maybe you have to learn from your own mistakes."

"I guess so." He let out a long sigh as they started coming into town. "Hopefully we'll both choose more carefully the next time around. At least you seem to be on the right track now, Mom."

"I hope so." The car got quiet as she navigated the city traffic, and finally she was back at his apartment complex. "Are you going to be okay?" she asked as he reached in the back for his duffle bag.

"Sure, Mom." He made what looked like a forced smile as she came around the car. "I just need to get through this afternoon, and then the next day, and the next."

"Keep me posted, okay?" She hugged him tightly.

"Yeah." He nodded as he stepped away. "I will."

"I'll be praying for you."

He chuckled. "Well, I guess that can't hurt."

"That's right. And in time you might figure out that it actually helps."

"Okay, Mom." He nodded in a tolerant way. She got back into her car and started driving west. Once again, as she drove, she prayed for Ashton, and this time she prayed for Leo, too. Part of her wanted to hate Leo, but she remembered that she was supposed to love her enemies and pray for them, too. Although it was not easy, she was trying.

She got home a little after three. Following a walk on the beach and a nice long nap, she decided to spend a couple of hours primping. It had been a long time since Marley devoted this much attention to her appearance, but it was actually kind of fun. She styled her hair, put on a bit of makeup, picked out a great outfit and jewelry, and was feeling much prettier than usual. The closer it got to seven, the more excited she became. Tonight was really going to be special!

As she drove to Jack's house, though, she started to question herself, wondering if she might possibly be mistaken. What if Jack really had invited her only to have a casual dinner with him—as a friend? After all, it was perfectly acceptable for a friend to have a friend over for dinner. And here she'd gotten all spiffed up, let her hopes run wild, and was probably going to end up looking like a perfect fool. She was halfway tempted to go back home, change back into her regular jeans, and tone it down, but it was already a few minutes past seven.

She parked in front of Jack's house, then used a tissue to soften her lipstick. She even considered leaving the bottle of chardonnay in the car as well, but then realized she was probably overreacting. A friend could bring a friend a bottle of wine for dinner without suggesting romance.

"There you are," Jack said as he opened the door. "You look lovely."

"Thanks." Relieved to see that he had dressed carefully too, she smiled nervously as he took the wine and helped her remove her coat. In dark woolen pants and a black turtleneck sweater that gave his gray beard a distinguished look, Jack looked more handsome than ever.

"Oh my!" she exclaimed as she noticed how many candles were lit. "It looks beautiful in here."

He chuckled. "I might've gotten carried away. But with the Christmas tree up, and with you coming … well, I felt like being festive."

She felt warm and tingly now, like romance was in the air. And yet her old skeptical self kept warning her to be careful. *Don't get swept away. Don't fall too easily.*

By the end of the meal, under the influence of good food, candlelight and wine, easy conversation, shared interests, and Jack's undistracted attention, Marley knew it was too late. She really was falling, and there was nothing she could do to stop herself.

"You know how long I've been waiting for an evening like this?" Jack said to her as they sat on the sofa in front of the fireplace, drinking their after-dinner coffee.

"How long?" she asked quietly.

"Since that first day you walked into my gallery."

She nodded. "Me, too."

"Seriously?" Jack looked a bit unsure. "You've been so cool these past few weeks. Every time I tried to engage you in a conversation, like when you'd drop off Hunter or a new picture or whatever, it always seemed you were keeping me at arm's length. Then you'd make some excuse to get away from me. I honestly thought I was losing you, or that something had soured between us. Until you invited me to join you and your friends on Thanksgiving, I was very concerned."

Marley thought about this for a moment, then laughed.

"What's so funny?" He looked slightly hurt.

She confessed some of Hunter's conversations to him. She didn't go into all the details, and she didn't mention the marriage word or Hunter's hopes that they'd all live together as one big happy family. But she did tell him about Hunter's haphazard attempts at matchmaking. "It just made me feel so uncomfortable, and then I'd see you and didn't want you to think I'd been putting her up to it."

Now Jack smiled. "If anything, I was probably putting Hunter up to it."

"Really?"

"Not directly, but after your Wednesday dates I would ask Hunter what you two had done together, and I'll bet that got her to thinking her grandpa was pretty pathetic. I'm sure she assumed I needed some help in the romance department." He laughed. "The truth is, I probably did need some help." He put his hand under her chin now, sweetly asking if he could kiss her. Naturally she obliged him.

By the time the evening ended, well after midnight, Marley felt certain that her relationship with Jack had taken a definite turn—a turn for the best. As she drove home, she felt like singing.

Chapter 29

JANIE

Early on Saturday morning Janie quietly let herself into the inn. After locking the door to the basement behind her, she tiptoed downstairs to her law office. Her goal was to finish putting everything away and be ready to open her office on Monday. She'd purchased ad space in the local paper and wanted to be set up and ready to meet with clients as soon as calls started coming in. Because her advertisement promised legal consultations at an affordable price, she expected to get results. However, knowing that Donna was still renting a room from Abby, she did feel uneasy about being in the house.

"How long is she going to be staying there?" Janie had asked Abby last night.

"On Thanksgiving I told Donna that I could only rent to her for one more week," Abby said.

"So she has to be out by ... when? Wednesday, Thursday, Friday?" Janie could hear the frustration in her own voice.

"I'm sorry. Maybe I should've said by Monday."

"It's just that I want to start using that space." Janie told her about the ad.

"Do you want me to throw Donna out?"

"No, of course, not. I would think she'd want to leave now that Victor has made himself perfectly clear."

Abby had told Janie about the conversation between Caroline and Donna on Thanksgiving night. "Caroline told me that Donna sounded hostile and angry—not just toward you, but all of us."

"And yet she's still here?"

"Apparently." Abby had apologized again, promising to do all she could to get rid of her unwanted guest. Today Janie knew she was probably asking for trouble by being here, but she wanted to get on with her life. If that upset Donna, so be it.

Janie had finished bundling up the wires to her computer and printer and fax machine when she heard someone knocking on the door at the top of the stairs. Trying to ignore it, she continued tucking the wires out of sight, but then she heard what sounded like Caroline calling out her name. So Janie crawled out from under her desk and hurried to open the door.

"I saw your car," Caroline said quietly as Janie let her in and then locked the door again. "I didn't want to disturb you, but I think Donna knows you're here. I have a bad feeling about that."

"A bad feeling?" Janie frowned.

"I think that woman is on the warpath."

Janie couldn't help but chuckle. "Really? Is she carrying a tomahawk?"

"I wouldn't be surprised." Caroline explained that Donna had gotten all dressed up. "I asked her if she was getting ready to head back to Chicago, but she said no, she still had some business to take care of here."

Janie sighed. "What is wrong with that woman?"

Caroline pointed to the side of her own head. "I think she's deranged."

"So what do you think I should do?"

"I don't know, but I just figured if you needed to sneak out, you know, while Donna was preoccupied, well, maybe I could help."

Janie nodded. "That's probably a good idea." She glanced at her watch, surprised to see that it was nearly noon. "I promised to meet Victor for lunch at The Chowder House, so I really do need to go."

"Okay. Let me run up there and distract her. Give me about five minutes, then get out of here as fast as you can go."

Janie thanked her. Waiting behind the closed door at the top of the stairs, she kept her eye on her watch, and after five minutes she quietly slipped out of the house and into her car with no problem. Feeling pleased with herself, she made it to the restaurant and was seated with Victor a few minutes past twelve.

"It's so good to see you." He reached over and grasped her hand, smiling warmly into her eyes.

"And you, too." But his smile faded when Janie told him about Caroline's escape plan. "Otherwise I might not have gotten here on time."

"I can't believe Donna is still in town. She promised me she would leave." Victor made a grim face. "Frankly she worries me a lot. She's been calling the house regularly. I don't answer when I see that it's her. It seems pointless to talk to her. But that kind of behavior is unsettling."

"Caroline seemed a little concerned too, but really, I think if we just ignore Donna and go about our lives, well, she should get the message. Eventually."

"You'd think. Just the same, it might not hurt for me to speak to her again. Firmly, of course. Somehow I need to make it perfectly clear that it's pointless for her to stick around."

"That might be good."

He squeezed Janie's hand. "Let's agree not to waste any more time talking about my ex-wife." They enjoyed lunch and each other's company, and because the sun was out, Victor invited Janie to walk down to the docks with him to check on the boat.

"I feel so badly about what Donna did to you that day, and how she took your key." He pulled out a new brass key and slipped it into her hand. "I had a locksmith come out and change the locks."

"Thanks." She pocketed the key and paused to gaze at his boat. "She's such a pretty boat, Victor." She wanted to add that it would be a shame if Donna did something to mess it up. Janie wouldn't have been surprised if Donna stooped to something that low.

He climbed aboard, then reached out to help Janie. "I also had a security system installed, both at home and here." He opened up a small metal box by the cabin door. "Hopefully I'm not getting unnecessarily paranoid, but it seemed a good idea." With her watching, he punched in the code. "Remind me to write down the numbers for you later, so you can finish outfitting the boat at your leisure. Of course, I want to compensate you for the things that Donna, uh, removed from here."

Janie shook her head. "I still cannot figure how she did that."

They went into the cabin, and to Janie's relief everything looked perfectly normal. Janie still felt sad to remember how Donna had sabotaged her, but losing some silly material things seemed insignificant compared to what might have happened if she'd lost Victor. They poked around the cabin for a bit, and Janie was just explaining an idea for sprucing up the small eating area when someone began pounding on the door.

"Oh no." Victor looked troubled. "I'll bet that's—"

"Let me in," Donna yelled. "I know you're down there!"

Alarmed and imagining the worst, Janie pulled out her cell phone. "Do you think we should call the police?" she whispered.

"No, not yet." Victor pointed to the bedroom as the pounding and yelling continued. "Go in there, lock the door, and be quiet while I try to reason with her. If it gets out of hand, go ahead and call 9-1-1. I hate to say it, but Donna is, uh, a bit unpredictable."

Janie didn't hesitate to do as she was told, but as soon as the door was locked, she had her phone ready.

"What are you doing here, Donna?" Victor asked in a firm tone.

"Looking for you," Donna snapped at him. "I know you're not alone."

"Donna," Victor said calmly. "I don't know why you're doing this. But you have to—"

"I'm doing this because I still love you, Victor. We belong together. Why can't you see that?"

"I've told you, Donna. It's over between us. You have to accept that."

"I know you still love me, Victor. How can you say you don't?"

"I don't want to hurt you, Donna, but the truth is I do not love you. My love for you died a long time ago. I've tried to be patient during your visit, but it's time for you to go home. There is no hope for us ever getting back together. You have to understand and accept that."

Janie could hear Donna beginning to cry. "But ... but ... Victor! How can I go on without you? I know I messed us up. But we can fix that. Why can't you just give me another chance?"

"I did give you another chance, but I can't manufacture feelings I don't have, Donna. It's over between us. Now please go back home. Get on with your life. And get some help."

Janie heard their voices getting quieter, and the sound of footsteps on the ladder. She waited for a several minutes, still hearing their voices on deck though she couldn't make out the words. Finally Victor returned. "It's okay," he told her. "You can come out now."

She cautiously unlocked and opened the door. Feeling uneasy, like she was actually doing something wrong by hiding in the bedroom, she came out and looked around. "Did Donna understand?"

"I hope so. I tried to be perfectly clear." He put his arms around Janie now. "I was tempted to tell her everything, including how serious I am about you, but I didn't want to make her too angry."

"I appreciate that."

He leaned down and kissed her. "I'm sorry this has been such an ordeal for you, Janie. I appreciate how patient you've been with me."

She smiled into his face. "I actually appreciate how understanding you've been toward your ex-wife."

He looked surprised.

"Okay, it took me a while to fully appreciate that, but after I gave it some thought, I realized it showed your integrity, and that you're a gentleman. I think your sons appreciated it too."

"I told Ben and Marcus the truth," he said. "As soon as they arrived last week, I explained that I could never go back to their mother. They understood."

"I'm glad."

"They're well aware that their mother is bipolar and—"

Janie blinked. "Donna is bipolar?"

He nodded. "I wasn't going to mention it. It's something she's always tried to keep private." He almost laughed. "Well, except when she's in a manic state and out of control."

"Does that happen a lot?"

"Not when she stays on her medication." He grimaced. "I asked her about it specifically just now. She confessed that she stopped taking them several months ago. She claims she doesn't need them anymore."

"Oh dear."

"I encouraged her to get back on them."

They quietly talked for a while longer, then, satisfied that Donna had gone on her way, Victor cautiously went up on deck. "Coast is clear," he called out.

Janie came out. Not because she didn't trust Victor, but because she knew Donna was unpredictable and possibly mentally unstable, she went around the backside of the cabin and peered out from behind a pole to be sure Donna was really gone. She noticed something glinting in the water below her. Thinking it was a fish, she bent over to see better, but then she spotted a broken shard of what appeared to be a plate. It was resting on a lump of concrete right next to the pier post.

"Victor," she called, "come see this."

He came around to join her and she pointed out the broken dish.

"What is it?" he asked.

"It's from the things I'd brought over here that day. The things Donna took."

He scratched his head. "You think she threw everything into the water?"

Janie couldn't help but chuckle. "I think maybe she did."

"That's so crazy." He hugged her close to him. "I'm just glad she didn't try to toss you overboard too."

Janie laughed. "I'm sure she wanted to. Poor Donna."

"I told 'poor Donna' to make an appointment with her psychiatrist when she gets back. He's an old family friend. In fact I think I might even call him and give him a little heads-up."

Janie actually felt sorry for Donna. "You know, Victor," she said quietly, "I can kind of relate to Donna."

"You?" He looked surprised and slightly worried. "Don't tell me you're bipolar too?"

"No. But I do remember how mixed up I felt when I lost Phil. It was almost like I was suffering a form of mental illness."

"You were grieving."

"I know, but I felt lost and confused just the same. My grief over losing him was probably similar to how Donna feels about losing you. Well, minus the bipolar factor. Grief does funny things to a person, and I'm sure I acted a little crazy."

"Maybe, but I doubt you threatened anyone."

"Even so, I do feel sorry for her, Victor. I hope she can get her life leveled out again."

He pulled Janie close to him. "I hope so too."

Chapter 30

ABBY

Tuesday morning Abby arrived at the coffee house early and told herself to be patient. She would not make her big announcement until all her friends were seated with their coffee and ready. Finally that moment arrived.

"Now, quiet everyone." She dinged her spoon on the side of her ceramic mug to get their attention. "I have an announcement."

"Go for it," Marley said.

"First of all, I'm sure you will all be happy to hear that Donna is on her way to Chicago right now."

"Really?" Janie looked hugely relieved. "Does Victor know?"

"I'm not sure about that," Abby admitted. "But I arranged Donna's ride to Eugene. She left the inn at 6:00 a.m., and it was confirmed to me shortly before eight that she made it to the airport just fine." Abby looked at her watch. "Her flight should've taken off about twenty minutes ago."

"So that's why she wasn't around this morning," Caroline said. "I thought it seemed awful quiet at the inn." She chuckled. "And there

I was, tiptoeing around like a mouse, trying to keep Chuck from making any noise so I could get out of there without having to have a conversation with her."

Abby grinned at her friends, suppressing the urge to laugh loudly.

"Nice work, Abby." Marley patted her arm.

"But I have even bigger news." Abby looked at her friends, determined to get as much enjoyment as possible out of this moment.

"Are you going to be a grandma again?" Caroline asked. "Is Jessie pregnant like you'd been thinking?"

Abby shook her head. "No, Jessie was simply having a regular bout of flu."

"Oh, that's too bad." Janie gave her a sympathetic look.

"It might be for the best. I don't think Jessie is ready for another child just yet."

"So what is your big news?" demanded Marley. "Spill the beans."

"Well …" Abby placed her hands on the table. "Apparently none of you was watching the *Live in the Morning Show* today."

"Huh?" Marley frowned at her. "What are you talking about?"

"You were on TV?" Janie asked.

"How's that even possible?" Caroline said. "That show's taped live in New York, and you're here."

Abby started to giggle. "Yes, yes, I know. But you see, I always watch that show. Almost every single day. Paul says I'm addicted. I always enter their contests, too. I have for years now. Today they called me from the show, live, at about six in the morning. At first I thought it was Donna's driver calling to tell me Donna had managed to mess it up somehow."

"Which would not be a surprise," Janie added. "Donna is an expert at messing things up."

"Or she might've hijacked the driver to take her over to kidnap Victor," Marley teased. "And then she could've hijacked the plane to take them both to some Third World country to—"

"Enough about Donna," Caroline interrupted. "Back to Abby's story. What happened?"

"So I answered the phone, and once I got over the shock that they had finally called me after all these years, they asked me the question of the day, and because I had seen the show on Monday, I knew the answer!" She paused to catch her breath.

"And?" Caroline urged her. "What then?"

"And then I won a seven-day Carnival cruise trip down to Mexico!"

"Congratulations!" Caroline reached over to give her a high five. "Awesome!"

"That's wonderful, Abby." Janie grinned. "When are you going to go?"

"After the new year. I think mid-January."

"Was Paul thrilled?" Marley asked.

Abby frowned now. "No, Paul doesn't even want to go."

"Doesn't want to go?" demanded Caroline. "What is wrong with that man?"

Abby shrugged. The truth was, she'd been disappointed too. At first she'd imagined a romantic second honeymoon, but her stick-in-the-mud husband had trampled all over that idea.

"Paul said no to a free cruise?" Marley looked truly disgusted.

Abby rolled her eyes. "Yes. He claimed he's got to finish the Armstrong house in January. Plus he said he can't stand the idea of being cooped up on a boat for a whole week. He's been before, and he really didn't like it much then, although I thought it was mostly the expense that he'd complained about. There's the food thing too—he's supposed to be watching his cholesterol and fat intake. So cruise food might not be such a good idea."

"So can you take one of your daughters?" Janie asked.

"Or your mom?" Marley suggested.

"I actually won *four* tickets!" Abby exclaimed. It was all she could do not to simply shout out her great idea, but she had promised herself to handle this just right, stringing out her story for as long as she could, enjoying the moment completely.

"Then you can take all three of your daughters," Janie suggested. "A mother-daughter cruise would be such a memorable trip."

"I thought of that," Abby admitted. "But it won't work. Nicole will barely be back from France, plus she'll be in school by then, and the other girls have their jobs and responsibilities." She smiled broadly at her friends now. "So I thought … why don't I just take my friends with me?"

"Your friends, as in *us?*" Caroline's eyes lit up.

Abby nodded eagerly. "Yes! Can't you just see it? The Four Lindas on a Mexican cruise together! Doesn't it sound perfectly delicious? We'll go midwinter when it's dull and cold and gray around here, and we'll do some shopping for cruise clothes, and everyone will be so envious of us when they hear that we're heading down there to enjoy the sunshine and—"

"And margaritas!" Marley added.

"And food and fun," Caroline said eagerly.

"With friends," Janie said finally.

"That's right," Abby said. "So what do you think? Are you guys all in?"

"You bet," Caroline firmly nodded.

"Count me in," Janie said happily.

"I can't wait!" Marley agreed.

Abby held up her coffee cup. "Here's to the Four Lindas hitting the high seas!"

The others held up their cups too, all clinking them together.

"Here's to the Four Lindas making a run for the border!" Caroline added.

"To *las quatro amigas!*" Marley frowned. "Or something like that. My Spanish is pretty bad, but I promise I'll work on it."

"You're sure Paul is okay with this?" Janie asked hesitantly. "He won't change his mind and decide he wants to go with you?"

"Or you won't change your mind and worry about leaving him alone?" Caroline asked.

Abby laughed. "Well, I will ask Mom to check in on him from time to time. And Paul informed me that cruises are for 'white-haired grannies and geriatric patients.' No, he definitely does not want to go."

"Well then." Caroline lifted her mug again. "Here's to four hot babes amongst a bunch of old-timers."

"What if *we* turn out to be the old-timers?" Marley asked with a furrowed brow. "I don't want to bum anyone, but I've seen those cruise ads on TV. The passengers always look young and fit—all tan and sleek in their string bikinis."

"Those are just actors," Caroline pointed out. "I even did an ad like that once, back in my thirties."

"Hey, even if we are the old-timers," Marley injected, "at least we're in good company, right? We have each other."

"That's right," Janie agreed.

"And if we're slow or forgetful," Abby said, "or sagging or lagging or hot-flashing or whatever—at least we're doing it together, right?"

"Right. All for one and one for all," Caroline proclaimed.

Abby nodded. "Here's to the Four Lindas cruising with the oldies!"

... a little more ...

When a delightful concert comes to an end,

the orchestra might offer an encore.

When a fine meal comes to an end,

it's always nice to savor a bit of dessert.

When a great story comes to an end,

we think you may want to linger.

And so, we offer ...

AfterWords—just a little something more after you

have finished a David C Cook novel.

We invite you to stay awhile in the story.

Thanks for reading!

Turn the page for ...

- **Discussion Questions**
- **Excerpt from The Four Lindas Book 4**

DISCUSSION QUESTIONS

1. There is a saying that married men live longer than single men because wives nag their husbands into good health. Do you think this is true? What's your opinion of the way Abby wanted to help Paul manage his health?

2. Victor's need for Donna to have a place to stay and Caroline's need for a home remotivated Abby to get her bed-and-breakfast up and running. Recount a time in your own life when a friend's need propelled you into a project that you found personally fulfilling.

3. How did you feel about Donna's desire to be reunited with Victor? If you were writing their story, how would you have wanted it to go?

4. How is romance in middle age similar to first-time love? What complications are unique to older couples, and what makes these easier or harder to overcome? Use examples from Marley and Jack's relationship, or Janie and Victor's, or Caroline and Mitch's.

5. Why was it important for Janie to understand what her father's war experience might have been like? Do you think her discovery was significant enough to overcome the unresolved pain of her relationship with him? Why or why not?

6. Because she deeply loves her gay son, Marley finds it challenging to reconcile the love and peace of her newfound faith with the judgmental attitudes about homosexuality among the women in her Bible study. Talk about a time when you've experienced a clash between your faith and your life circumstances. How did you cope with the tension?

7. How would you characterize Marley's relationship with Ashton (e.g., nurturing, enabling, healthy, unhealthy, and so on)? What decisions and attitudes allowed Marley to empathize with her son even though she couldn't relate to his experience firsthand?

8. What aspects of Caroline's experience caring for her mother made her a stronger person? How did Michael's abusiveness threaten to weaken her again? Was Caroline appropriately gracious toward him, or would you have counseled her to take a harder stance against him? Explain your answer.

9. Marley and Abby had a grand adventure and told a few lies while trying to track down whether Joan Wilson was a smoker. Were they being noble or reckless? Have you ever done something you normally wouldn't think of doing in order to help a friend? If so, what were the positive and/or negative outcomes of that choice? How were you changed?

10. If you won four tickets for a weeklong cruise in any part of the world, who would you take, and where would you go?

An Excerpt from

THE FOUR LINDAS BOOK 4

═Chapter 1═

ABBY

Trying to catch her breath, Abby shuffled her way into the women's locker room, barely able to put one heavy foot in front of the other. Feeling twice her actual age, she eased herself down onto the only unoccupied bench and gazed around the steamy room. Women with firm, sleek, healthy bodies paraded themselves around in various stages of undress, as if trying to rub it in.

Lowering her eyes in defeat, she stared down at her pudgy white thighs and found herself craving cottage cheese. Without a doubt, she had lost her ever-loving mind. Why else would she have allowed Janie and Caroline to talk her into this? And why would she have bragged to Paul about her grandiose plan to join the fitness club?

"I'm starting tomorrow," she'd boasted to her husband last night. "After I become a member, I'll start off by taking ... what's it called? A circuit-something class. I think that's what Caroline said."

"You're starting with a circuit-training class?" Paul frowned at her. "You sure you want to do that?"

"Janie and Caroline said it's really fun, a bunch of women working out together with upbeat music. It's probably like aerobic dance. I loved doing that back when the girls were little."

His mouth twisted to one side. "Yeah, but circuit training is hard work, Abby."

"Are you saying I can't do it?"

He shook his head. "I'm saying you should start with something easier. When I joined the club, I started with a trainer and a special—"

"Yeah, well, you were recovering from a heart attack, Paul. I'm in a lot better shape than you were."

He looked skeptical.

"I've been walking three or four times a week. I've even lost a little weight this fall."

"Yeah, but starting out with circuit training—"

"Why do you always have to rain on my parade?"

"Because I *know* you, Abby."

"Meaning?"

"Meaning if you start out with something too tough, you'll give up."

"I will not!"

"I'll bet you don't last a week."

"I will!" she insisted. "You'll see. I'm going to join the club and take that class. And maybe I'll go five days a week at first, to jump-start things. I could swim on Tuesdays and Thursdays and—"

"Why don't you just use that a free one-week coupon I gave you?" he suggested. "Make sure you know what you're getting into before you plunk down all that dough."

"I *know* what I'm getting into. Janie and Caroline swear by that class. They go three times a week—and love it."

He looked like he wanted to say something but stopped himself. "All I'm saying is that the club is pretty expensive, Abby, and I think—"

"You think I'm not worth it?" She shook her fist at him. "Sure, it's fine for you to belong to the club, but poor old Abby doesn't deserve—"

"That's not what I'm saying." His brow creased. "You're worth it. I just don't want to see you pay all that money up front and then change your mind." Of course, he took the opportunity to list all the activities Abby had started but never finished. But instead of falling for that old bait and getting into a ridiculous fight, Abby took their counselor's advice and the high road.

"If you love me," she calmly informed him, "you will support me in this. I'm making a healthy decision for my life, and you should respect that, Paul."

He held up his hands in surrender. "Fine. Just take it easy, okay? Don't kill yourself on the first day. Remember, slow and steady wins the race. Pace yourself."

"That's exactly what I plan to do."

But Abby's plan, like the best-laid schemes of mice and men, had fallen by the wayside after she joined the club and paid her membership fees in the morning. It wasn't that she was trying to impress anyone in the circuit-training class. She knew better than that. But as she went from station to station, attempting to figure out the confusing machines and determine the realistic weights and master the forms, she understood she'd bought more than she'd bargained for. Trying to stay one step ahead of the perky energetic woman who followed Abby in the circuit was no picnic either. The petite blonde kept nipping at Abby's heels. "You know there's a *special* class for people who don't know how to properly use the equipment," she sniped as Abby untangled herself from one of the machines.

As she tried to hurry along, Abby decided to call this snippy woman Trixie, after an ill-tempered Chihuahua Abby's daughters had begged her to get for them long ago. Fortunately Paul got fed up and found the feisty dog another home.

"Maybe you should try out the pool aerobics," Trixie said in a snarky tone. "I hear the *older* ladies really enjoy the *slower* pace." She folded her toned arms across her flat abdomen, leaning against a pole and scowling as she waited for Abby to move to the next machine.

The last straw came about midway through the class. Abby knew it was midway because she'd kept one eye on the lethargic clock the entire time. She'd never seen a minute hand move so slowly. Trixie laughed loudly upon discovering that Abby had been using the biceps machine without weights attached.

"You gotta be kidding," Trixie said. "You'll *never* get into shape doing that."

Fed up and worn out, Abby had released the handle and let the bar slam back into the machine, which she knew was a no-no. Glaring at Trixie, she'd turned on the heel of her frumpy walking shoes and stormed out. No doubt Trixie was hugely relieved. Right now, she was probably telling everyone how hopeless and out-of-shape Abby was—and how fat old women like her should be banned from circuit training and maybe even the entire fitness club. So humiliating.

At least Caroline and Janie, who were stuck in a bank appointment regarding Caroline's mother's estate, hadn't been there to witness her embarrassment. That was something Abby could be thankful for. What had made her think she could pull off something like this? She felt like crying. Paul was right—she had wasted their money. She really was a failure.

As she slowly stood, searching the room for some sort of a stall or private area where she could discretely disrobe, she wondered how hard it would be to convince the club to refund her membership fee. Maybe there was some sort of twenty-four-hour cancellation clause. She would have to find out. But first she needed to find a place to change.

"Excuse me," she asked one of the only women with clothes on. "Where are the changing rooms?"

The woman laughed, waving her hand around the open area. "This is it."

"Oh." Abby nodded stiffly. "Yes … okay … I'm new here." Wondering why she hadn't noticed the insane lack of privacy during the tour of the club, Abby picked up a white towel from the neat stack and sniffed it. At least it smelled clean. And it was actually rather soft and thick. Nice. As were many of the other amenities that had distracted Abby from noticing the absence of dressing stalls.

It figured that she'd been too busy checking out things like attractive tile designs and chic light fixtures and rain-shower heads, too distracted by fluff to be concerned with function. She reminded herself that she'd arrived in her workout clothing (which, like her, was out of style and out of shape) and had no need for a changing room then. Really, she should just get over herself and strip down and not worry about what anyone else thought. That's probably what Caroline and Janie did when they were here—why couldn't Abby?

"Janie and I have so much fun at the club," Caroline had said when the Four Lindas club met last week at the Clifden Coffee House. Abby, Janie, Caroline, and Marley—who as schoolgirls had all shared the first name of Linda—were discussing their upcoming cruise to Mexico. They talked about spray-on tans, waist-trimming swimsuits, and how they only had six weeks to get into shape. Motivation was high, especially with the holidays upon them. But for Abby, the initial thrill of winning her Mexican cruise for four was quickly turning into high anxiety. She hadn't purchased a new swimsuit since her three daughters were kids. And the sorry threadbare thing she wore in the hot tub at home was not fit for public viewing. Neither was her body!

"You and Marley really should come try out the club," Caroline urged Abby. "We can get you free passes."

"I know," Abby said. "Paul's always telling me that."

"But if you guys joined, we could do classes together," Janie said. "We could encourage each other to get fit."

"And the club's running a special until the end of the year," Caroline told them. "If two people sign up, the second membership is half off. You and Marley could split the difference."

"I don't know." Marley shook her head with a doubtful expression. "I've never really been a fitness-club sort of girl. I think I'd rather do yoga or Pilates."

"They have those classes too," Janie told her.

"Yeah, but I like working out on the beach. I take my iPod filled with my own music and just do my thing. I guess I'm still just a free-spirited hippie at heart. Kind of a lone wolf. Well, except for my Lindas." Marley smiled. "Count me out."

"I wish I had that kind of discipline," Abby admitted. "Even walking regularly is a challenge for me, unless I have someone to go with me."

"That's why you need to join the club," Janie insisted. "It's more fun to work out with your friends by your side."

"That's right," Caroline agreed. "You can do this, Abby."

So Abby had decided to trust her friends and, like the Nike ad said, just do it. But now that she'd "done it," she was sorry. She should've listened to Marley. And even to Paul. Abby should've known she wasn't a "fitness-club sort of girl" either.

Finally Abby decided that a shower stall could perform as a dressing room *and* shower. Safely behind the translucent curtain, she peeled off her sweat-soaked clothes and dumped them on the floor, where they got drenched while she showered. Relieved to be away from the curious stares of onlookers, she had to admit she was a complete misfit here. That was ironic, because she remembered a time when she was the kind of girl who thought others were misfits, including old friends like Janie (who'd turned into a geek in high school). Not that Abby picked on anyone. But she had been one of the "cool" kids, a cheerleader even. She'd been the kind of girl who never got teased in any locker room.

Now Janie was fit and beautiful. Someone like Trixie wouldn't think of picking on Janie. Or Caroline either. As Abby shampooed her hair, she realized that in this club, she wasn't only a misfit; she was a sideshow freak. She could probably charge admission. Maybe that would help to recoup her wasted membership fee. Because she knew she was never coming back here. Never.

That's how Abby comforted herself as she took a very long shower, utilizing endless hot water and generous handfuls of the club's luxurious soaps and shampoos. At least she'd get some of her money's worth! By the time she finished, she felt marginally better and squeaky clean. As she dried off, feeling a bit more like her old self, she was almost rethinking her previous resolution to become a fitness-club dropout on the very first day.

But as she attempted to wrap the fluffy white towel around her fluffy white body, she was reminded of reality. The towel was too small to wrap around her body! Staring at the six-inch gap where the ends of the towel refused to come together, she wanted to scream. *What is wrong with this place? Can't they afford bigger towels?* Or perhaps this was the club's subtle message. They didn't want any overweight, out-of-shape, fitness-challenged people to join their ranks. Of course, that was why it was called a "fitness" club. You had to be *fit* to join. Perhaps what Abby needed was an *unfit* club—a place with queen-sized towels, easy-to-use machines, no skinny naked bodies, and donuts! A place where someone like Abby would fit in.

Finally, struggling to hold the loose ends of the towel as well as her soggy workout clothes, Abby emerged from the shower stall and made her way back toward the locker area. The room was a bit less crowded now. At the lockers, she dropped her wet clothes on the tile floor, still trying to cover her backside with the mini-towel as she extracted her clothes from her locker. Then she

went to a relatively quiet corner. Just a few feet away, two partially dressed young women chatted amicably over the pros and
cons of—*give me a break*—colon cleansers. Huffing and puffing,
Abby bent over, hurriedly tugging her clothes onto her still damp
body, trying not to listen to the sordid details of these women's
bathroom habits.

As Abby sat down to put on her shoes, she also tried not
to stare at the young brunette who had just stepped up to the
sink area. Wearing nothing but a contented smile and some very
skimpy panties (or maybe just dental floss), this woman positioned
herself in front of the brightly lit mirror. Happily blow-drying her
short hair, she seemed oblivious to the fact that she was only two
feet from the door, and that anyone in the hallway on the other
side would see her standing there, topless, if it swung open. Was
the girl nuts, or simply an exhibitionist, or maybe a porn star?

Maybe Abby was a prude or old-fashioned or just plain uncomfortable in her own flabby skin, but she just did not understand this
sort of thing. She had raised her three daughters on the principles
of modesty and propriety and sensibility, and she hoped they knew
better than to run around buck naked in public.

The door flew open and Caroline and Janie burst into the locker
room. "There she is!" exclaimed Caroline. Naturally, they didn't even
give the nearly naked brunette a second glance as they came over to
join Abby.

"So how was it?" Janie asked Abby. "Are you sore yet?"

Abby shrugged. "A little."

"Wow, you're fast," Caroline observed. "The class only got out a
few minutes ago. How'd you even have time for a shower?"

"Because she *skipped out* on class," someone from behind them announced.

Abby turned to see Trixie swinging a sweat towel in one hand and looking smug.

"Hey, Serena," Janie said in a friendly tone. "How's it going?" Trixie, aka Serena, smiled at Janie. "Pretty good. I had a nice little workout." She snickered. "Unlike *some* people."

Caroline frowned at Abby. "Did you really skip out on the circuit class?"

"I did half of it," Abby assured her. "A full thirty minutes. Besides, Paul warned me to take it easy today."

"You can take it easy and still do the full hour," Janie explained. "Just go slower and—"

"Go slower?" Abby growled. "When you've got a Chihuahua nipping at your heels?"

Janie frowned. "There were dogs in the class?"

"Just the female kind," Abby retorted.

"Huh?" Caroline looked confused.

"Never mind." Abby picked up her wet workout clothes, wondering what to do with them.

"What happened?" Caroline pointed at the soggy mess.

"Did someone hose you down?" Janie asked wryly.

"No." Abby held her head high. "I was multitasking."

"What?" Janie studied Abby curiously.

"Changing, showering, and doing my laundry," Abby proclaimed. "All at the same time."

Caroline laughed. "Hey, I saw that in a *Seinfeld* episode once. Kramer was—"

"Never mind," Janie told her. "Back to the circuit training," she said to Abby. "It's better to do the full hour and just go slower and use lighter weights and—"

"*Lighter* weights?" Trixie snickered. "Like that would even be possible." She'd already stripped down to her underwear, revealing a set of abs that would make a six pack jealous. "She wasn't using *any* weights."

"Really?" Janie looked disappointed.

"Oh, don't pick on her," Caroline said. "At least she showed up. That's the first step."

"That's true," Janie conceded. "Getting started is always rough, Abby. At least your first day is behind you now."

Abby made a weak smile as she dumped her wet clothes into her gym bag, right on top of her shoes. She'd sort that mess out later. Mostly she just wanted out of this place.

"Good job!" Caroline slapped Abby on the back. "Just wait until we're in class with you. We'll bolster up your spirits."

"And by January, you'll be in the best shape ever," Janie said optimistically.

"You really think so?" Abby tried not to sound too negative as she picked up her heavy bag, but she could not imagine working out with her energetic, trim friends urging her to try harder. No, today had opened her eyes. It was hopeless.

"You'll see. Next time will be better," Caroline said kindly.

Abby wanted to tell them there was not going to be a next time, but she had no intention of confessing her failure in front of all these women, especially Trixie. More than that, she wondered how she would break the news to Paul. Even if he didn't say, "I told you so," he would be thinking it. She would see it in his eyes. He would add today's failure to his already long list of her shortcomings. Then he'd stick it in his pocket and save it for the next time he wanted to give her a reality check.